The Mother Road

"With a compelling, fresh voice, Jennifer AlLee blends Americana with the trials of a modern-day family. *The Mother Road* is a simply smashing story. Not to be missed!"
—PATTI LACY, author of *Reclaiming Lily*

THE MOTHER ROAD

Jennifer AlLee

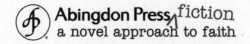
Abingdon Press fiction
a novel approach to faith
Nashville, Tennessee

The Mother Road

Copyright © 2012 by Jennifer AlLee

ISBN-13: 978-1-4267-1312-5

Published by Abingdon Press, P.O. Box 801, Nashville, TN 37202

www.abingdonpress.com

All rights reserved.

Library of Congress Cataloging-in-Publication Data

AlLee, Jennifer.
  The mother road / Jennifer AlLee.
    p. cm.
  ISBN 978-1-4267-1312-5 (pbk. : alk. paper)
  I. Title.
  PS3601.I39M68 2012
  813'.6--dc22

                                                              2011034543

Printed in the United States of America

1 2 3 4 5 6 7 8 9 10 / 17 16 15 14 13 12

To my sisters, Kelly and Chrissy. It took us a while, but I'm so glad our roads finally crossed!

And to my mother, Rose-Marie, who gave me the best map she could and pointed me in the right direction. I love you.

ACKNOWLEDGMENTS

Writing a book is a journey, one that isn't traveled alone. Some very special people went down this road with me and deserve to be recognized.

To my awesome agent, Sandra Bishop: You're that rare person who cares about not only an author's career but about her heart as well. Thanks, Sandra, for creating a family of writers who support each other in every area of life.

To everyone at Abingdon Press: There were so many people involved in bringing this book to life; I know I'll leave someone out if I try to name you all. Let me just say that the Abingdon team rocks my world. I adore working with you all!

To Lisa Richardson, my best friend and sister in all things writing: You've been right there with me on every dip and rise of this never-ending roller-coaster ride. You are a rock, an amazing woman, a fabulous writer, and one of the coolest chicks I know!

To the Monday Night Bible Study gang: Billy, Lynn, Nate, Cora, Coleen, Carol N., Pius, Judy, and Carol C. You've bathed my life and writing in so much prayer; you all get to claim a piece of this book. We may need to celebrate with Blizzards.

To my husband, Marcus, and my son, Billy: I could get all mushy here, but I'll spare you and just say thanks for putting up with my craziness. I love you both very much!

Most important, thanks to God for filling my life with so much love, so much joy. Even though my own personal road has taken more than a few detours, I know His hand is on me, and I can't wait to see where I end up.

1

I cannot get divorced.

"I want a divorce."

Tony repeats himself, speaking slower. Does he think I didn't hear him the first time? That somehow I missed his startling proclamation? Oh no, I heard every one of those ugly words. I just can't believe they came out of my husband. Not him. Not the man I've been so blissfully, ignorantly joined to for the last eighteen years.

"Natalie, say something."

I try to swallow, try to push down the shock that clogs my windpipe. This day started out so normal. How did it go so wrong?

When Tony arrived home from work, late as usual, I didn't complain. In fact, I had everything ready for a beautiful evening. Dinner warming in the oven, a special bottle of wine breathing on the table, and me, ready to celebrate. But when I greeted him at the door, my welcoming arms wrapped around a statue of a man, his arms hanging straight down at his sides, his torso cold and hard.

He's anything but statuesque now. Pacing like an agitated animal, he rakes his hands through his hair as he looks back at me. "Come on, Natalie. Don't give me the silent treatment."

Is that what he thinks I'm doing? Punishing him with my silence? What I wouldn't give for more silence. How I wish I could turn back time and press my hand against his mouth, forcing his lips closed so the words couldn't spill out.

But there's no going back. No undoing the news that all these nights I thought he was working late, he was actually getting cozy with his administrative assistant.

I stare back at him. What does he want me to say? What is there to say?

"When did it start?"

He stops pacing and sighs. I bet now he wishes he hadn't encouraged me to speak. "In Omaha."

Omaha? "I thought you went there alone."

"I was going to. Bringing Erin along was a last-minute decision. I needed a hand."

I'll bet you did. Facts bounce around my brain, banging into one another as I try to grasp what my husband is telling me. That trip was only three months ago. How can he already be certain that our marriage is over?

"We can get through this. We can go to counseling." The words squeeze out of me so thin and garbled it sounds like I'm talking through the speaker at a fast-food drive-through. Humiliation burns my cheeks, the back of my neck. Basically, I've chosen to ignore the fact that he's been unfaithful and am begging him not to leave me. If I have to swallow my pride to work things out, I will.

Because I cannot get divorced.

Tony closes his eyes, jerks his head hard to the left. "It's too late for that."

"It's never too late." I grab his arm, my fingers digging into his shirt sleeve, twisting into the cotton. Now that I'm touching him, I'm desperate. Desperate to keep contact. If I can just hold on, I can fix this. "We can work it out. Remember our vows? We're a threefold cord, you, me, and God. Together we—"

As soon as I say "God" his eyes cloud over and he yanks his arm away from me. "No. I can't do this anymore."

"But Tony, I—"

"She's pregnant."

Pregnant. That one word sweeps away anything else I might have said. Pregnant. And after only three months. I put my palm flat against my own stomach and sink onto the couch. Well, now we know.

There's no fight left in me. I can't look at his face, but I see his feet step closer.

"I'm so sorry. I didn't mean for it to happen this way."

This way? In other words, he did mean for it to happen, just in a nicer, more humane way. Finally, my mind clears and I know exactly what I want to say.

"You need to leave now."

He doesn't answer at first. But then his shoes back away and he says, "I'll have my lawyer contact you."

The absurdity hits me, jerking my head up, pulling me off the couch so I'm standing upright, hands balled into fists at my side. "You already have your own lawyer?"

His face is a mixture of sadness and pity. *Poor Natalie*, it seems to say, *how could you not see this coming?*

He scoops his car keys off the hall table and walks out the front door. He pulls it closed behind him so gently I barely hear the click of the latch.

So this is how it ends? Eighteen years of love, work, planning . . . over after a fifteen-minute confession.

The ding of the oven timer calls me to the kitchen. On my way there, I pass the dinner table, set so beautifully with our good china, a centerpiece of fresh flowers in the middle of a midnight blue tablecloth. And there, between Tony's seat at the head of the table and my seat to his right, is the reason I was so ready to celebrate. The contract for the next three books in the *Happily Married* series.

I cannot get divorced.

I'm a romance novelist. And not just any romance novelist. One of the top-selling Christian romance novelists in the country. I also write nonfiction books about—get this—marriage. I've put my life under a microscope and written about it, bared my soul, and now I'm considered an expert in the field. I make a living from couples who live happily ever after, or are at least trying to.

A cold numbness spreads through my body as I walk into the kitchen. I turn off the timer. Turn off the oven. Pick up the oven mitts from the counter. Open the oven door. Pull out the roast.

It looks perfect, but I pinch my lips together as the aroma sets my stomach to rolling. I don't even like roast. I only made this stupid thing because it's Tony's favorite.

So much boils up inside me—anger, grief, nausea—that I explode. I hurl the hunk of meat, roasting pan and all, against the wall and release a scream that comes from somewhere beyond my toes. Dropping to my knees on the floor, I weep as meat drippings and carrots and onions slide in slow motion down the wall and ooze across the floor.

My whole adult life has been about happily ever after. And now, it's over.

I'm getting a divorce.

2

How did I get in this bed?

I push up on my elbow but freeze, squeezing my eyes tight. Too fast. Slower this time, I kick off the covers and sit up, clenching my jaw against the throbbing in my temples. My feet hit the ground, toes crunching into an empty Oreo bag in the middle of a field of used tissues. That explains the aching in my head. I have a sugar hangover.

I remember very little of what happened Friday night after Tony left. Apparently, I cried a lot, went on a cookie bender, then crawled under the covers with all my clothes on.

Across the room, sun streams through the open window coverings. How totally inappropriate for the day after my life is torn in half. The sky should be gray and cloudy. Even thunder would be acceptable. Instead, I get sun, and somewhere outside, a bird is being so overly chipper that I want to track it down and shoot it.

I stumble into the bathroom and reach for my toothbrush, but my eyes stray across the blue-gray granite countertop to Tony's side of the double vanity. His electric toothbrush stands in the charger, flanked by his razor, comb, and a Costco-size bottle of Listerine. The fact that he walked out of this house without personal hygiene items means only one thing: somewhere, he has duplicates to all of it. Somewhere, he has a new toothbrush, a new comb, a new bottle of mouthwash. Probably at the same place where his new woman and new baby wait for him.

My stomach rolls. I jerk toward the toilet, yank up the lid, and promptly spill my guts. Thinking of them making a home together is too much. So are all those Oreos I gorged on last night.

I peel off the clothes I slept in and drop each one—chino slacks, white-silk shell, sea foam–green sweater—into the trash can. There's no way I can wear any of it again without remembering the night I got dumped. Too bad. That sweater was one of my favorites.

Once in the shower, I stand as still as a hunk of granite, chin to chest, letting the hot water beat down on my back. Maybe, if I stay in here long enough, the pulsating jets will pound the knots out of my shoulders, the steam will melt the fog from my mind. But when I step out of the shower twenty minutes later, my fingers and toes shriveled like prunes, I'm no less tense or confused.

How does a marriage of eighteen years end in one evening?

I grab a towel off the bar and wrap it tight around my body. Of course, it didn't just end last night. Tony and Erin have been sneaking around for the last three months, but she's worked for him for almost two years. Long enough for them to become friends, to form a close bond. Not that I'm giving him an excuse. Lots of men are friends with their assistants and it never goes beyond that. Never turns into an affair that ends with a choice between the loyal wife and the pregnant girlfriend.

Pregnant. After three months. The thought almost knocks me off my feet. That kind of thing doesn't usually happen so fast. I should know. For me, it's never happened at all.

The closet door creaks as I pull it open. I flip the light switch, illuminating the cavernous walk-in space. It's so unlike our first apartment, with such a tiny closet that all our clothes had been smooshed together. Now, there's at least three feet of space between my side and Tony's side. We've come so far. Not even our clothes touch anymore.

I stand in the doorway, staring at the neat rows of blouses, slacks, skirts, all organized by color and season. Part of my job is to look put together whenever I step out of the house. You never know who you might run into. But today, I don't want to hassle with zippers, buttons, or binding fabric. Today, I need elastic and soft, stretchy cotton.

By the time I head down the stairs wearing the oldest, most comfortable sweats I own, I'm starting to feel like I can do this. Tony may have blindsided me, he may have pulled the rug out from under my feet, he may have done every awful cliché in the book, but that doesn't mean I have to let him win. I can survive without him. It's like creating my own personal twelve-step program: one day at a time. One minute at a time. One breath at a time.

But when I enter the kitchen, the physical manifestation of last night's trip off the deep end is waiting for me. Beef, vegetables, and congealed meat drippings are everywhere, and the odor is beyond ripe. My stomach turns in on itself. I will never eat a roast again.

Donning rubber gloves, I attack the mess. I scoop the solid pieces into a grocery bag, tie it off, and dump it in the trash. It takes half a roll of paper towels to soak up the jellied juices. Then, armed with a spray bottle of ammonia-fortified cleaner, I hit my knees and start scrubbing. It's while I'm on the floor, rubbing a sponge back and forth across fat-covered tiles, that I finally start to pray.

"Why?"

That one word falls from my lips, over and over and over, asking God to explain this to me. But instead of divine revelation, more unanswerable questions crowd my mind—What did I do wrong? Did I push him away? Could I have stopped this?—but *Why?* is the only thing I can vocalize.

I don't know how long I'm down on the floor, scrubbing and questioning myself. Questioning God. When I finally sit back on my heels, I'm drenched with sweat, my cheeks wet with tears. The floor gleams. Now it's time to tackle the huge grease stain on the wall.

I scrub. And scrub. And scrub some more.

Nothing.

Rummaging under the sink, I find a more abrasive brush and a more powerful cleaner. Minutes later, I step back from the wall and sigh.

It's no use.

No matter how hard I scrub, a shadow of the stain remains. With the exception of the spot where I started to rub the paint off the wall, it's still there. Nothing—not expensive cleaners, not hours of elbow grease—will erase that mark. The only way to make it go away is to paint over it, but the stain's still going to be there, hidden.

Like the pain of Tony's betrayal. It might fade. I might be able to cover over it. But nothing is going to erase it from my heart.

Nothing.

"Help."

The truth pushes me backward until I make contact with the kitchen island, and I send up a new prayer.

"Help me. Help me. Help me."

3

So that's it? It's over just because he says so?"

My assistant, Jade, sits on the couch beside me, her round cheeks flushed red, her silky black hair quivering in indignation. It's almost laughable. You'd think Tony walked out on her too. I guess he did, in a way. Jade's livelihood depends on my selling books, being a sought-after speaker, and needing someone to keep my life organized. Once news gets out about Tony's affair and my offers start drying up, Jade may have to work somewhere that doesn't allow her to come in at 10:30 a.m. wearing yoga pants and a USC T-shirt.

Thinking of losing Jade turns my urge to laugh into a need to cry. Back when my writing took off and it became clear I needed help keeping all the bits and pieces of my career organized, I posted a flyer at the community college. Jade was the only one to call about it, and when she showed up for her interview, flyer clutched in her hand, I understood why. It was just as well, because we clicked right away. But she isn't just my employee—she's my friend. Sometimes she's the daughter I will never have. The idea that I might have to lose her too makes me want to find something of my husband's—

something small, fragile, and precious to him—and throw it against the fireplace bricks.

Does Tony have any clue how much damage has been done thanks to his raging hormones? If he did, would he care?

I motion to Jade, then pat the seat cushion beside me. "Come. Sit."

Her hands slice through the air even as she drops down on the couch. "I can't believe he'd do something like this. Is he crazy? Is he—"

With the reflexes of a kung fu master catching a fly with chopsticks, I grab Jade's hands and hold them still, enfolding them in my own. "He is a man," I say quietly, "who decided to change the direction of his life. It's lousy, and I certainly don't understand it, but there's nothing I can do about it."

Jade tilts her head to the side, eyes narrowing. "How can you be so calm?"

I give her hands a final squeeze before letting them go and falling back onto the sofa. "I've had a few days to process everything."

By "process" I mean completely fall apart and then drag myself together.

The opening notes of "Stayin' Alive" fill the room as my cell phone vibrates on the coffee-table top. Tony's ring, assigned to him because Tony Marino sounds so much like Tony Manero, the John Travolta character in *Saturday Night Fever*. I've got to change that ring to something else. Maybe "Love Stinks."

I reach for the phone, but Jade gets to it first. She snaps it up and holds it in both hands, pleading with me. "Oh, please let me get this for you."

It's juvenile to avoid his calls, but she's giving me an offer I can't refuse. "Be nice," I warn her.

Responding with a sideways eye roll, she pushes a button and puts the phone to her ear. "Natalie Marino's cell. How can I help you?"

A pause, during which time Jade sticks her tongue out at the phone.

"No, I'm sorry, Mr. Marino. She's unable to speak to you now."

Pause.

"That's right. She told me."

Tony's voice goes up a level and snippets of his side of the conversation travel out of the earpiece and over to me. "No reason . . . difficult . . . act like adults . . ."

Now it's my turn to stick out my tongue. Act like adults. What does he know about acting like an adult? Acting like an *adulterer*, maybe.

"Just a minute." Jade covers the mouthpiece with her thumb and leans toward me. "He wants to come over and get the rest of his stuff," she hisses. "What should I tell him?"

Oh, there are so many things I wish she could tell him, but I restrain myself. So he wants to get his stuff. I could put him off, could make him wait just to inconvenience him as much as possible. But I don't want to put Jade in the uncomfortable position of relaying that kind of information.

"Tell him to come by tomorrow after ten. I'll be out of the house."

I wonder what he'll take. His toiletries and clothes, obviously, and anything that's used only by him. But what about our communal objects? Will he want any of the photos from our vacations, birthdays, time with friends? Our wedding pictures? Then again, now that my marriage has crumbled in a deceitful heap, do I want to keep any of those things?

Jade ends the call and holds the phone out to me. "He'll come by tomorrow. Stinking sack of—"

"Jade." Even though I agree with her, my tone says *Step lightly.*

"Sorry. So where are you going to be while he's here?"

I sigh and take the phone from her, rubbing my thumb across the top of it. "I don't know yet. I'll figure out something." It might be a good time to find an attorney of my own.

"You're going to let him come in here unsupervised and take whatever he wants?"

While the idea of letting him pick and choose what he wants to salvage from this relationship is like sandpaper on my skin, the alternative is even worse. I refuse to stand by and watch him do it. My shoulders jerk in a defeated shrug. "Do you have a better idea?"

"Actually, I do." Jade twists a piece of hair around one finger, her mouth sliding up into a sly grin. "Why don't we make it real easy for him?"

4

While I was tempted by Jade's idea of gathering all of Tony's belongings and dumping them in a heap in the middle of the lawn, I vetoed it for several reasons. First off, it would draw way too much attention from the neighbors. Not that they won't notice Tony carting his stuff away, but why give them anything more to chatter about? Second, as much as I hate the idea, I'm heading into divorce proceedings with this man. Antagonizing him before we start divvying up our assets would be just plain stupid. Satisfying, but stupid.

Instead, I sent Jade off to purchase packing supplies. We'll box it all up and put it out on the porch. The neighbors will still talk, but perhaps it will be about how giving I am. *My goodness, did you see the large donation Natalie Marino left out for the Salvation Army? That woman is such a giver.* If they only knew the half of it.

I'm standing in the middle of the family room, staring at the entertainment center and wondering which one of us should have custody of the VHS copy of *Indiana Jones and the Last Crusade*, when Jade returns. We go back and forth through the door that connects the garage to the kitchen, and I help her carry in several six-packs of collapsed cardboard banker's boxes and two bags of miscellaneous supplies. It looks like she picked up everything we'll need: a tape dispenser, rolls of packing tape, Sharpie markers, and a little something extra.

"Really, Jade?" I hold up a huge bag of M&M's. "Five pounds? Don't you think that's a little much?"

She looks up from the kitchen floor where she's wrestling to assemble the boxes and shakes her head. "Nope. I almost bought two bags."

I turn to leave the room, then look over my shoulder. "I'm going to start in the bedroom. Pray for me."

"Already am."

Rather than stuff Tony's clothes into boxes, I decide to put what I can in his suitcase and garment bag. Except that the garment bag is already gone, along with most of his suits. Somewhere along the way, he snuck them out without my noticing.

I toss the suitcase on the bed and flip open the top, releasing a residual hotel-room smell. He's taken a lot more business trips this year than usual. He said things started with Erin in Omaha, but is that when it really began, or is it just the first time they had sex? How many of his trips were actually for business, and how many had been excuses to spend time alone with her? Suddenly, I want to know everything. I want proof, concrete proof that my husband isn't the man I always thought he was.

I open every zipper and pocket on the case, running my fingers through them, searching for what he might have left behind. Other than a handful of lint and an extra set of earbuds, I find nothing.

His clothes are next. Before putting them in the case, I thoroughly inspect every item. If it has a pocket, I check it. But again, I find nothing. Doubt and hope start to churn in my stomach. Surely, a man having an affair would leave some evidence behind. Maybe this is all a big mistake. Maybe Tony's just confused. Maybe Erin tricked him, and the baby isn't his. Of course, for him to believe it is his would mean he'd been unfaithful at least once. It would still be awful, but if it was just once, maybe there's a sliver of hope for us. Maybe we can work through this. Maybe . . .

My hand freezes as my fingertips brush against a piece of thin cardboard in the pocket of a pair of brown Dockers. I pull it out. It's a movie ticket stub. Just one, hardly proof of an affair. Except that I remember sitting at the breakfast table barely a month ago, telling Tony about this exact same movie and asking if we could go see it together. He'd lowered the newspaper far enough to look at me over the top of it, his face puckered up like he was sucking on a lemon drop.

"You know how I feel about those sappy romantic comedies. You couldn't drag me to one."

Now, the ticket stub mocks me. *You couldn't, but she could.*

Ice-cold reality falls on my shoulders, chasing away my need to search for further proof. Now, I'm fueled only by a need to get this over with as soon as possible. Folding and neatly stacking is no longer an issue. I snatch clothes from hangers, wad them up, and toss them into the suitcase. My breath comes faster as T-shirts, old tennis shoes, and a pair of flip-flops encrusted with year-old sand from the last time we ventured to the beach are mixed in with silk ties, cashmere sweaters, and Brooks Brothers shirts. Finally, when the mound in the middle of the suitcase is impossibly high, I smash it all down, swing over the soft lid, and practically sit on top of it to force the zipper closed.

My eyes burn as I pull the case off the bed and let it thud to the floor. I turn to drag it from the room, but stop short when I see Jade. She stands in the doorway, her nose red and lower jaw jutting forward, holding the open bag of M&M's in her hand.

At this point, I have two choices. I can give in to the tears that are pushing against the back of my eyeballs, in which case Jade will most likely lose her composure too, leaving us both emotional, soggy messes. Or I can decide that enough tears have been shed over this situation and begin moving forward.

Abandoning the suitcase, I step up to Jade, pat her cheek, then sink my fingers into the bag of candy. Pulling out a handful, I smile. "Such a wise girl."

5

So you just piled all his things on the porch, eh?"

I nod at Pastor Dave who sits on the other side of his desk, hands clasped over his stomach. Poor man. He looks more than a little stunned after all the information I just dumped on him.

If he thinks hearing about it is bad, he should try living through it.

After Jade and I finished all the packing and stacking yesterday, it struck me that I still hadn't made plans to get me out of the house the next day. It was far too late to start looking for an attorney, let alone make an appointment with one. Which was probably for the best. I hadn't taken the time to consider it before, but it made sense to seek spiritual counsel before sitting down with the legal kind.

I've been a member of Grace Community for fifteen years, and in all that time I haven't asked for much. But this morning, I not only asked, I stooped to bribery. When Sarah, the church secretary, arrived to open up the office she found me standing on the doorstep holding a bag of warm muffins and a full coffee carrier. "I know he's probably super-busy," I said, handing her a cup before she could stutter out a hello, "but I'm in the middle of a crisis. Please, I really need to talk to him."

Sarah is not new to the church secretary gig. She's been doing it long enough to know who's in desperate need and who just craves a little extra attention. I had no doubt that my haggard appearance would telegraph just how dire my situation is. Sure enough, one sympathetic smile later, she ushered me inside the office and told me to have a seat until Pastor Dave got in. Ten minutes after that, he walked through the door, looked at me and my bag of bribes, then asked Sarah, "Do I have some free time this morning?"

Now we sit in his office, our muffins barely touched but our coffee cups drained. Other than the initial "What can I do for you?" he hasn't said much as I spilled out my tale of Tony and the shambles my life has become. Apparently, my pastor can relate to the pain of a man finding his belongings piled up outside the house because this finally gets an audible reaction out of him.

"Do you think I went too far?" I ask.

He purses his lips and moves his head slowly from side to side. "Oh, no, I wouldn't say that. On the topic of taking things too far, Tony is the clear winner."

He's got that right.

"I'm just wondering . . ." His voice trails off. He leans forward and gives the muffin a poke, as if a tactful way to say whatever he's thinking might reside within the banana-nut treat. "This all seems to be moving very quickly."

I sigh and immediately regret making such a weak and hopeless sound. "It feels quick to me, too, but that's because you and I just found out about the whole thing. It's not quick to Tony. He's been living this other life for quite a while."

"And you're absolutely sure you want to give up on reconciliation?"

Am I sure? No, of course I'm not. Marriage is a lifetime commitment. I believed that when I said my vows, and I believe it now, despite Tony's betrayal. If there were a way to fix this, I'd try. I really would. But Tony made it quite clear that he's only interested in moving on, not in repairing our marriage.

"What I want doesn't matter. Tony's made the decision to leave. He's chosen to be with . . . her. And now that she's pregnant—"

Pastor Dave bows his head for a moment. "I remember how you and Tony struggled."

Thanks to my book, *Just the Two of Us: How to Remain Happily Married While Struggling with Infertility*, the whole world knows about it. Of course, that's an exaggeration, but *my* whole world knows the details. More women than I can count, faceless women I'll never meet, have sent me e-mails and letters recalling their own stories and telling me how much the book meant to them. That they would share their hearts in such a raw, open manner touched me, and I wrote back to most of them with encouragement. But Pastor Dave is one of the few people who walked through the actual experience with us.

Tony and I met with him before we started looking into medical treatments. We had so many questions. Were we wrong for doing everything we could to conceive a baby? After all, if God wanted us to be parents, wouldn't He do all the heavy lifting? We truly wanted to know. Pastor Dave prayed with us, asking that we'd feel God's peace and know what to do.

For a week, Tony and I prayed. We prayed together. We prayed on our own. And finally, we both knew we'd gotten an answer from the Lord.

Unfortunately, we didn't get the same answer. Tony felt certain that we needed to do things the old-fashioned way. If God wanted us to have a baby, we would. But Tony was wrong. I was sure of it. We were supposed to do everything we could, follow every medical lead, to have our baby. And we would have a baby. I knew that in the same way I knew how to breathe. We just had to have faith and walk through the wilderness first.

I shared my revelation with Tony. Gently at first. When he didn't come around right away, I became a bit more forceful. I showed him Scripture. I cajoled. I cried. And then I pulled out the biggest gun in my arsenal: the best-selling author and oft-requested teacher gun. If thousands of women turned to me for marital and spiritual guidance, then shouldn't Tony trust me too?

Remembering that now, I'm ashamed of how far I went to get my way. If I hadn't pushed, if I hadn't made us go through endless rounds of tests, shots, taking body temperatures, and making love to a schedule, would things have turned out the same? If I hadn't made my husband feel like I heard God and he didn't, maybe he wouldn't have stopped talking to God completely.

Pastor Dave knows about all of it. He knows that after the final round of in vitro, the one when the doctor essentially pronounced us a lost cause, Tony pulled back from the church. He stopped going to the men's group. He suddenly had to work more on the weekends than ever before. And when he did attend Sunday services with me, he was sullen and withdrawn the rest of the day. I'm sure Pastor Dave's made the connection, but he's kind enough now not to bring it up. Instead, he tends to my wounds.

"This woman's pregnancy," he says, "has to be the unkind-est cut of all."

"You know, it is." My nose tingles and tears start to leak from the corners of my eyes, but I don't care. "It would be bad enough if he was just leaving me for another woman. But to leave me for another woman and *their baby* . . . there's no going back after that."

Pastor Dave reaches behind him for a box of Kleenex, which he then sets in front of me. I pluck two tissues from the top when I hear him mutter under his breath, "Dirty dog."

My hand freezes in midair. I can't believe my loving, even-keeled pastor has just called my philandering husband a dog. As I stare, the hint of a blush colors the skin around his ears. "Sorry about that. My pastor hat fell off for a second."

I burst into this crazy sort of half-laughing, half-crying sound punctuated by a hiccup. After mopping up my face and blowing my nose, I muster a smile. "Thanks. I needed to laugh at something."

"Glad to be of help. But we both need to remember that no matter how heinous Tony's actions are he's still a child of God. He still needs our prayers. Now more than ever."

"You're going to have to handle that part, Pastor. I'm doing all I can to hold myself together."

"I'm sure it's the last thing you want to think about now, but forgiveness is a vital component of your own healing process. Eventually, you're going to have to forgive Tony."

He's absolutely right. Forgiveness is vital. It's the corner-stone of my faith. Not only have I studied it in the Bible, I've taught it too. How many times have I stood in front of women's groups and encouraged them to let go of the hurt and anger from their pasts? Told them unforgiveness is a poison that will eat away at their souls? Too many times to count. It's one of my most popular speaking topics. And now, it's one more thing Tony has destroyed. Because how can I teach others to do something I can't do myself?

6

When I pull back into my driveway, Jade is waiting for me on the porch, a porch that is now completely empty of everything but the white wicker rocker in which she sits. My stomach does a little flip beneath my seat belt. Did Tony pick up his things, or did he send someone else to do it? Was *she* with him? I cut the engine and shake my head hard. No, even Tony wouldn't be that insensitive. Still, it's probably better not to ask. I don't even want to know the details. I want to move on as if nothing out of the ordinary happened today.

I exit the car, sling my purse over my shoulder, and plaster on a big smile as I walk up the porch stairs.

"Was he here?" The question pushes past all my good intentions and posturing. I'm pathetic.

Jade looks up at me and nods. "Yes, he was."

I bite my lip and look at where the boxes used to be. I can't stop myself. "Did he . . . was she . . ."

From the expression on Jade's face, I think she's trying to decide whether to slap some sense into me or hug me. Thankfully, she does neither. "No. He was alone." Her mouth twists to the side. "And I made him do all the work. Didn't help him load a single thing."

"Good for you."

"Yoo-hoo!" A bright voice calls from the end of the drive-way. Shading my eyes, I see my retired next-door neighbor waving as she nears the porch.

Forcing a smile, I wave back. "Hi, Mrs. Hernandez. How are you?"

"I'm well. But how are you, dear?" Her voice is earnest, and I immediately know she saw Tony pick up his things today. "I saw the boxes this morning, and I said to myself, I certainly hope they're not moving away. Such a nice young couple."

"No, we're not moving. At least, I'm not." Is this how it's going to be from now on? Fumbling for the right words to answer well-meaning questions? "Tony's moving. We're getting a divorce."

There's no reproach in her eyes. No judgment. Only genuine sadness. "I'm so sorry to hear that. I'll leave you alone, then. But if you need anything, anything at all, dear, you let me know." She gives my arm a gentle pat, then walks back down my driveway and up her own.

"That's it," I say, squeezing the back of my neck with one hand. "Now the whole neighborhood will hear about it."

Jade cranes her neck, watching as Mrs. Hernandez shuffles down the sidewalk, up her walkway, and into her own house. "You think she's going to gossip about you?"

"No, not gossip. But people talk." Mrs. Hernandez is one of the nicest women I know. She's also the very definition of a social butterfly. I imagine at her next Red Hat Society outing, or over coffee with friends, someone will say how sad it is that people can't seem to stay married anymore, and she'll mention the nice couple who lives next door. She won't share my story to be malicious. She may even ask people to pray for me. But the word will spread just the same.

Jade stands up and I notice a large, brown envelope wedged between the side of the rocker and the seat cushion. Happy to change the subject, I point at it. "What's that?"

Her eyes follow my finger. "Oh, man. I forgot about that." She plucks it up with two fingers and holds it out to me. "I really wish I wasn't the one giving you this."

"What is it?" The question is unnecessary. There's no doubt what's in the envelope, and I don't want to take it yet. I just look at it hanging in midair between us.

Jade's head flops to the side. "He didn't tell me, but I think it's pretty obvious. What else could it be?"

Indeed. It can only be one thing. Divorce papers.

Natalie Marino, thank you for playing the Marriage Game. Sorry you didn't win, but here's your consolation prize.

I take the envelope, pull up the flap, and look inside without bothering to remove the contents. Enough of the first few lines are visible that I confirm they are indeed divorce papers.

"He didn't waste any time, did he?"

"Neither did I." Clearly, Jade is done talking about Tony. "I found you a divorce attorney of your own."

"You did?"

"Yes. And she comes highly recommended."

"By whom?" Jade is twenty-two years old. Her parents have been married for almost thirty years. I doubt she runs into many divorce attorneys in her day-to-day comings and goings.

She looks at me like I'm mental. "Uh, by my best friend's mom. And by her sister. And her sister's best friend. And—"

I hold up my hand. I get it. She knows a family whose relationship issues have probably paid for this lawyer's summer home. "What do you know about her? The attorney, I mean."

Jade crooks her finger, motioning for me to follow. As we walk into the house, she keeps talking. "Her name is Wendy Willows."

"Sounds like a stripper."

Jade glares at me over her shoulder.

"Sorry. Gut reaction. Humor as a defense mechanism, you know." We've made it to the living room where I collapse onto the couch. "Continue."

She sits in a deep-red, wingback chair. When Tony and I found it in a thrift store years ago, it was threadbare, but it worked for our first apartment. After it got too ratty, we made a slipcover for it out of a bed sheet. When we bought this house, the chair stayed in the garage until I had it reupholstered and presented it to Tony as an anniversary present. Huh. I wonder if he looked for it amid the stack of his possessions on the porch. It never crossed my mind until now that he might have wanted it.

Too bad if he did. Let him find his own chair.

The coffee table is strewn with papers. Jade picks one up off the top. "Ms. Willows is a highly regarded lawyer. And not just by my friend's mom. I Googled her, checked her background and her references. She's known for being ethical and doing extremely well by her clients."

"Is she Christian?"

"I didn't ask. But she's *ethical*. That's the most important thing. I'd hate to find you a Christian lawyer with an ethics problem. And I'm sure there are a few of those out there."

Excellent point. And I'm sure she's right. Just because someone calls himself a Christian doesn't mean he acts like one. Not if husbands are any indication.

"Besides, if she's not a Christian, you can always witness to her. Consider it a bonus."

A bonus for whom? Right now, I don't feel like I could lead anyone to salvation from sunburn, let alone eternal salvation. "I'm sure Ms. Willows will do a fine job. Go ahead and make me an appointment with her."

"I already did."

Jade digs her phone out of her pocket and starts tapping on the screen. "It's set for Thursday at 9:30 a.m." Her eyes scrunch tighter and tighter as they follow her finger up and down the phone screen. Then she stops and mutters, "Uh-oh."

I hate *uh-oh*. "What?"

"You've got a speaking engagement tonight."

Uh-oh.

7

Usually, I take all day to prepare for a speaking event. I'll pray for the people I'm going to speak to. I'll ask God to give me the right words to say. I'll go over my notes, even if I know my topic backward and forward, which I usually do. And I'll start getting dressed and made up at least two hours before it's time to leave, because I know I'll change my mind about what to wear more than once.

Those are all the things I do. Now, for all the things I don't do: I don't eat any rich or heavy foods; I don't skimp on sleep the night before; and above all else, I don't engage in any high-stress activities prior to the event.

I am in such trouble today.

It's three in the afternoon when Jade finds the forgotten notation: *Mt. Olive Marriage & Family Conference, 6:00 p.m.*

Jade jumps to her feet. "Don't panic. There's plenty of time."

"Plenty of time?" My voice squeals like rubber-soled shoes on a linoleum floor. "It starts in three hours." Jade's got me by the arm now and is dragging me across the room and up the stairs. "I need to shower, and get dressed, and—" I stop dead in my tracks. "What town is it in?"

Jade puts on a big smile, like she's about to tell me something fabulous. "Santa Monica."

"Santa Monica? That's at least an hour's drive. More if the traffic's bad."

"Piece of cake," she says as she tugs on my arm again.

Who's she kidding? This is Southern California. The traffic's always bad. I follow her, muttering the whole way. "I'm never going to make it. How did this happen? How could I forget?"

"You've had a lot on your mind the last few days." We're in the bathroom now. Jade leans into the shower and turns on the water. "I should have remembered though. I can't believe I slipped up like that."

I'm in a daze. "You're right. You should have remembered. Why didn't you?"

She gives me an are-you-serious? look, then wiggles her fingers under the faucet, testing the water temperature. "You can fire me later. Right now, I'm going to get you to your event." Hands on my shoulders, she speaks directly toward my nose. "I want you to take the quickest shower ever. No dawdling."

She leaves the bathroom and pulls the door shut behind her. I immediately hear the sound of plastic hangers squeaking across the closet bar and clunking together as she rummages around. I continue standing there, frozen by the immensity of the task at hand, until she calls through the door. "Are you in the shower?"

I jump like a little girl who's been caught playing with her mother's makeup. Fast as I can, I strip off my clothes, step gingerly beneath the spray of water, and then call out my answer. "Yes!"

Just under five minutes later, I stand on the bath mat with a towel wrapped tightly around me. Water drips from my hair, running in rivulets down my bare shoulders, as my teeth chatter. There are two staccato raps on the door, then it opens and Jade's head pops through. "Good. You're out."

Without waiting for an answer, she walks in, grabs a dry towel from the rack, and starts rubbing it over my hair. "I put your clothes out for you on the bed," she says.

"You did? Don't I have anything to say about it?"

"Believe me, right now, you don't need choices."

Good point. Jade's much more stylish than I am anyway. I'm sure whatever she picked out will be fine. The most important thing is to get to this event on time. After that, I can go on autopilot and it should be smooth sailing the rest of the way.

❧

Jade gets me to the church on time, but just barely. She pulls up to the back entrance and tells me to go in ahead. As she drives away to find a parking spot, I feel a moment of panic, akin to an unwanted kitten dropped on a stranger's doorstep. But panic quickly turns to damage control when a woman dressed in a long, brown, cotton dress swoops out of the building and runs up to me.

"Mrs. Marino?" Her eyes are hopeful, but at my nodded agreement, they turn stony and reproachful. "You're late."

Words catch in my throat. "I . . . I'm supposed to speak at six."

"That's right, which means I have two minutes to get you inside, put on your mic, and make sure you're ready." The corners of her mouth pull down severely. "You *are* ready, aren't you?"

"Absolutely." Not.

She pulls me inside and we go through a zigzag of corridors to what I assume is the church office. A bearded man with headphones ringing his neck descends on me as soon as I'm through the door.

"You've used one of these before, right?" He clips a tiny microphone to my lapel, then looks toward my waist, mic-pack in hand.

I nod and take the pack from him. "Let me take care of that." I clip it to the waistband of my pants, far enough back so it's hidden by my jacket. Performing this simple act, something I've done countless times before, provides an oddly calming effect. Maybe I can survive this night, after all.

"Thanks." The man gives me an encouraging smile, then adds, "Nice blouse. Great color."

Before I have a chance to respond, the woman in the brown dress has me by the arm again. "It's time." She leads me across the room. "Good luck," she says. With a final pat on my shoulder, she goes up a small set of stairs, opens a door, and stands back. Now I can hear what's being spoken through the sound system.

" . . . like to introduce tonight's main speaker. She's a nationally acclaimed author and an expert on marriage and family relations. Please welcome Mrs. Natalie Marino."

I have time for one quick prayer. *Lord, get me through this.* Then I plaster on a smile, climb the stairs, and walk out onto the platform. I give a hearty handshake to the man who introduced me, turn to the crowd in the sanctuary, and keep that smile plastered on my face, even as women turn to whisper to one another. The applause sputters a bit, and I make a horrific discovery.

I am the only woman in the room wearing slacks.

Well, that's not exactly true. Jade—who stands behind the last row of pews and mouths the words *I'm sorry*—is also wearing pants. Jeans, to be exact.

At least my slacks are extremely nice. They're black crepe and part of a tailored, two-piece set that I wear with a hot pink silk shell. I've been told the color is a perfect complement to my skin tone and hair. Which would be great, if it weren't the brightest color in the room. No wonder the soundman noticed it.

Turns out, the ladies of Mt. Olive Congregational adhere strictly to the Scriptures about modesty. And hair length. And keeping your head covered. Without thinking, my hand goes to the top of my naked head and ruffles the layers of my short, sassy hairstyle.

This isn't the first time I've spoken to a group with dress and grooming standards different from my own. Normally, it's no problem. They don't expect me to mirror them, but I try to be sensitive. If I'd had time to think about tonight, I would have chosen a simple dress in a muted tone, and I probably would have covered my hair with a hat or a head scarf. I certainly wouldn't have worn the brightest, silkiest top I own, acting like I don't care about their traditions.

I feel like an idiot.

"Thank you." The words fall away as soon as they leave my mouth, and I realize I didn't turn on the microphone. I flip a switch on the pack on my hip and repeat myself. "Thank you!" This time, my greeting blasts through the room. I smile and motion for everyone to sit down.

An opposing movement in the rear of the sanctuary catches my eye. A young woman with dark streaks of burgundy dyeing her blond hair is headed toward the back door. She reminds me a bit of my sister, Lindsay, except that Lindsay wouldn't waste her time in a church. Especially a church that had invited me as a speaker. There's a sad twinge in the pit of my stomach as the door swings shut behind the woman. I don't know if it's because she made me think of my sister, whom I haven't seen

in years, or because she was a kindred spirit in her apprecia-
tion of color, but I wish she hadn't gone.

Once the audience is seated, I launch into my talk.
Thankfully, I've spoken on the topic of marriage so many
times, it's like turning on a faucet: I open my mouth and the
words pour out. My initial misgivings about how this group
would receive me were way off the mark. They listen intently,
laugh at my jokes, and take notes of key points. Eventually,
I'm comfortable enough to venture out from behind the safety
of the podium. If my slacks and bright shirt continue to give
them pause, they certainly don't show it.

This is turning out to be a good evening, after all. We've
all learned something about judging others by appearances or
doctrine. I feel I've made great strides in the area of interfaith
relationships.

"And now," I say with a big smile, "I'll open it up to questions. Is there anything you want to know?"

In the back, Jade stands up and shakes her head, her eyes
wide as Frisbees. She obviously thinks the Q&A is a bad idea.
But it's too late to take it back now.

I point at the first person I notice with her hand raised.
"Yes?"

A woman in a dark blue dress stands up. "I have four children, and I feel like I'm always doing things for them.
Sometimes, I think my husband feels . . . left out." She smiles
shyly, a blush coloring her cheeks. "How can I take care of the
house and the kids and still see to his needs?"

A fire ignites in my gut. As the woman sits down, I think of
the answer I'd like to give her: *how can you see to his needs? Well,
sometimes you can't. Because sometimes he needs someone younger
and more fertile than you are, and there's nothing you can do about
it. You won't even see it coming.*

But I can't say that. Instead, I walk back behind the podium and lean on it for strength. "I find that organization is a key factor in a happy marriage and a happy family." I talk about calendars and schedules, a place for everything and everything in its place, and the wonders of Post-it Notes. There's truth to my words, but it's dry and boring, and not at all what these women came to hear. They want to know something that's going to make a difference in their lives. They want to know how to hold onto the spark they experienced when they were dating. They want to know that when they leave here tonight, the man they left at home will still be there, waiting for them. And that he'll be there the next night, and the next.

They want hope and romance. I'm giving them the kind of tips you'd give an office manager.

I take a deep breath and force on my smile again. "But the most important thing you can do is tell him you love him." Murmurs of agreement and nodding heads encourage me to continue. "No matter how crazy life gets, you must keep the lines of communication open with your spouse. Ask him about his day. Go for a walk and hold hands. Pray together. If your hearts are knit together, everything else will fall into place."

What a pretty sentiment. I even sound like I believe it.

More hands wave in the air, but before I can pick one out, a woman in the third row stands up. "Is it true that your husband filed for divorce yesterday?"

The room becomes so quiet that for a moment, I fear I've gone deaf. Then the buzzing starts in my ears. I don't know what to say, so I do the worst thing possible and ask, "Excuse me?"

She's more than happy to repeat herself. "Did your husband file for divorce yesterday?"

How does she even know to ask that question? I take a close look at her. At first glance, I thought she was wearing a long, black dress, but now I see it's a long, black tunic over black leggings. From the waist up, she could almost pass for one of the Mt. Olive ladies, if not for the digital microrecorder she holds in her manicured, blood-red taloned fingers.

She's a reporter.

"I'm sorry, but how—"

"How did I know? All divorce cases are part of the public record." She glances at the women around her. "So I guess I don't really need to ask you if he filed for divorce. We know he did. The real question is why?"

"That's none of your business." I look to Jade for help. She's talking to two men and pointing. They leave her and walk down the center aisle toward the reporter.

The reporter glances back and, realizing her time is nearly up, gets out another zinger. "I think it is my business. You claim to be an expert on marriage, but your own just fell apart. I think you owe me, and all these ladies, an explanation."

When the men reach her pew, they exchange a few quiet words, then she exits without a fuss. They follow her back up the aisle and out the rear door. The whisper of voices swirling around the sanctuary picks up speed. Left unchecked, it will be a roar of confusion. The reporter was right about one thing. I've spent the last hour with these women, giving them advice about keeping a happy home. I owe them the truth. Or at least part of it.

I hold up my hands, motioning for silence. "It's true, my husband filed for divorce yesterday. It was his choice, not mine."

"Why?" A voice calls from the crowd.

How much should I say? How much will that reporter be putting in her story? If the divorce is public record, isn't the rest of my life, too? "He had an affair. That's all I want to say about that."

What I really want to do is leave the podium, but another voice calls out, angry and accusing. "How could you come here tonight?"

It's the wrong reaction, but I laugh. "Because I thought I was doing the right thing."

"By lying?"

"No, by keeping my commitment." Now I'm angry. Angry at the reporter for outing me. Angry at Tony for not keeping his commitments. Angry at these women for judging me. And angry at myself for everything else. "You're right, I shouldn't have come. But by the time I remembered I had this event, it was too late to cancel."

There's a collective gasp as every woman in the room makes the next logical leap: if I forgot about the event, then I forgot about the people too. Now it's become an even more personal affront.

Jade is on her way up the side aisle. She probably hopes she can pull me off the stage before I say anything else I'll regret. But she's not walking fast enough. My mind is already whirling, trying to come up with some way to repair the damage.

I fall back on my old standby: humor.

"I guess now you understand why I'm dressed this way. If I'd had more time to think about it, I would have dug out my funeral clothes from the back of the closet."

Now I've done it. A few women stand up to leave. Jade is running. She vaults up the stairs to the platform and grabs my arm. "Thank you all for coming!" she yells to the audience. "God bless you!" And she drags me back through the office.

"I'm sorry," I mutter. "I never meant to insult anybody. I just wanted to make a joke, to lighten the mood. But it's hard to be funny when you just found out your husband's been banging his assistant and now she's pregnant and—"

"Turn it off! Turn it off!" The woman who greeted me upon my arrival runs into the room. "The mic is still on. They can hear everything you're saying!"

"I'm so sorry." I pull the pack from my waistband and the mic from my lapel. Before I turn it off, I put it to my mouth and say one more time, loudly, "I'm so sorry."

I hand it to the soundman, who has the good grace not to say anything. Then I turn to the woman, ready to apologize again. But the most amazing thing happens. Her face softens, transformed by compassion. Patting my shoulder, she says, "We'll be praying for you, dear."

There's actually sympathy in her eyes. I don't know if it's for my dead marriage or my ruined career, but she and I both know I shouldn't expect to be booked for more speaking engagements anytime soon.

8

Jade and I don't speak as we get in her car and drive away. It's pointless, really. I mean, what is there to say? We both know I've just kissed my career good-bye.

In the world of motivational speakers, particularly Christian ones, there is a very active communication system. It will probably go something like this: one of the ladies at tonight's event undoubtedly works in the church office. During casual conversation tomorrow, she'll mention the debacle to the pastor. He in turn will use it as a funny anecdote when talking to a colleague over lunch. Said colleague will share it with his wife, who realizes that her friend—a pastor's wife at a church in the next town—mentioned booking me for their ladies' convention. She'll call her up to double check that I am indeed the scheduled speaker, and to suggest that perhaps they might want to rescind the invitation. For the good of all concerned, of course.

Good news may travel fast, but scandal rides a bullet train. Between the old-fashioned gossip network and the reporter, I fully expect a slew of cancellations within the next few days. But just in case . . .

"You'd better go through my calendar and cancel everything."

Jade exhales a breath so deep, I wonder how long she's been holding it in. "Are you sure?"

"Positive."

She balls her fingers into a fist and pounds the side of the steering wheel. "I don't get it. Tony's the one who did everything wrong, so why did that reporter go after you?"

"Because it's my name on all the books."

"Well, it's not fair."

"No, it's not." I look at Jade. She keeps her eyes on the road, her bottom lip clenched between her teeth and her jaw jutting forward. Poor thing. This is almost as hard on her as it is on me. And I know she's blaming herself for most of what happened tonight. I really should say something to her, something comforting and wise.

Bad things happen to good people.

We live in a fallen world.

When life gives you lemons . . .

I turn away from Jade and press my forehead against the glass of the passenger-side window. All I have are clichés and worn-out platitudes. What makes me think I have anything worthwhile left to share with anybody?

Did I ever? Or has my entire life to this point been one giant mistake?

Still, I've got to try. For Jade's sake.

"It's not your fault," I tell her. "None of it."

"What?" She sounds completely befuddled, as if the thought had never occurred to her. "I know it's not."

"Oh. Well, you were so deep in thought. I just assumed—"

Jade barks out a laugh. "You assumed I was berating myself. I probably should be after tonight, but I wasn't. I'm not nearly as nice a person as you are, Nat."

"Then what was going through your mind?"

The corner of her mouth quirks up. "I was thinking of all the ways to inflict pain on Tony without leaving any visible evidence."

Jade wanted to come inside with me once she got me home, but I wouldn't let her. "I just want to go straight to bed," I told her. What I really wanted was to go straight to the freezer, but she didn't need to know that.

"Okay," she agreed, even though I could tell she didn't want to. "But I'll be back tomorrow at ten. We'll do damage control."

I nodded, waved good-bye, closed the door behind her, then ran to the kitchen. I pulled open the freezer door and—crud. No ice cream.

Which is why I now find myself standing in front of the freezer section of the closest 7-Eleven, trying to decide which flavor of overpriced ice cream would be the best balm for my bruised ego. Jade's words from earlier this evening replay in my mind: *the last thing you need right now are choices.* How true.

My fingers are half-numb by the time I get my selections to the counter. The cashier takes one look at my four pints of Ben & Jerry's and shakes his head. "Hard night, huh?"

"You have no idea."

"I hope you're not driving."

"Don't worry. I live just a few blocks away."

After the shock of seeing my total pop up on the register, I pay the man. "Want this?" He holds up a plastic-wrapped spork.

I shake my head and wonder how many women he's seen slinking in under the cover of darkness for a sugar fix. "I can control myself until I get home."

He puts the ice cream in a plastic bag and hands it to me, but when I grab it, he doesn't let go right away. Before he does, he says, "He's a jerk, you know."

"Who?"

"Whoever drove you to this."

The young man is just that . . . young. Probably a college freshman. He could be my much-younger brother. Which makes his kindness even sweeter.

"Have a good night." A tiny smile settles on my lips and stays there as I walk out to the car. Tossing my snack-stash on the seat beside me, I feel a surge of satisfaction. Maybe I won't even need to eat any of it. Maybe it was enough just to leave the house by myself. It's almost as if I took control of my destiny and was greeted by an affirmative soul.

I snap on my seat belt and start up the engine. Maybe things are going to be okay after all. But then I push the button on the radio. Big mistake. "Just the Two of Us" blares through the speakers, transporting me back to my wedding day. Tony and I are dancing, our first dance as man and wife. His cheek is warm against mine, and his breath caresses my neck as he croons the song in my ear. Just the two of us, he promised. You and I.

A sob forces its way out of my throat. I drop my head in my hands, but misjudge the distance in this small space and accidentally push against the horn. Jumping back, I say something not at all nice to myself. I have got to pull myself together. I'm acting like an idiot.

I turn off the radio and close my eyes, trying to collect my thoughts. It's not until a minute later that I realize I've ripped the lid off a container of Half Baked and am holding it beneath my nose. Just the aroma starts to calm me. Something moves in the distance. I look up and through the store's front window-wall I can see the cashier. He's looking right at me, wiggling the spork in the air.

My mouth twists into a sheepish grimace and I shake my head. Great, here's something else that's been ruined. I'll never be able to come back to this store again. My emergency junk food source has just been cut off.

With a sigh, I back out of the parking space, gun the engine, and beat a hasty retreat away from the store and back to my empty house.

9

When Jade arrives the next day, she finds me sitting at the kitchen table nursing a mug of green tea and nibbling on saltine crackers.

She immediately frowns and shakes her head. "You fell off the wagon again, didn't you?"

"I didn't fall off. I dove."

"What was it this time?"

"Ben & Jerry's."

She perks up. "Is there any left?"

I wave at the fridge. "Deliver me from temptation." The thought of eating ice cream right now makes my stomach turn in on itself. "Leave me the Vanilla Caramel Fudge, though." Just in case.

A minute later, she's sitting at the table with me, digging her spoon into the ice cream. She savors it, and I can't help thinking of the injustice of it all. She could eat that entire pint without affecting her athletic build. Not me. After what I ate last night, even my bathrobe feels tight.

"I got up early and did some research about that reporter," she says.

"How did you find her?"

"I did Google searches until I dug up the article."

Groaning, I drop my forehead against my crossed arms on the table. "Oh, no. She already wrote something that was published. What did it say?"

Jade shakes the spoon at me. "That doesn't matter. What does matter is that she's a local reporter who writes for one of those Internet article data banks. I wouldn't even call her a reporter. More a writer of local human interest stories."

Jade can call her what she wants, the woman is still reporting information. But it's some small comfort that she's not a staffer for the *Los Angeles Times*. "People can still read what she wrote."

"Sure, if they know where to find it. The question is how many people will try to find it?"

I don't want to venture a guess. "I appreciate you finding all that out. But I still think it's best to cancel all my upcoming events."

"That's what I figured. So I started calling people this morning." She opens the paper planning calendar I force her to keep—despite protests that it's a duplicate of the information on her phone—and pushes it toward me. There are about fifteen appointments written into the month of May. Only five of them don't have a big red X scrawled across them.

"Are those the ones that still want me to come?" Maybe people are more understanding than I expected. Maybe there's hope.

"No. Those are the ones I couldn't get hold of. I don't want to leave any details on voice mail, so I need to call them back."

"I see." I take a bite of my cracker and it falls apart in my fingers, showering crumbs on the front of my robe. Could I be any more pitiful?

"Don't let it get you down." Jade finishes one more spoon of ice cream, then slaps the top back on the carton. "Even if a place still wanted you to come, I canceled the event."

"Why?"

"Because you need some time for yourself. Period." She gets up, puts the pint back in the freezer, and drops the spoon in the sink.

"So there really were places that still wanted me to come?"

"Oh, sure."

"How many?"

She hesitates, then sits and pulls the planner back toward her. "At least one. It was . . . " Her voice trails off into a flat hum as she moves her finger across the pages. "This one!"

I lean over and look at the box she's jabbing. My heart sinks. "That one doesn't count."

"Why not?"

"That's my church."

"Oh. Yeah."

When I sold my first book, Tony and I were living in a one-bedroom apartment with two dead bolts and a chain on the door. We celebrated the signing of my contract by walking to McDonald's and getting hot fudge sundaes. "This is just the beginning," he said to me. "I'm so proud of you." Then he smiled, reached across the table, and rubbed his thumb over the corner of my mouth. "Mmm, chocolate." As he put his thumb to his own lips, my insides went all warm and mushy. We finished our sundaes in a hurry, then went back home, where we continued the celebration.

That day, I felt like the entire world was spread out in front of us. We were on a great adventure, Tony and me. We had each other, and soon we would have success in our careers. It never occurred to me then that I could lose it all in the course of a week.

I pull the calendar in front of me and flip the pages, looking at months of booked dates that haven't been crossed out yet. Even if they still want me, how can I go to any of these events and speak to women about being fulfilled and happy in marriage when I don't even know what that means anymore?

The answer is crystal clear: I can't. Like it or not, this part of my life is now over. I can either crawl back in bed with another pint of ice cream, or I can do something positive. *Which is it going to be?*

"Cancel everything," I tell Jade.

"Everything?"

There is so much substance wrapped up in that little word. I nod slowly. "Yes. Everything."

She closes the book and pulls it to her chest. "And what are you going to do?"

I stand up, dust off the front of my robe, and let the crumbs fall to the floor. "I'm going to start from scratch."

⸉⸌⸍

Sometimes, a girl needs her daddy. Even if the girl is just this side of forty and her daddy lives halfway across the country.

"How's my Sugar Plum?" I snuggle into the cushions of the couch and close my eyes as his deep voice rumbles through the phone line and wraps around me in an audible hug. My mother told me he started calling me that when I was two years old and I'd twirl and twirl whenever they put on Tchaikovsky's "Dance of the Sugar Plum Fairy." I don't remember it, but I like the idea of a time when all it took to make me happy was an open space and pretty music.

"Well, Dad, I've been better."

Instead of responding, he gives me the open space I need, and I pour out the whole story. I manage to get through it without crying. We even laugh a little when I tell him about the convenience store clerk waving the spork in the air. But then, when I have nothing left to say, he lets out a deep sigh.

"Honey, I'm so sorry."

"Yeah. Me too." My spirit is still bruised and battered, but I feel a strange sense of relief. As though the mere act of sharing my burdens with my father has lightened them somehow. "I don't suppose you have some incredibly sage advice for me, do you?"

"Absolutely." His response is so immediate he must have been waiting for me to ask. "Come home."

"Home? To Illinois?"

"Why not? It's been too long since we've seen you."

My dad's not the kind to play the guilt card, so I know that's not his motive. Still, the emotion gnaws at me. I meant to go back for a visit last Christmas, but a big event came up and I couldn't get away. Just like the year before. And the year before that. It's amazing how quickly *next time* turns into *you haven't been home in nearly four years.*

"I'd love to, Dad, but . . ." But what? Tony's schedule and the fact that he wants me to be with him no longer apply. I just told Jade to cancel all my existing speaking events. There isn't even a doctor's appointment on my calendar. All the buts are gone.

"It would mean a lot to me." He clears his throat before continuing. "Natalie, there's something you need to know about your mother."

No. Not more bad news. "What?"

"She's getting worse."

My mother has Alzheimer's, so *worse* is not something she'll rebound from. "What's going on?"

"She's been forgetting people's names. People she's known for years. And she's been blanking out on familiar tasks. The other day, I found her sitting on the couch, staring at the TV remote. She had no idea which buttons to push."

My throat constricts. "With all the buttons on the new remotes, anybody would get confused."

"Honey," he says gently, "she's the one who taught me to use it in the first place."

"Oh, Dad." My mind whirls, trying to reconcile what he's telling me with memories of the sharp woman I knew. Yes, she was always a bit on the forgetful side when it came to things like where she left her keys, but she never forgot a face. When we'd look at photo albums, she could rattle off the names of every person in every picture, even if she'd only met them once.

One of her favorite pictures was the one taken when I was a week old. "Four generations of Tuttle women," she'd say. Mom is sitting on a bench, holding me in her arms. Her mother stands behind her, looking over her shoulder and down at me. And next to Mother on the bench is her grandmother, my great-grandmother. But instead of looking at me, she's staring straight at the camera, her brows furrowed, as if she's trying to remember something.

My grandmother had Alzheimer's, and that picture always made me suspect my great-grandmother had it too, even though she was never diagnosed. Still, despite the family history, I never considered it might also happen to my mother. When she was diagnosed, I refused to believe it. To acknowledge that it really was happening to her made it more real that, one day, it might also happen to me. But it looks like I can't deny it anymore.

"I really think you should visit her soon."

While she still remembers who you are. He doesn't have to say it for me to get the message. "You're right. This is the perfect time for me to come."

"Wonderful. If only I could convince your sister."

"You've talked to Lindsay?" Not only have I not seen my sister in years, I don't even know where she lives. For reasons I've never understood, Lindsay does not like me. But when she stopped communicating with me, I just assumed it extended to the whole family.

"She calls every now and then. I spoke to her a few weeks ago."

Apparently, I was wrong. "Oh."

"I told her what was going on with your mother, but she won't come."

"Why?"

"She absolutely refuses to get on a plane."

I snort into the phone. "She's probably just afraid of running into me."

"Now, Natalie." His voice is reproachful, but in a kind way. "You know your sister loves you."

No, I really don't. But there's no use making Dad feel worse. "I'm sorry she won't come. If I knew where she was, I'd get her myself and bring her to you."

"You would?" Dad's voice goes up a decibel. "Sugar Plum, that would be wonderful."

What is he talking about? I was just making a grandiose gesture, something to make him feel better. Like saying, "I'd give you the moon on a silver platter." No one really expects you to do that, but they're awfully happy when you say it.

"Well, if I *could*, sure. But I don't even know where she's living now."

"I do. In fact, she doesn't live far from you. Hold on." I hear papers rustling in the background, the muffled scrape of the mouthpiece rubbing against his chin. "Ah, here we go. She lives in Santa Monica."

After my fiasco at Mt. Olive Community Church, I doubt the wisdom of venturing back into Santa Monica, especially to retrieve my prodigal sister. But Dad is so excited. How am I going to get out of this?

"Wow, that is close. But if she won't fly, how am I supposed to get her home?"

"Well," he pulls the word back like a rubber band before it's shot, "you could drive."

"Drive? All the way to Illinois?"

He laughs. "It could be fun. There's nothing like a road trip to give you lots of time to clear the cobwebs from your mind. You said yourself, you've got the time."

Zap! His words sail at me, landing square between my eyes. Talk about a sneak attack. I've just been cornered into taking a road trip with my sister.

Either God has a twisted sense of humor, or I've been cursed. Possibly both.

10

Wendy Willows is, thankfully, nothing like her stripper-sounding name. She's probably in her fifties, although she could pass for mid-forties. Her wheat-colored hair is pulled back into a neat chignon, not severe enough to be scary, but practical enough to inspire confidence. And her navy blue, impeccably tailored suit probably cost more than all the clothes in my closet combined.

I sit on the other side of her desk, watching her skim the divorce papers from Tony. She holds a gold Cross pen, and alternates from running the end of it down the document to pressing it against the corner of her mouth. I wonder if, in the days before she became the high-powered attorney she is, she would have chewed on the end of her plastic stick pen.

"There's no mention of children." Her statement intrudes on my daydreaming. "I take it you don't have any."

"No. We don't. But not for lack of trying." The laugh that comes out of me is so fake, it makes me cringe.

Wendy flashes me a quick, sympathetic smile. "At a time like this, it's actually a blessing. Makes it much easier for us to work out a settlement."

Of course, if we'd had children, there might not be a time like this. But why argue?

"Have you read over this yourself?"

I shake my head. "No. I started to, but it didn't make much sense. I was hoping you would break it down into simple English."

"That's what I'm here for." She pushes her glasses higher up on her nose and leans back in her chair. "It's pretty straightforward. He's not asking for anything crazy, like spousal support. Essentially, he wants a clean split of the assets."

"That sounds . . . fair." Funny how I can't say the word *fair* without it sticking in my throat.

"What about alimony?"

"I don't want it."

Her pen hovers over a notepad on her desk. "Are you sure?"

"Positive." This is something I've already thought about. Over the years, Tony and I both contributed financially to our household. For a while, he made more money than I did. Then, after my books took off, I made more than him. Then, when he became a partner in the architecture firm, we were about even. So a half-and-half split of our current savings and retirement accounts is only right. But I certainly don't want to be tied to Tony after this fiasco is over, even if it's only through a monthly alimony payment. What I'm not sure about is how I'm going to earn a living going forward. But that's a whole other issue.

"Okay." Wendy's pen glides smoothly across the paper. "Then the only major hurdle will be selling the house. After that—"

"The house? I don't want to sell the house."

"But he does. It's right here." She flips a few pages and starts reading. "Both parties agree to sell the property located at 529 West Oak. Profits to be split evenly."

"But it's my house."

Wendy's eyebrows lift. "Is the deed in your name alone?"

"No. It's in both our names, but . . ." *But he's the one who left.* "It's my home."

"I'm sorry. But if you own the home jointly, he has every right to make this request."

"Can we contest it?"

"Yes, of course. But it will slow things down considerably."

Smug satisfaction coils around me. I'm in no hurry to move on to someone else. He's the one who wants to play house with a new partner. Why should I make this easy on him?

I lean forward in my seat, feeling in control for the first time in weeks. "Contest it."

―――――∞∞∞―――――

On the way home from Wendy's office, I stop at an Automobile Club office. I haven't talked to Lindsay yet, but I figure it's best to have everything planned out before I tell her what a great idea this trip is.

When it's finally my turn, a gal named Alice calls me up to the front desk. As soon as I tell her I need road maps to get me to Illinois, she lights up.

"Oh, do you want to take a trip down the Mother Road?"

"The what?"

"The Mother Road. Route 66. Just a sec."

She scurries away and starts pulling maps and books out of a cubby against the far wall. Of course, I know what Route 66 is. I grew up at one end of it and now live at the other. It just never occurred to me to take the old highway home. I was thinking more along the lines of four-lane freeways with comfy hotels right off the exits.

Alice comes back and dumps her armload on the counter in front of me. "Now, you can't drive the whole thing from start to finish anymore," she says, barely taking a breath, "but I can help you plot out a trip that will take you along the most interesting parts of what's left of it."

"That's sweet of you, but I was hoping to take a faster route."

She deflates a bit. "Oh. Well, of course there are faster ways to get there. But I can promise you won't enjoy it as much. Are you driving alone?"

I wish. "No. My sister and I are going home to see our parents."

Alice perks back up. "Oh, that's perfect. Two sisters making a memory together. Think of how much fun you'd have."

"It's hard to imagine." I have no doubt this trip will be memorable. Whether or not it's a good memory remains to be seen.

"You know what else you could do? You could make a video diary of your trip. I'll bet your parents would love that."

What she's suggesting is insane, the kind of thing I would never come up with on my own in a million years. But when she mentions making a video, something clicks into place and it feels like the right thing to do. If my mother really is starting to slip away, then Lindsay and I have a lot of time to make up for. Taking this trip and sharing it with our mom is a good way to start.

I smile at Alice, who I'm now certain is an angel sent from God to point me in the right direction. "You sold me."

The woman is so excited, she actually yelps and claps her hands. You'd think I just invited her to come along.

Her enthusiasm is contagious and I laugh. "Are you getting some kind of commission for this?"

Alice covers her mouth with her hand, but she can't hide the grin behind it. "You'd think so. Truth is, I love the Mother Road. My husband and I used to drive it on our vacations. He passed last year, God rest his soul." She glances up at the ceiling as she crosses herself. "We had a lot of good times on that road. So whenever I get the chance, I like to encourage other folks to do the same."

Tears well up in my eyes as I listen to this woman. It took death to separate her from her husband, yet she remains full of life and enthusiasm. She has no idea how much I envy her.

"I hope you know I'm counting on you," I say, wagging my finger. "You need to tell me all the best spots to see."

Her eyes sparkle as she uncaps a highlighter pen. "I'll tell you everything you need to know."

As Alice draws out a yellow line that stretches from one map to the next, I wish she could tell me the one thing I need to know most of all: if my sister has gone out of her way to avoid me all these years, how will I ever convince her to make this trip with me?

11

Maybe showing up on Lindsay's doorstep unannounced wasn't the best plan. But nothing about my sister has ever gone the way any of us expected.

When I was growing up, my mom and dad talked about having another baby all the time, but it never happened. When I was thirteen, they'd stopped talking about it, and I figured they'd given up on the idea. Perhaps it was because I was such a spectacular daughter. Why mess with a good thing, right? Which is why I was shocked when they sat me down to have the birds-and-the-bees talk and punctuated the whole awkward thing with "And that's why we're having another baby!"

In an effort to make me feel included, they drug me along to all kinds of things I didn't want to do, like picking out nursery furniture and shopping for baby clothes. But the absolute worst was ultrasound day. Since it was the middle of summer and I was out of school, my parents made an event out of it. First we went shopping (which left me asking how much clothing one little baby needed), then to lunch, and then to the doctor's office. By that time, all I wanted to do was go home and climb up into my favorite tree with a book. Or better yet, with my journal so I could write things like "My parents are acting so lame." Instead, I sat in the waiting room while my mom and dad went in to see the doctor. I was flipping through a two-year-old copy of *Ladies' Home Journal* when I heard someone call my name.

"Natalie?" A nurse held open the door from the waiting room, grinning like she had an orange wedge stuck in her mouth. "We've got something to show you."

All the other women in the waiting room turned to look at me, wearing the same kind of crazy grins. Even now, just thinking about it, I can feel the hot flush of blood rushing to my cheeks. I did not want to go with the nurse, but I did. I didn't want to have to look interested when they showed me the sonogram picture, which looked nothing like a baby, but I did. And when the nurse asked me, "Do you want to hear the heartbeat?" I wanted to say "No," but I didn't. My mom and dad were so excited, I knew they expected me to be excited too. So I said, "Sure."

Here's the thing about hearing the heartbeat of a yet-to-be-born baby: it sounds nothing like a heartbeat. It's more like a series of whooshing sounds, like meteors hurtling through space. So I said the first thing that came to my mind. "Whoa. Sounds like *Star Wars*."

All the adults in the room laughed, and I realized with relief that I'd passed the test. They thought I was just as into the whole baby thing as they were, even though nothing was further from the truth. Come to think of it, that may have been the day when I learned the power of a well-placed joke to deflect true emotions.

By the time my sister was born, I was determined to have as little to do with her as possible. It didn't work out that way, though. In that doctor's office, she had only been an idea. Just a bunch of white squiggles on a monitor and weird whoosh-ing sounds. But when she was right there in front of me, she became an actual person; a little person with lips that exposed toothless gums when she smiled and stubby fingers that reached for anything dangling in front of her, like my hair or earrings. The kid grew on me.

Lindsay was four when I graduated from high school, so it only makes sense that we wouldn't be as close as your average sisters. But for some reason, when she was in junior high, her whole attitude toward me changed. That year, Tony and I came to my parents' house for Christmas, and Lindsay was like a different person. She was quiet, sullen, and when she did say something, it dripped sarcasm. When I was able to get my mom alone, I asked her about it. She shrugged it off and laughed, "I wouldn't worry about it, dear. I think it's just the age." But the smile on Mom's lips was forced, and I knew Lindsay's attitude bothered her too.

After that, things just got worse. Lindsay got in trouble at school. Her grades slipped. Worst of all, she was causing a lot of grief for our parents. Still, I thought that being her sister gave me an in of sorts. I figured she'd listen to me. So I made a point of stopping by in the middle of a book tour to talk to her. Big mistake. She ended up screaming at me instead.

"Did you ever stop to think that maybe I don't want the same things you do? Just because you're the perfect daughter doesn't mean I'm going to be!"

That was six years ago. I can count on one hand the number of times we've talked since then. So as I park my car in front of the Shangri-La Apartments in Santa Monica, my heart is trying to pound its way out of my chest. I don't know what kind of reaction to expect from Lindsay. She's back in touch with our parents now, which is a good thing. But she didn't bother contacting me, even though we live only about an hour away from each other. That's not so good.

The complex is pretty big, so I have to look at a map posted by the front gate to figure out how to get to Lindsay's unit. After several wrong turns, I stand outside her front door, trying to gather some clues from what I see outside. There's a mat on the ground, but it doesn't say *Welcome*. Two potted plants sit under the window sill, but they're half dead. I don't know if it's because they're nearly spent annuals, or if they've been neglected. No, there's nothing out here to give me the slightest hint about the kind of woman my sister has become.

When I can't put it off any longer, I inhale deeply and ring the doorbell. Exhale. Wait for what seems like an eternity. Stuff my hands in the pockets of my jeans and shift my weight from one foot to the other. Fight off the urge to press my ear against the door.

Is she out? Or is she home and ignoring me? Did Dad tell her I was going to stop by? Unlikely, but possible. I purposely came by on a Saturday morning because I figured she'd be home. But I don't know anything about her life now. She could be at work. Or she could be out with friends. Or she could be sleeping in. Maybe I should ring again.

My finger is halfway to the button when I hear the dead bolt knob being twisted. The door opens, but it's chained, so all I can see is one side of Lindsay's face. But it's enough.

We stare at each other. She probably wonders if she's hallucinating, and if not, why I'm on her doorstep. And I take in the bit of her hair that I can see peeping through the slit in the door. Blonde hair with burgundy streaks. The same as that lady at the Mt. Olive event.

It was her. She came to see me, but she left before I started talking. I don't know what to make of that.

"Hi, Lindsay," I say. "Can I come in?"

She sighs, shuts the door, and removes the chain. When she opens it up all the way, I get a good look at her. The part of her face that I couldn't see before sports a nasty bruise on the cheek below her left eye. And her belly protrudes in such a way that I know my sister hasn't just gained weight. She's pregnant.

Shock takes control of my vocal cords, producing a word I instantly regret.

Lindsay rolls her eyes and ushers me into the apartment with a wave of her hand. "Nice to see you too, Sis."

Oh yeah, I definitely should have called first.

12

The inside of the apartment tells me a little more about what my sister's life has turned into. It's a dichotomy of thrift store mixed with high-end. A battered coffee table sits in front of a threadbare couch that takes up one wall of the living area. On the opposite wall is a state-of-the-art sound system, complete with speakers that look like they could be used on a concert stage. Propped up in the corner is an electric guitar. Either Lindsay's become a musician, or she lives with one.

Then I notice the moving boxes. There are about six of them, and the one on the top of the stack is open.

"What are you doing here?"

The chill in her voice brings me back to the matter at hand. I did come here for a reason, after all. But now, I've got so many other questions. Are the boxes hers, or someone else's? Moving in, or moving out? Is she married? Most important, how did she get that bruise?

I turn back. Her crossed arms only emphasize the baby bump beneath her baggy, white T-shirt. And the iciness in her pale, blue eyes is a startling contrast to the purple and blue around the left one. I touch her cheek with my fingertips. "What happened to you?"

She backs away, swatting at my hand. "I ran into a door. It's no big deal."

No big deal? She just gave me the universal response of battered women across America, and she's telling me it's no big deal?

"Lindsay," I say as gently as possible, "you can tell me the truth. You don't have to be embarrassed."

"The only thing I have to be embarrassed about is being a klutz. If you came here to call me a liar, you might as well leave."

Obviously, she's not ready to talk about it yet, so I won't push her. "Sorry."

She nods. "Why are you here?"

"Let's sit." We take opposite ends of the couch. "It's about Mom."

"Dad sent you, didn't he?"

I wish I could say, *Oh no, I missed you so much that I tracked you down all by myself.* But even if I tried, she'd see right through it. "Yes."

"I don't know what he expects me to do. If Mom's getting worse, my being there won't change anything."

I know exactly what she means, because I've thought it too. No matter how much time we spend with Mom now, it won't mean a thing to her after the Alzheimer's takes over. As the disease progresses, it will all slip away. We'll slowly become strangers to her. A big, selfish part of me wants to stay far away, to remember Mom the way she was the last time I saw her: vibrant and connected to her family.

I wish I could squeeze Lindsay's hand and tell her I understand, but the way she's pressed herself into the corner of the couch makes her personal boundaries clear. Instead, I lean in as close as I dare. "It may not change anything for Mom, but it will for Dad."

She looks away. "Poor Dad."

"Yeah," I say with a laugh, realizing how right she is. "All the women in his life are a mess."

Her head whips back in my direction and she shoots me a look that could burn a hole through plaster. "Thanks a lot."

Silly me. I thought I was stating the obvious. "Hey, I included myself. In case you haven't heard, I'm getting a divorce."

Her eyebrows shoot up as her chin drops to her chest. "How would I have heard?"

"Beats me. How did you know I was speaking at that church?"

Her cheeks flush. She must have thought she ducked out before I noticed her. "Someone in the complex put a flyer on the bulletin board. Morbid curiosity drew me there."

So much for my fantasy that she tracked me down out of a yearning to create a sisterly bond. Looks like neither one of us have felt that way. "You left before I started talking."

"Guess I wasn't that curious after all." She looks down at her fingers, picks at one of her cuticles, then looks back up at me. "So why do you want a divorce?"

"I don't. Tony does."

"Oh."

How did this conversation get so far off track? "Look, the reason I'm here is because you and I need to spend some time with Mom and Dad. Are you coming or not?"

"Not."

"Why? Is it your job? Maybe if you tell them it's a family emergency—"

"I don't have a job." At my silence, she makes a face. "Not anymore. I was a waitress in a bar. The boss told me I couldn't work the floor as soon as I started showing, so I quit."

"Sorry."

"Just as well." She puts a hand to her stomach. "The smoke wasn't good for either of us."

Good for her. At least I know she's capable of making rational decisions. "So what's the problem? Why won't you come with me?"

She shakes her head. "I already told Dad. I won't fly."

"How far along are you?"

"Six months."

"I'm no expert, but I'm pretty sure it's safe for you to fly."

"Finally, something you're not an expert at." She pushes herself off the couch and walks to the small kitchen. "Look, it has nothing to do with whether some book says it's safe or not." She takes a glass out of the cupboard, opens the fridge, and grabs a bottle of orange juice. "It's my choice. I don't want to get on an airplane right now. I won't do it. End of discussion."

"Okay. I get it. No airplanes." And no juice for me, either. Not that I wanted any, but it would have been nice if she'd offered. "I have a better idea, anyway."

She comes back to the couch, her eyes narrowed. "What's that?"

I pull one of the maps out of my purse and wave it like a fan. "Road trip."

Lindsay flops back against the cushions, nearly spilling her drink. "Shoot me now." She's obviously not thrilled about the idea, but she hasn't said no either. All things considered, this part of the conversation is going much better than I expected.

13

They say God works in mysterious ways. I am living proof of that, because right now, my life has become one long string of those weird, mysterious ways.

Lindsay doesn't fight me much on the road trip idea, but only because she doesn't have a lot of options. Turns out those boxes are hers, and she's moving out.

"Things have been bad with Ben and me ever since I got pregnant," she says. "He doesn't want a baby, and I do. So now we fight all the time. It finally got to be too much for me."

Yeah, getting punched in the face will do that. The bruise on her cheek catches and holds my eyes like Velcro on a knit sweater. "The most important thing is that you and your baby are safe."

A frustrated growl rumbles in her throat. "I told you, he didn't hit me. He's selfish, but he's not violent. He's a musician. He feels things so deeply that—Oh, forget it. You're not going to believe me, anyway."

She's right about that. Sooner or later, I hope she feels she can tell me the truth, but it doesn't matter now. I just need to get her out of this apartment and away from that thug. Thank God I came when she was alone.

"Is there anything else we need to pack?"

"We? Why?" She cocks her head to the side, and for a second, I see the little girl she used to be. Despite the streaks in her hair. "You want me to go with you now?"

"Why not? Do you have a better place to go?"

"I have no place to go."

Her unexpected moment of honesty shoots a pang of sympathy through my heart. She packed all her boxes not because she knew where she was going, but because she couldn't stay where she was. Something we have in common.

I stand up and rub my palms against my thighs. "Then there's no point in waiting. And it'll be easier if we do it now while Ben's out."

"Ben's not out."

I whirl around as if I expect to find him standing behind me. "He's here?"

"Yeah," she says slowly. "He's sleeping. He played a late set last night."

As if on cue, the bedroom door opens and a man stumbles out, rubbing his eyes and wearing only boxer shorts. "What have we got to eat? I'm starving."

"Ben!" Lindsay shouts. "Put some clothes on."

"What?" He drops his hand and gapes when he sees me. "Why didn't you tell me someone else was here?" He mutters all the way back into the bedroom and slams the door behind him.

I'm shocked, but not because I just saw Lindsay's boyfriend in his underwear. Even though I've only known of Ben's existence for about fifteen minutes, a picture of him had already developed in my head: tall, muscular, with long, jet-black rocker hair and a tattoo on each bicep. Boy, was I off target.

A minute later, Ben comes back out wearing frayed jeans and a T-shirt with a beer logo on the front. He's not much taller than Lindsay, and now that she's pregnant, she probably out-weighs him. His short, sandy hair sticks up in all directions, and as far as I can tell, his biceps are tattoo-free.

He frowns at me. "Who are you?"

Well, he's as surly as I expected him to be. "I'm Lindsay's sister."

"You got a name?"

Yeah. Just call me Your Worst Nightmare. "Natalie."

"Huh. She never mentioned you." He scratches his head, and I notice that he does have tattoos, after all. Letters below the middle knuckle of each finger on his left hand, placed so that if he made a fist, you could read what was coming at you. Before I can make out the word, he shuffles into the kitchen.

Lindsay doesn't bother explaining to me why her boyfriend thinks she's an only child. "I'm leaving, Ben," she says in his direction.

He turns to her, his hand still on the open refrigerator door. "Seriously?"

"Don't act so surprised. I told you I was moving out."

"Yeah, but you've been saying that for two weeks. I didn't think you meant it."

"The moving boxes didn't give you a hint?" Lindsay waves her hand toward the stack.

Ben shrugs. "Figured they were for effect." He shuts the fridge door and goes back to Lindsay. He takes her hand. "I can't believe you're really leaving me."

Oh, this guy is good. His voice has gone all sweet and oozy, like warm molasses. For a second, I see Lindsay waver. See doubt in her eyes. I want to jump in and speak for her, but I know that would push her in the wrong direction. Instead, I send up a silent prayer. *Give her strength, Lord. Help her.*

She pulls her hand away from Ben and places it protectively on her stomach. "*We're* leaving you, Ben. If you don't want the baby, then you don't want me."

"I do want you." He takes a step backward. "Man, this sucks. Everything was so great for us. Why did you have to go and get pregnant?"

I can't keep my mouth shut any longer. "Don't put the blame on her," I say. "You were at the party too."

Ben looks in my direction. His jaw is set, and even though he doesn't say a word, the accusation is in his eyes. He blames me for taking her away. Forget the fact that I didn't know about any of this mess before I arrived today. She's leaving with me, therefore, I'm responsible. Well, that's just fine. I'm happy to be his honorary scapegoat, if he needs one.

"Look," I say, crossing my arms over my chest, "I'm going to get Lindsay and her stuff out of here. All you have to do is stay out of our way. Are we clear?"

"Like crystal, doll." His jaw shifts sideways, and I wonder what else he's trying to keep from saying.

I expect him to leave the apartment, or at the very least go in the kitchen and eat his noontime breakfast, but he does neither. Instead, he grabs the guitar from the stand in the corner, plunks himself on the couch, and begins to play. With gusto.

My hands instinctively fly to my ears. "What's he doing?" I yell at Lindsay.

"He plays when he gets upset. It's how he lets off steam."

I guess I should be thankful he's chosen to express his displeasure through music. If you want to call it that. It's so loud and discordant, I feel like I'm in the bowels of a horror movie.

Below my feet, I feel more than hear a thumping. "What's that?"

"The downstairs neighbors." Lindsay yells. "They get kind of cranky."

It's no wonder.

Speaking over the noise is too much trouble, so I don't. I nod toward the bedroom, indicating that Lindsay should pack her clothes, and I go to the stack of boxes. Picking up the first one, I decide it's full of books. Or bricks. Maybe I shouldn't have dismissed Ben so quickly. It would sure help if he pitched in.

But one look at him convinces me otherwise. He's attacking the guitar with such intensity, I fully expect the strings to snap. He's useless.

As I wrestle the box out the front door and downstairs to my car, I can't help wondering . . . is any man ever worth the heartache and trouble they put us through?

14

First stop, the Santa Monica Pier."

Lindsay flops her head from side to side against the seat's headrest. "We're not taking a boat to Illinois. Why are we going to the pier?"

"Because it's where Route 66 begins."

That's not really true. The pier has become known as one of the symbolic ends of 66, even though the road terminates about a mile from there. But it will make a great backdrop for the beginning of our video diary.

I don't intend to stick strictly to 66 the entire way. After poring over all the information Alice gave me, it became obvious that it was impossible, since not all of the old road has been maintained. And if we tried to drive every bit that still exists, it would take us about a month to get to Mom and Dad's. That was out of the question even before I knew about Lindsay's . . . condition. Thankfully, Alice gave me a list of must-sees, the easiest pieces of the road to navigate with the most interesting sights. The first of which is the Santa Monica Pier.

Fifteen minutes later, we're at the pier. Ten minutes after that, I find a parking spot. Since it's Saturday, the place is packed, which brings on a new round of whining from Lindsay.

"Why did we have to get out of the car? I've seen this place a billion times."

"I haven't." Even though I've lived in California most of my adult life, I've never been much of a beachgoer. This has saved me untold hours of torture by allowing me to avoid shopping for swimsuits. "Besides, if we didn't get out of the car, we wouldn't have a very good video."

"Video?" Lindsay stops so suddenly she's nearly plowed into by a dreadlocked man on Rollerblades. "You never told me we were making a video."

"That's because I didn't expect it to be a big deal." I put my hand on her elbow and propel her forward. "I thought it would be cool to involve Mom and Dad by showing them a video diary of our trip. Won't that be fun?"

"Tons," she intones. "Especially when Mom wants to know who those two women are and why we're showing it to her."

"She's not that bad. She still knows who we are."

"Yeah, for now. But one of these days she's going to look at us and there will be nothing there."

I hate to think about how disconnected Mom's gotten, so I usually don't. Which is exactly why I haven't been home in such a long time. But pretty soon, when I'm standing right in front of her, there'll be nothing left to deny.

We walk a bit farther and then I steer her to one side. "I want to get you with the pier sign in the background. Then you can get me."

"Why don't you just ask someone to film both of us?"

For a moment, I'm encouraged that she wants to record the memory of us together; two sisters setting off on a great adventure. But she starts fidgeting, and I realize her ulterior motive. If we do it together, we'll get out of here faster. Which is fine by me.

I pull my brand new Flip camera out of my purse. I've had it just long enough to figure out how to work it, so I'm not thrilled about the idea of handing it over to a stranger. "I don't know . . ."

"What about him?" Lindsay points to an elderly gentleman using a similar camera to record his wife.

"Good choice." He's probably more tech savvy than I am. And if he tries to run off with it, I think I can catch him.

I wait until they're done, then approach the couple. "Pardon me, I was wondering if you'd mind making a short video of my sister and me?" I hold up my camera, and the man smiles.

"Sure thing. Stand where you want and let me know when you're ready."

Tucking a strand of hair behind my ear, I position myself next to Lindsay. I start to put my arm around her, but her crossed arms and tight lips convince me otherwise. "Okay, we're ready."

Our cameraman nods and starts recording. Oops. I probably should have thought about what I was going to say before I said I was ready.

"Hi Mom. Dad. Lindsay and I are here at the Santa Monica Pier. We're about a mile from the official start of Route 66."

"End." Mrs. Cameraman pipes up.

"Excuse me?" Does she want us to stop?

"It's the end, dear."

"If only," Lindsay mutters.

"Behave," I hiss at my sister, then turn back to Mrs. Cameraman. "The end of what?"

"The end of 66. It starts in Chicago, and it ends here in Santa Monica."

"So we're starting off at the end of the road." Lindsay uncrosses her arms and puts one hand on her hip. "If that isn't just dripping with symbolism."

"I guess it's the end, technically, but so what? The road goes both ways." I put a finger in the air and try to sound wise. "One man's end is another man's beginning."

"That's lovely, dear," says Mrs. Cameraman.

"You sound like a fortune cookie." Lindsay scowls.

Mr. Cameraman taps his foot to get someone's attention. "Are we done? Do either of you have anything else to say?"

Oh, boy, he's been recording this whole time. Our tapes are going to need a ton of editing before I show them to Mom and Dad. I'm about ready to tell him he can turn off the camera, when Lindsay interrupts me.

"Wait. I've got something to say." She beckons with her fingers. "Come in closer."

Mr. Cameraman takes a step toward her. Lindsay leans in his direction, cups her hand around her mouth, and says in a stage whisper, "This woman is not my sister. She's Mexican Mafia and she's taking me over the border to sell my baby on the black market."

Mr. Cameraman almost drops the recorder. Mrs. Cameraman presses her hand against her chest and sucks in all the surrounding air. They're obviously shocked, and by the way they look from Lindsay, to me, and back to Lindsay, it seems they don't know whether or not to believe her. Thankfully, Lindsay breaks into a face-splitting grin and waves her hands in front of the camera. "I'm just kidding. This really is my sister. That's why she's such a pain in the—"

"Lindsay! I think we've imposed enough on these nice people."

The man's hand shakes a little when he gives me back the camera. "You two ladies have a nice day." His words are slow, cautious. As he and his wife turn away from us, he crooks his arm through hers and I hear him say, "Let's get out of here, Evelyn."

78

I turn back to my sister, ready to give her what for. But I can't. This is the happiest I've seen her all day. Instead, I just shake my head. "Come on. Let's get back to the car."

She rubs her hands together. "Oh, goody. I can't wait to see what other adventures await us."

Translation: *I can't wait to see what other ways I can come up with to torture and torment my sister.*

Fifteen minutes later, we're standing in the parking lot, looking at the empty space where my car used to be. "Is this the kind of adventure you had in mind?" I ask.

It takes Lindsay a moment to find her voice, but once she does, she's a verbal geyser. "I don't believe it. They stole all my stuff!"

For a flickering instant, I want to grab her by the shoulders and shake her. *Yes, selfish girl, they stole all your stuff. And the container it was in, which just happened to be my car.*

While Lindsay continues her tirade, I take my phone out of my purse, dial 911, and console myself with a platitude: after this, there's nowhere to go but up.

Otherwise, we're in a whole mess of trouble.

15

Lindsay and I are sitting on the edge of a concrete planter in front of the Santa Monica Police Department when Jade pulls up and honks her horn.

"Finally." It's the first word Lindsay has uttered in over two hours. She stopped talking to me after I lost my temper back at the pier and yelled that the loss of her iPod didn't qualify as a catastrophe.

I clutch my purse close to me, thanking God one more time that I chose to carry it on the pier rather than leave it in the car, and get into the front seat. Lindsay is already sulking in the back.

"Thanks, Jade."

"No problem." She puts on her blinker and pulls smoothly away from the curb. "I should warn you, though. If you plan to make a habit of this during your trip, you're on your own. One police station visit a year is plenty."

"That won't be an issue. I have no intention of doing this again anytime soon."

My stomach rumbles and I look down at my watch. Three o'clock. No wonder. "I'm starving."

"Do you want to stop and get something?" Jade asks.

"Yeah, I do."

"What sounds good?"

"Hmm. I don't know. What about you, Lindsay?" I look back at her. "What sounds good to you?"

"Nothing," she grumbles, her face pressed against the cushioned backrest.

Fine. Then we'll just get what I want. "Anything sound good to you, Jade?"

She laughs. "If you're feeling brave, we could head over to Taco-Rama. Thirty-four percent beef can't be beat!"

I sigh and shake my head. "I used to love those tacos. Now I can't go near them."

"Aw, come on. You ate them for years. What's the difference now?"

"Well, now I know that only 34 percent of the ground beef actually is beef. So what's the other 66 percent made of?"

"You don't want to know."

"That's my point."

I catch motion out of the corner of my eye. Lindsay is waving one hand in the air, while holding the other up to her mouth.

"Ruby!" she calls.

"It's Jade."

"Whatever. Pull over."

Jade addresses Lindsay through the rearview mirror. "You don't look so good."

"I'm gonna be sick."

Jade pulls over. The car barely comes to a stop before Lindsay pushes the door open, stumbles out, and loses it on the side of the freeway.

"Your sister's a real charmer," Jade says with a smirk.

I should jump to Lindsay's defense, but all I can do is nod. I stare through the front window, trying to ignore the sound of retching from outside the car, but it's impossible. "Do you think I should go out and help her?"

Jade purses her lips. "I think she's doing just fine on her own."

"I'm serious."

"So am I. What could you possibly do to help?"

"I could give her moral support. Let her know I'm there for her."

"Trust me, she'll just feel worse if you're watching her toss her cookies. There are some things a person has to do all by herself."

And there are some things a person wishes she could do all by herself. Right now, I wish I could drive to Illinois alone. It was bad enough when I thought I just had to share the car with my sister's lousy attitude. Now, I've got her delicate stomach to worry about too.

Not funny, God. Not funny at all.

16

It's another three days before we're ready to leave on our trip. Not only did I have to arrange for alternate transportation, I had to take Lindsay shopping to replace her clothes and other essential items. During that time, Lindsay has stayed at my house, bunking in the guest bedroom. She locks herself in there for hours on end. She says she just wants to be alone, but from the muffled sounds coming through the door, I can tell she's on her phone, most likely talking to Ben.

Every morning I half expect her to be gone. And every morning when she opens the door to her room and comes out for breakfast, I feel a twinge of disappointment. Followed swiftly by guilt.

But this morning is different. The loaner car sent over by my insurance company—an amazing convertible that I'm sure was supposed to go to some car-less celebrity but was mistakenly delivered to me—is packed and ready to go. Jade, who will be house-sitting while I'm gone, sits at the kitchen table, her hands cupped around her Starbucks cup, a frown indicating her displeasure at getting up so early. It's a look mirrored by Lindsay as she shuffles in with her purse slung over her shoulder and a backpack of sundries hanging from the crook of her elbow.

That's okay. Let them both be grouchy. I have no idea what this trip holds in store for us, but I'm itching to find out. For the first time in a long time, I'm excited about something. And no one is going to bring me down.

"I must have been crazy to let you talk me into this."

Not even my crabby sister.

Jade stands up and I walk into her open arms. "Have a safe trip," she says against my hair.

I pull away and blink back the unexpected emotion of the moment. "I'm going to miss you."

She waves the thought away. "Are you kidding? You won't even think about me. Not with Little Miss Sunshine keeping you company."

I laugh, despite the glare Lindsay shoots at us. "If you need anything, call me."

"I will."

"And if Tony gives you any trouble—"

"I'll sic your lawyer on him. I've got it. Now get going."

Quickly, I take a last look around the kitchen. Even though I'm coming back, there's something final about leaving this time. It's one more door I'm closing on another part of my old life: the meals I cooked here, the times Tony came up behind me as I stood at the stove so he could poke a finger into whatever pot I was stirring and tell me it needed more salt, how I'd laugh and tell him one cook in the kitchen was more than enough. Moments like those will never come again.

I wonder . . . does Erin cook? Does she hold out a wooden spoon for him to take a taste? Does he pull her to him for a kiss, their unborn baby sandwiched between them?

"Natalie." Jade's voice breaks in on my reverie. "Everything's going to be fine. Have fun."

Have fun. A tall order. The excitement I felt earlier has dissipated, leaving nagging dread in its place. What am I doing with my life? Am I throwing it all away? Was Pastor Dave right? Should I have fought harder to save my marriage?

Lindsay puts her free hand on her hip with a grunt. "Are we leaving or not?"

There stands my sister, so different from the girl I thought she'd be. Maybe I've made a mess of my life, but it's not too late for Lindsay to turn hers into something she's proud of. And the first step is to get her far away from her abusive boyfriend.

"You bet we're leaving." I head to the garage door, motioning for her to follow. "Adventure awaits us."

⸺⸺

Lindsay falls asleep in the car as soon as I pull out of the driveway. It's entirely possible she's faking in order to avoid talking to me. I don't really care. In fact, having her in a state of unconsciousness, be it real or put on, is a blessing I plan to savor.

I push the button on the stereo, thankful for a car with satellite radio. The next time my insurance company sends me a survey I'm going to give them five stars for service. I may even remember to put it in the mail this time.

The first leg of our journey is made up of roads with which I'm extremely familiar. From Foothill Boulevard, down Shamrock, then east on Huntington Drive until it turns into another segment of Foothill Boulevard, I try to look through different eyes. The eyes of an adventuresome explorer, seeing things she's never seen before: the Aztec Hotel in Monrovia, looking like it was left behind by a lost tribe; the Route 66 Memories antique shop in Rancho Cucamonga, guarded over by a menagerie of metal dinosaur sculptures; and lots of Historic

Route 66 signs. All unique and interesting, but nothing worth disturbing my sleeping sister. Until we reach Fontana and the giant orange.

As I pull the car over to the curb, Lindsay peeks through one eye. "Please tell me we've made it to Illinois."

"Nope. Just the first of many great photo ops." I hop out of the car, camera in hand, but she makes no move to follow. "Come on out so I can get a shot of you with the orange."

"The what?" Both of her eyes are open now as she turns to look at the structure behind me. "You've got to be kidding."

I turn on the camera and, holding a guidebook off to the side where I can still read it, start narrating. "This is Bono's Historic Orange in Fontana, California. Built in 1936, it was saved from demolition in the 1990s by the Fontana Historical Society and moved three miles to this location in 1997." I swing the camera to the right. "It sits beside Bono's Restaurant and Deli, which, sadly, appears to be out of business."

Behind me, the car door closes. I turn around and point the camera at Lindsay. "What do you think?" I ask her.

"It's big. And it's orange."

Thank you, Captain Obvious. "Yes, it is. They used to sell orange juice out of it. But now, it's a reminder of a simpler time."

"A simpler time when men made drink stands shaped like fruit."

I laugh, and am rewarded by the glimmer of a smile playing at the corner of Lindsay's mouth. Maybe this trip won't be so bad after all.

She looks around, whipping her head from side to side. "Is there a bathroom around here? I've got to pee."

Ah, another beautiful moment recorded for posterity. I shut off the camera and move toward the car. "Come on. There's a gas station on the corner."

While Lindsay takes care of business, I fill up with gas and ponder just how scenic this trip should be. I had been planning on seeing as many sights as possible, but that was before I took into account the demands of a pregnant woman's bladder. Now I'm thinking it might be better to take a more direct route.

When Lindsay pops back in the car, she's carrying a bag of potato chips and a huge soda cup with "thirsty-two ouncer" emblazoned on the side.

"This should hold me until we reach the big banana," she says, then takes a slurp through the straw.

"What banana?"

"I don't know. I just figured there'd be more enormous fruit along the way."

Oh, yeah. It's looking like the shorter this trip is, the better.

17

Nothing makes my sister happy.

When I stay on the highway, she complains there's nothing to see. When I venture off onto old 66 and stop at what I think is a fun and interesting sight, she complains about how lame it is. The hotel we stayed at last night was, I hoped, a compromise. It had authentic old-time charm, but the sign out front boasted air-conditioning and color TV. Unfortunately, the TV only got three stations and the air conditioner rattled like a rock tumbler. Chalk up one more bad choice for me.

This morning, after our complimentary breakfast of cold cereal and instant coffee for me, milk for Lindsay, I gave her control of the radio. At least if she chose the music, she'd have one less thing to complain about. That's what I hoped, anyway.

"I can't believe this." She punches a button, listens to five seconds of a song, then changes the station. Again. And again. "There are like, fifty stations, and nothing good on."

I want to slap her hand away from the controls, but I restrain myself. Maybe, if I sing a song in my head, I can tune her out. The first thing that comes to mind is less than ideal, but once it starts playing in my brain, I can't get rid of it.

I've got a lovely bunch of coconuts . . .

"I wish I still had my iPod."

. . . there they are all standing in a row . . .

"But no, you had to be all Steven Spielberg on the pier."

. . . big ones, small ones, some as big as your head . . .

"If we hadn't stopped, my stuff wouldn't have been stolen. I should never have come with you in the first place."

"That's it!" With a squeal of tires I jerk the car to the side of the road, gravel spraying out from beneath our tires. "Get out."

"What?" Lindsay clutches the dashboard with one hand, her shoulder strap with the other.

"You heard me. Get out. If you're so unhappy, get out of the car."

"Are you nuts? We're in the middle of the desert."

"Fine. Then I'll get out."

I've completely lost my mind. I push the car door open, slam it shut behind me, and start walking down the road. As luck would have it, I picked part of old 66 on which to have my mental breakdown. There are no other cars around, no sign of life that I can see. But I don't care. I need to get as far away from my sister as I can.

"Natalie!" She calls after me. "Natalie? Where are you going? You can't just leave me here!"

Oh, can't I? Tony left me. Just up and walked away. He didn't care how much it hurt, how he broke my heart, destroyed my career. Why should I care about anybody else now?

With every step, emotions churn faster, hotter. Is it too much to ask that I be appreciated by somebody? Tony doesn't need my love. Lindsay doesn't want it. The sun beats down, but a chill sweeps through my body, freezing me to the cracked pavement beneath my feet.

I'm a failure. I failed in my marriage. I failed at my career. I'm even failing at being a sister.

Who am I now? Who have I ever been?

The gravel crunches behind me and a hand grasps my arm. I turn to see Lindsay, her blond and burgundy hair blowing in the breeze, her face white as a surrender flag. "Natalie, I'm sorry. Please come back to the car."

Please. Say the magic word, Mom used to tell us. Back when we were kids, saying please would get us almost anything. Funny how well that word still works on me.

"Okay."

An SUV roars past as we trudge back to the car. Once we're sitting down, I take a swig from my water bottle. Then I look at Lindsay. "I can't fight with you anymore."

Her eyebrows furrow. "We weren't fighting."

"Maybe I wasn't fighting with you, but you were fighting with me." She opens her mouth, but I put my hand up before any words come out. "Since the minute I got to your apartment, you've been unhappy and hostile toward me. Everything I've done has been wrong."

"You have to admit, the trip's been kind of bumpy so far."

She's right about that. But I can't help thinking the bumps would be less annoying if she weren't so crabby. "Look, I know I'm not perfect, but I'm doing the best I can. It would help if you'd try too."

"How do you know I'm not?"

"Doing the best you can?"

"Trying."

It hadn't occurred to me that, after all these years, maybe this was the best Lindsay could do with me. With thirteen years separating us, we'd barely known each other as children. As grown women, we don't know each other at all. Not in any way that matters. Essentially, we are two strangers who decided to take a very long, potentially life-changing drive together.

I reach over and pat her hand. For once, she doesn't roll her eyes or make a face at the contact. "I guess all we can both do is try."

"Does that mean you're not going to ditch me on the side of the road?"

"No." I turn the key in the ignition, bringing the car back to life. Now that we've established a shaky rapport, I can't resist teasing her just a bit. "Not today, at least."

18

"Welcome to Oatman." A grizzled fellow calls out with a wave as I park the car in front of an old, wood-frame building. One strong wind could probably blow the place over.

Lindsay gives him a halfhearted wave in return, then whispers to me, "Are you sure you want to get out here?"

"Positive. According to Alice, Oatman is a must-see town."

"Alice?"

"My automobile club advisor."

Her lips form a silent "Oh" and we get out of the car.

Oatman, Arizona, is busier than I expected. Young couples, families with kids, and older folks who I assume are retired, stroll up and down both sides of the street. But the most interesting visitors in Oatman are the four-legged kind.

Lindsay keeps her back plastered against the car. "There's a donkey on the sidewalk."

I tap her shoulder and point behind us. "There are a few in the street too. And one's about ready to walk into the general store."

The animals are everywhere. Lindsay wrinkles up her nose. "Is it always like this?"

The man who welcomed us to town barks out a laugh and slaps his thigh. "You bet it is. Them are gen-u-ine descendants of gold rush–era burros. When the gold ran out, so did the miners. But they left their asses behind."

I'm struck speechless by his colorful turn of phrase, but Lindsay is warming up to the fellow. She takes a step forward, looking at a big, dark-gray burro walking around the corner of the building. "Are they friendly?"

"Depends what you consider friendly," the man says. "Mostly, they're big beggars. Sometimes they bite, but usually only cuz they're in a hurry to eat whatever's being handed out."

Lindsay grins. "Can we feed them?"

"No," I say.

At the very same time, the stranger answers, "Yeah!"

Okay, the animals are kind of cute, but they have really big teeth. And more than a few germs, I'm sure. "We don't have anything they'd like."

"No problem, there. Every business in town sells burro chow."

Lindsay looks at me and I shrug. "What's burro chow?" she asks the man.

"Feed pellets. Lots of places have carrots too. In fact . . ." The man reaches into the deep pocket of his baggy jeans. "Here you go. This one's on me."

Lindsay takes the limp carrot he hands her. "Thanks."

It's the most unappetizing vegetable I've ever seen, and I can't imagine it interesting any of the burros. But the steady *clop-clop* of hooves tells me otherwise. Three of them are walking straight at Lindsay.

Two of them poke at her with their muzzles while the other shakes his head up and down, his upper lip pulled back to offer a toothy grin. With a yelp, she drops the carrot on the ground. She backs away from the trio as they ignore her and fight halfheartedly over the discarded treat.

The man laughs. "See. They're harmless as a bunch of hungry kittens. You ladies enjoy your stay now." He nods us a farewell, then saunters away, already waving and calling hello to a family on the other side of the street.

The smallest burro, the one who was not victorious in his quest for food, turns in my direction. He stretches his head toward me and blows out a big, warm breath.

I hold my palms out. "Don't look at me."

Satisfied that I'm not holding out on him, he walks away, no doubt in search of an easier mark. "What do you think?" I ask Lindsay.

She looks at the store behind her, then back at me. A grin blooms on her face. "I think we need to buy some carrots."

"Did you know that Clark Gable and Carol Lombard spent their honeymoon in the Oatman Hotel?" I look up from the pamphlet in my hand and point across the street. "Right over there."

"Cool." Lindsay is poking through a bin of costume jewelry. She puts on a ring with a big purple stone in a flower-shaped setting and holds her hand up to admire it. "What do you think?"

"Pretty, but kind of big." She nods and tosses it back in the bin. I continue reading about the hotel. "It says they've restored the room so it looks just like it did when the couple stayed here. I've got to see that."

"Sounds kinda la—uh, lovely."

I appreciate her attempt to cover over her disinterest. I guess it is kind of lame that a woman on the brink of divorce would want to see a honeymoon suite. But I have to believe romance is still alive and well somewhere in the world. Even if it's only in the faded memories of a long-gone celebrity couple.

But I know how to grab Lindsay's interest. "There's a restaurant in the hotel. We can eat first then take the tour."

"Deal."

We leave the gift shop and walk down the sidewalk. Up ahead, a family has made friends with the cutest burro I've seen yet. It's tiny, probably not full grown, and has pale beige markings. A little girl stands in front of him, clutching a carrot close to her chest. Her mother stands behind her, giving her full attention to the squirming toddler in her arms. Off to the side, the dad has a video camera up to his face, capturing everything.

"Hold out your carrot, honey," he calls.

Honey smiles at her father. There's so much love and trust in that smile, it breaks my heart. If Tony and I had had a daughter, would she have looked at him the same way? I'll never know. I'll never have a child of my own. Not now. But Tony will. He's the one who broke our vows, broke the rules, yet he's the one who's going to have precious moments like this. Suddenly, I'm not so excited about seeing the honeymoon suite anymore.

Lindsay and I reach the family just as Honey holds out her carrot. The burro is not as docile as he looks, and he lunges forward. The girl drops the carrot, emitting a shriek loud enough and high enough that it scares the donkey away. Since her dad is following the animal's movement with the camera, and her mom is still trying to calm down the baby, neither one of them notice Honey's quivering lip and downcast eyes. But my sister does.

Squatting down on the balls of her feet, Lindsay picks up the carrot and hands it to the girl. "Here you go."

Honey looks at Lindsay, looks down at the carrot, then back at Lindsay. "It's dirty now."

She shrugs. "That's okay. These guys eat off the desert floor. A little dirt won't bother them."

"It's dirty," Honey insists. "I can't give dirt to the pony."

Now she's got her mother's attention. "It's a donkey, honey, not a pony. Now tell the nice lady thank you."

"Thank you," she says loudly. Then she leans in to Lindsay and whispers, "It's a pony who was turned into a donkey by an evil witch. But this is a magic carrot."

"I see," Lindsay says gravely. "And this carrot will break the spell."

"Yes."

"But only if it's clean."

Honey's eyes grow wide, as if amazed to find an adult who understands. "Yes."

"Then there's only one thing to do." Lindsay fishes her water bottle from her purse and rinses off the carrot. She wipes it dry on her jeans and hands it back to the girl. "How's that?"

"Perfect." Honey beams, then turns to her father and yanks on the tail of his T-shirt. "Daddy, we need to find that donkey-pony."

Dad laughs, Mom smiles and thanks us, and the family walks away.

My chest grows tighter and tighter as I watch my sister interact with the little girl. I was so sure God wanted me to be a mother that I tried everything I could to get pregnant, but nothing worked. Lindsay and Ben definitely didn't plan to have a baby, yet there she stands. Not only is she pregnant, she's just shown me a tender, maternal side I never knew she had. It strikes me that maybe, in the grand scheme of things, there was a reason for how it all worked out.

But what? What is it that makes me unsuitable to be a mother? Is it a character flaw? Some genetic oddity I don't even know about? What's wrong with me?

Lindsay stands up, wiping her hands together. "I'm going to need a washroom before we eat."

I don't answer. I just stare until she finally looks at me, her brows drawn together.

"What's wrong with you?"

"Nothing," I say. "I was just thinking."

"About what?"

I wish we had the kind of relationship where I could tell her anything. It would feel so good to share my pain with someone and receive some support. Some encouragement. But Lindsay and I aren't at that point yet. I don't know if we ever will be. So I smile and only tell her the good part. "I was thinking you're going to be a great mother."

For a moment, it seems that she's trying to decide whether or not I'm being serious. Then her facial muscles relax, her brows return to their natural level, and the pucker leaves her lips. She doesn't say anything in return, but when I link my arm through hers to lead her across the street, she lets me.

19

"That may have been the best burger I ever ate." Lindsay gives her fingers one last lick before swiping her mouth with a napkin.

"When you're starving, everything tastes good." I couldn't tell you what the darn thing tasted like. It could be the most delicious burger in the world, or it might be made out of cardboard. Since we sat down, I haven't been able to concentrate on much of anything except for how unfair life is.

The waitress, Sharon, comes over and lays the check and a Sharpie marker on the table. "In case you ladies want to sign bills for the wall." She picks up our plates and walks away.

"What do you say?" Lindsay asks. "Want to leave your mark?"

The inside of the restaurant is full of dollar bills. They cover the walls, frame the doors, and hang from the ceiling like stubby stalactites. Each bill bears the name of the person who left it. A few hours ago, I would have been eager to add mine to the collection, and Lindsay would have rolled her eyes at the suggestion. Now, I just want to get in the car and drive.

"Don't you think it's kind of lame?" I ask, fiddling with the straw in my half-empty soda glass, concentrating on the *clink clink* of ice against the sides.

Lindsay leans back in her chair with a frown. "What bit you on the hind quarters?"

I can't help laughing. We've only been in town a few hours and she's already talking like a local. "Nothing. With the exception of some stubborn cellulite, my hind quarters are perfectly fine, thank you."

"Then snap out of your funk and let's have some fun." She puts her purse in her lap and pulls out her wallet. "Look, at least I'm trying. If we're going to show Mom and Dad all the stuff we did on this trip, this is the kind of thing they'll want to see." She puts one dollar bill on the table and waves the other in my face. "I'll even donate the bills."

"How can I pass that up?" I snatch the dollar from her before she can change her mind.

She writes across President Washington's face, her name big and bold. Just like Lindsay. Then she writes something under it that I can't read from where I'm sitting.

"What's that say?"

"It's just some words of wisdom. Now it's your turn."

I take the pen from her and write my name in neat, precise letters off to the side of Washington. But when it comes to words of wisdom, I'm stumped. What do I have to share with weary travelers who might pass by?

Watch out for hungry burros.

Stay hydrated.

Don't trust men.

No, none of those will do. Finally, something comes to mind. Something that sums up the reason for this trip, my hope for what it will be. I write it down, then hand it to Lindsay.

"Enjoy the journey," she reads. "Nice. Worthy of a bumper sticker."

"What did you write?"

She smirks and hands me her dollar. She drew a donkey head next to her name. Written under it in all caps are the words WATCH YOUR STEP.

It's perfect on so many levels.

We go up to the counter, pay for our meal, and hand our signed dollar bills to Sharon. I pull out the camera and record her as she reads them and laughs. "These need to go where people can see them."

She tapes them right on the back of the cash register. I get a close up of them, then tell Lindsay to get in the shot. She argues until Sharon comes around and takes the camera from me.

"You two both need to be in the picture. Get on over there." She motions where she wants us to go. "Good. Now try to look happy."

Miracle of miracles, Lindsay puts her arm around my shoulders. I smile and snake my arm around her waist. Then I feel something on the back of my head and Sharon laughs.

"Are you doing bunny ears on me?"

"Who? Me?" Lindsay feigns innocence, but from the speed at which she removes her arm, I know I was right.

"Thanks, Sharon." I take the camera back and give a little wave. "Have a nice day."

"Wait a minute," Lindsay says. "Didn't you want to see the honeymoon room?"

I shake my head. "It's okay."

Now Sharon blocks my way. "You haven't seen the room? You can't leave without seeing it."

"We really should get back on the road."

"But it won't hardly take any time at all. It's right upstairs. Amy!" Sharon calls toward the kitchen. Almost immediately, a teenager with a blond ponytail bounds through the half double doors. Sharon points at us. "We've got two for a tour of the Gable Suite."

"Great. Follow me."

Lindsay gives me a shrug. "I guess we don't have a choice. Come on."

Sharon was right. The tour doesn't take long. We go up a wide flight of wooden stairs, down a hall, around a corner, and there we are. Amy opens the door with a flourish and ushers us into the room.

As Amy launches into a prepared speech about the popularity of Gable and Lombard and how he loved to visit Oatman, Lindsay and I walk around the small space. Most of it is taken up by a white iron-frame bed. The patchwork quilt covering it looks homemade, but I doubt it's old enough to be the one the famous couple slept under.

"What's the deal with the coins?" I point at the spare change lying here and there on the quilt.

"Visitors toss them there."

"Why?" Lindsay asks.

Amy shrugs. "I guess they think it's lucky. Like coins in a fountain. We collect all of it and donate it to a children's hospital."

In each corner of the room are wooden chairs that look like they came from someone's dining room. An old lace dress has been carefully draped on one of them. Age has given it a slightly yellow tinge, but I imagine it's supposed to be a stand-in for Lombard's wedding attire.

Lindsay goes to the window and touches the edge of a faded curtain. "It's not the Ritz, is it?"

No, it's not. There's something sweetly sad about this room. As though the reality of the couple's love story wasn't enough of a testimony, so it's been preserved in an embellished time capsule. I think back on the budget-conscious hotel room where Tony and I spent our honeymoon. The only thing special about it had been the two of us. Fool that I was, I thought that was enough.

Judging from the excitement in Amy's voice, she's just gotten to her favorite part of the speech. "Gable had to get back to Hollywood where he was filming *Gone with the Wind*, so they only spent the night here. But they would return often in the years to come."

"You've got to be kidding!" Lindsay shouts.

"No, really." Amy holds her hand up as if giving an oath. "He liked to play poker with the miners."

But Lindsay's not even paying attention to the girl. She hasn't taken her eyes away from the window. I walk up beside her. "What's wrong?"

She points down at the street. "He followed us."

He's not hard to spot. In his black T-shirt, low-slung jeans, and silver studded belt, he looks completely out of place among the tourists and the burros.

It's Ben. Lindsay's boyfriend has just become her stalker.

20

How did he know we were here?"

Lindsay turns defensive. "How should I know?"

"Who?" Amy asks.

"Her ex-boyfriend." I turn back to Lindsay. "You told him, didn't you?"

"No."

"Lindsay!"

"Okay, I told him we were on 66. But I never said where."

She didn't have to. Oatman's one of those can't-miss spots on this route. There's one road in and one road out. The fact that he's here isn't so surprising, but his timing is darn near miraculous.

I pinch my forehead. "When did you call him?"

"I didn't."

"But you just said—"

"She texted him." Amy interrupts, her tone asking *What century are you from?*

Lindsay frowns at Amy. Amy shrugs. I grab Lindsay's wrist and pull her toward the door. "We've got to get out of here."

"Why?" Amy asks. "Is he dangerous?"

"Yes," I say.

"No," Lindsay says.

I glare at her. The bruise around her eye has mostly faded, and what's left of it she's covered with makeup. Maybe no one else can see it, but I know it's there. I remember what it looked like when I first saw her. And whether she admits it or not, I'm convinced Ben gave it to her. And now he's followed her into the desert.

"We're not taking any chances," I say to her. "Amy, will you help us?"

Apparently, this level of intrigue doesn't come through Oatman very often. The girl's eyes are practically snapping with excitement. "Of course. What do you want me to do?"

"Distract him and give us time to get to our car."

"You got it. Where are you parked?"

Lindsay shakes her head. "This is so stupid."

I shush her and answer Amy. "Across the street."

She leads us back down the stairs, then motions for us to stop. "You should go out through the kitchen," she says in the loudest whisper I've ever heard. "Go around the building and wait 'til I lure him inside. Then you can run to your car."

"Lure him how?" Lindsay asks.

She shrugs. "I'll think of something."

After a quick thank-you hug, Lindsay and I go the way Amy pointed. The cook staff doesn't seem bothered that strangers are running past the fryers and grill tops. Once we get outside, we run up to the corner of the building and come to an abrupt stop. Ben is walking across the street, heading straight for the hotel.

My heart pounds in my chest. It's like being in the middle of a made-for-TV movie . . . a down-on-her-luck novelist risks everything to save her sister from the maniacal ex-boyfriend who won't let her go. The ex-boyfriend who at this very moment has a burro nibbling at his back pocket. I have to admit, right now, Ben looks more confused than crazed. Behind me, Lindsay laughs, and Ben looks in our direction.

I hold my breath. Does he see us? He squints. Is the sun in his eyes? *We need some help here, God.*

Amy dashes outside, her hands cupped around her mouth, and yells, "Free beer for the next two minutes!"

Several people follow her straight into the restaurant, including Ben. From inside, I hear a woman bellow, "Amy! Have you lost your mind?" God does indeed work in strange and mysterious ways.

"Come on."

I run across the street. Lindsay walks behind me. I'm elated. What an adrenaline rush. In a game of cat and mouse, we are victorious!

I should have spent a little less time reveling in our victory, and a little more time looking where I was going. The next thing I know, my foot slides out from under me as it connects with a little burro present in the road. I hit the pavement hard, knocking the air from my lungs with a whoosh.

Lindsay looks down at me, hands on her hips. "Didn't I tell you to watch your step?"

"Very funny."

Watchful of where I put my hands, I push myself off the ground. But one step forward tells me I'm not going very far. As soon as I put weight on my right foot, a pain shoots through my ankle and I almost go down again.

Lindsay grabs my arm and helps me to the car. I move toward the driver's side, but she drags me forward. "Oh, no. Let me drive for a change."

I want to argue with her, but I have no good reason. After all, she's pregnant, not incapacitated. "Okay." A moment later, we're speeding out of Oatman and heading down the hairpin curves of 66.

Whether it's the speed of the turns or the smell emanating from the bottom of my shoe that makes my stomach lurch, I don't know. But Lindsay is having the time of her life. The convertible top is down, and her hair whips around her face like a glorious red and yellow flag. "Born to Be Wild" comes on the radio, and for a heart-stopping second she removes her hand from the steering wheel to turn it up.

"Sing with me, Nat!" She yells over the music, then breaks into full-throated song.

This is just the right song for her. Perhaps she was born to be wild, or maybe she's grown into her wildness. In any case, there's a sense of abandon about Lindsay that I've never had. All my life, I've wanted to please people. Lindsay just wants to please herself. Somewhere, between the two of us, a happy balance exists. But for now, I'll humor her and try to embrace my inner wild child.

I open my mouth and sing.

21

When we reach Kingman twenty-eight miles later, the pain in my ankle has subsided to a dull throb. I turn down the radio volume to get Lindsay's attention. "Let's park somewhere and get out for a while."

Originally, I'd planned to spend the night here, but Ben's appearance is a good reason not to. In fact, I decide we need to veer off 66 for a bit to put as much distance as possible between us and him.

We stay in town long enough to use a restroom, take some quick shots of interesting sights, and replenish our water and junk food supply.

"How's your foot?" Lindsay asks as we walk down the sidewalk to the car.

"Much better. I think it will be back to normal by tomorrow."

"Good." She pauses. "I can keep driving, though. If you want to rest it. Just to be on the safe side."

Seems my unexpected injury has given her an excuse to become a more active participant in this trip. I wish she'd just admit she's having a good time, but at least she's not still griping about every little thing. I bite the inside of my lip to keep from smiling. "You sure you don't mind?"

"Naw."

"Okay. Thanks."

I stow our purchases in the backseat and jump into the car as Lindsay revs the engine. "Top up or down?" she asks.

There are all kinds of practical reasons to put it up. It would keep the bugs out, for one, and it makes sense we'd have better gas mileage. But the simple fact that she asked my opinion pushes me to give the answer I think she wants to hear.

"Down."

She smiles. "Cool."

As we near the end of town, I pull one of Alice's maps out of the glove compartment. "Veer right here," I tell Lindsay.

"But that's Interstate 40."

"I know. We're getting off 66."

"What? Why?"

She's so incensed I don't know how to take it. Is she upset because I changed plans without asking her? Or because now it will be harder for Ben to follow us?

"It's just for a little while. I want to get to Seligman before dark, and 40 is the fastest way there."

This explanation seems to work for Lindsay. She follows my directions without further argument.

Interstate 40 is a long, fairly uninteresting stretch of road. With no signs proclaiming the next tourist trap or rickety buildings and roadside art to catch my eye, my mind starts to wander. It meanders back through the sights we've seen so far, glosses over the possible threat of Ben—I do not want to think about him right now—and lands squarely back at the other irritating male in my life: Tony.

What is he doing now? Is he picking out nursery furniture with his girlfriend? Are they debating the safety features on different car seats? Or is he alone, maybe in his own car, taking a drive through the foothills and wondering if he made the biggest mistake of his life?

"What are you thinking about?"

Lindsay's question surprises me. Since when does she care about my thoughts? I'm tempted to brush off her question with a breezy, *Oh, nothing* . . . but then I reconsider. This opening may never come again. She's reaching out. The least I can do is reach back.

"Tony," I say, trying not to sound too wistful.

She makes an affirmative noise in response, but nothing further. Until about a mile later when she says, "So. What happened with you two?"

"It's a long story."

"It's a long road."

I laugh. "True. Well . . . he had an affair. And he left me." Guess it's not such a long story, after all.

"That's it?"

"Isn't that enough?"

"Is it? You tell me. You're the marriage expert." The way she says the word *expert* makes it clear just how little she thinks of my expertise. "I mean, sure, it sucks. But you just let him go?"

"What was I supposed to do? Chain him to me?"

"Put up a fight at least. I mean you've been married for what . . . seventeen years?"

"Eighteen."

"Eighteen years. Seems like you'd fight to save that."

"She's pregnant."

This little bit of information finally shuts my sister up. I think she gets it now, but it's not enough for me. I want her to truly understand the depths of my suffering. "Tony and I tried to have a baby for years. I went through hormone shots, special diets, everything. I even stood on my head. Literally."

A memory that is both comic and tragic. "But we couldn't conceive. Or should I say, *I* couldn't conceive. Turns out the problem's all mine, because he's obviously fertile."

She glances over at me, and for the first time I see a new emotion on her face. Guilt. Her hand goes to her stomach, and I know I've made my point.

I turn on the radio, but neither of us sings. We spend the rest of the drive to Seligman ignoring each other.

22

There are a few different hotels to pick from when we get to Seligman, so I leave the choice up to Lindsay. When she pulls into the parking lot of the Supai, I give her a questioning look.

She removes the key from the ignition and drops it in my hand. "It has the best sign."

I'm not sure exactly what makes it the best—its cool, retro-neon design or the word *WI-FI*. Either way, I'm glad she made the decision. Now, if she doesn't like it, she has no one to blame but herself.

Our room is simple but clean. Like most inexpensive hotels, there's a separate room with the toilet and bathtub, leaving the sink in the main room with the beds. While Lindsay goes straight to the bathroom, I make my customary mattress inspection for bedbugs or suspicious sheet stains. She comes out while I'm straightening the spread on the bed nearest the AC unit. She pauses with her hand on the water faucet and looks at me over her shoulder.

"How do they look?"

"All clear."

"Cool."

One thing Lindsay and I both agree on is cleanliness. It may not be next to godliness, but it's right up there in the top ten. This gives me hope that maybe she and I can find common ground in other areas too.

Lindsay points at the bed I'm standing next to. "Can I have that one?"

"Sure." This is another thing that's worked out surprisingly well. Lindsay likes to be close to the air-conditioning, while I can't stand having it blow on me in the middle of the night. Most of these motels have wall units, so I let her take the bed closest to them. If there was a way to sleep through this trip, we'd be in great shape.

A few minutes later, we head out of the motel and onto the streets of Seligman for some exploring. There are a lot of the usual touristy things. Vintage cars sit here and there along the road. Some even have eyes painted on the windshields and mouths on their grills, as though they're ready to have a conversation with you at any moment. A mannequin dressed like Elvis in a red, white, and blue jumpsuit sits on the rear bumper of a pink Cadillac. The way he's positioned, he seems to be flirting with the mannequin seated beside him, who vaguely resembles Marilyn Monroe. Seligman's version of a mini-strip mall sports a second-story balcony lined with mannequins. Dressed in clothes from the fifties and sixties, they look like they're ready for an anachronistic sock hop.

I take some scenic shots with the video camera then hand it to Lindsay. "Want to indulge your inner Spielberg for a while?"

A faint blush colors her cheeks. Maybe it's from the walking. Maybe she remembers insulting me a few towns back. Regardless, the blush is followed by a smile. "Thanks."

I've found that the more things I let Lindsay control, the happier she is. And the happier Lindsay is, the more peaceful my experience is.

She takes in our surroundings, looking for interesting subject matter. "This is kind of how Spielberg got his start, you know."

"Strolling the streets of the Mother Road?"

"No. Making amateur movies when he was a kid. Only he did it with an eight-millimeter camera and sold tickets to his family and friends at a quarter a pop."

I laugh and shake my head. "He sure has come a long way."

"He had a dream and he never wavered. He knew exactly what he wanted to do with his life."

Her tone is determined and wistful at the same time. Like she has a dream of her own, but it's been crushed. "Lindsay—"

"Come on." She cuts me off and walks away, waving for me to follow her. "We're losing daylight."

As we head down the street, she starts giving me directions: stand next to that car, pretend like you're reading that sign, put your arm around the cardboard figure of James Dean. I'm a little self-conscious at first, until I realize that no one is paying any attention to us. All the tourists are in their own little worlds, doing their own touristy things. So I ignore everyone else, and when Lindsay tells me to kiss James Dean on his gritty cheek, I do.

Then I make a face and pretend to blow dust from my lips. "Yeesh, James needs a bath. And I need a drink."

Lindsay lowers the camera. "I could use some food. Want to grab dinner?"

"Sure. Have you seen any place that looks good?"

Shading her eyes with one hand, she almost turns in a complete circle before coming to a stop. She points down the street. "We've got to go there."

I squint and read the sign on the building. "The Road Kill Café." I look back at her. "Seriously?"

"Absolutely. Talk about local flavor."

There are some flavors best left alone. Especially at a diner whose motto is "You kill it, we grill it." But in the spirit of adventure, I'll give it a try. Besides, she's already halfway there. For a pregnant woman, she sure can hustle when she wants to. I have to hurry down the street to catch up with her.

The clientele inside the cafe seems to be an even mix of locals and tourists. I figure this is a good thing, since the local folks wouldn't frequent a place with bad food. A waitress leads us to an open table, and hands us menus as soon as we sit down.

"What can I get you gals to drink?"

"An ice tea," I say. "No lemon."

"Just ice water." Lindsay looks over the choices. "So, what do you recommend here?"

The gal points down at the menu with her pen. "The Tire Tread Teriyaki. Comes with a side salad, vegetables, and loaded baked potato."

Tire tread? From the look on Lindsay's face, she got stuck on the name of the dish too. "It's good, huh?" I ask.

She gives me a wink and a nod. "It'll make you want to slap your grandma. I'll be right back with your drinks."

As soon as our waitress is gone, I lean across the table and whisper to Lindsay. "It's not too late to leave."

"Come on. This is an adventure, right? Let's find the least lethal-looking thing on the menu."

Turns out, the scary names are just a clever cover for basic roadside café fare. Tire Tread Teriyaki is, in fact, grilled shrimp skewers. After debating between two other options, I decide to go with the petite steak.

The waitress comes back, sets our glasses on the table, and takes her order pad from her apron pocket. "Have you ladies decided?"

"I'll have the Long Gone Fawn," I say. "Medium rare, please. And a house salad."

Lindsay hands over her menu. "And I'll have the Chicken that Almost Crossed the Road."

"How do you want your potato? Mashed, baked, or fried?"

"Mashed. And ranch on my salad. Thanks."

"Great. I'll be right back with your salads and some rolls."

I take a moment to peruse the taxidermied heads on the walls. There's a buffalo, an elk, and several types of deer. Mounted on a shelf in the corner is some kind of small, spotted wildcat, ready to pounce. I pity the stuffed mouse who might wander by.

"Here you go." Lindsay gives me the camera. "You'd better record this place."

I take pictures of all the animals I can, pivoting in my seat. As I turn back to the table, a black leather vest over a light gray T-shirt fills the viewfinder. Lowering the camera, I see the shirt belongs to an older fellow who stands by Lindsay's chair. His weathered face has more lines than the road map in my purse, and his long, gray hair is pulled back into a ponytail. I bet there's a Harley out in the parking lot with his name on it.

"Hi," I say.

"You ladies want an interesting story for your video?"

That's it. No "hi" back, no "let me introduce myself." Just the offer of a story. How can I turn that down? If it's bad, I can always erase it later.

"Sure." I train the camera on him and start recording. "Go ahead."

"See those dollar bills hanging up in the bar?"

I follow his pointing finger with the camera and Lindsay looks over her shoulder. "Hey, just like in Oatman," she says.

"Yep," Harley Man answers. "Do you know how it started?"

"No," Lindsay and I say together.

Harley Man grins. "Back when this was still the Wild West, it was ranch country. Folks only got paid once a month then, so before the cowpokes rode the herd out to market, they'd stop by the saloon, write their name on a dollar, and nail it to the wall. That way, they knew when they got back, they'd at least have enough money for beer."

"No kidding," Lindsay says.

"It's the honest truth. You could call it frontier money management." He nods to us. "Enjoy your stay."

As he walks away the waitress scurries up with our salads and a breadbasket. "I hope Lou wasn't bugging you."

"Oh, no," I say. "He told us about the money on the walls. Fascinating history."

She laughs. "Lou does like to enlighten our guests. Lucky for you he wasn't in a talkative mood today or else you'd never get to eat your dinner." She gives the table a once-over. "If you need anything, just holler." Then she rushes to the next customer, pen and pad in hand.

The food smells great, but before I eat, I point the camera right at Lindsay. "Is there anything you'd like to say?"

"Yes." She picks up a roll and tears it in half. "Even though Natalie basically kidnapped me and then someone stole all my stuff—"

"And my car."

"And your car. Even though this trip got off to a pretty lousy start, it's getting better. I'm glad I came along."

A warm rush of emotion flows through me and I look at her over the top of the camera. "Do you really mean that?"

"Sure." She takes a bite out of her roll and talks around her half-full mouth. "Now I can honestly say I've eaten road kill. And I have you to thank for it."

23

The next morning starts off with a bang. Literally.

As soon as I turn the water off in the shower, I hear a voice in the next room. Hopefully, Lindsay turned on the TV. I strain to listen closer, and my heart sinks. That's no TV show.

"I told you, it's me and the baby or nothing. You can't have one without the other!"

Then something slams. And something else slams. I grab a towel off the top of the toilet tank and hurry into the other room before Lindsay can destroy anything. "What are you doing?"

Her face is red, her breath coming in short, hard bursts. "Making sure we don't leave anything behind in the dresser." She opens a drawer and then bangs it shut without even looking inside.

"We didn't put anything in the drawers," I remind her.

"Well . . . good. Then we can't forget anything." She opens one more drawer, bangs it for good measure, then throws herself on the bed. "Men are slime!"

I can't argue with her there. What puzzles me is why she was talking to Ben again.

"Did you call him or did he call you?"

"I called him." With her face pressed against the pillow, I can barely make out her words.

"Oh, Lindsay. You didn't tell him where we are, did you?"

"No, I didn't."

"Then why did you call him?" I pull the pillow away from her, and she sits up.

"I wanted to know why he followed me. If you hadn't hustled us out of there in such a hurry, I could have asked him yesterday."

I wondered how long it would take before her troubles became my fault again. "Well, what did he say? Why did he follow you?"

"He misses me." Lindsay's eyes are shiny, like two big, blue, wet marbles. Her eyelids flutter and she looks down at the bedspread. "He said he's been miserable since I left, and he wants me to come home. But—" The rest of the sentence is choked off by a sob.

I give her a moment before encouraging her to continue. "But?"

"But he still doesn't want the baby. He wants me, but no baby."

"He wants you to terminate the pregnancy?" It's a terrible thought to put into words.

"He never came out and said so, but what else could he mean?"

"Maybe he wants you to give the baby up for adoption." An image pops into my mind: me holding a chubby, squirming infant. It could be the perfect solution. For me, at least. Maybe not for Lindsay. Without the baby, there'd be nothing to keep her from going back to Ben. And how would she deal with watching her sister raise the child she gave away?

"He doesn't understand. I *want* this baby. I know we messed up, I know we did things out of order, but that's not the baby's fault."

That answers my question.

She falls over on her side, recovers the pillow, and curls her body around it. "It's not like I got pregnant all by myself. He's responsible too."

I wish I could help her. I wish I could tell her that everything will be all right. That one day, she'll meet the perfect man, the man God's been saving just for her, a man who will love her and her baby. I wish I could tell her not to give up on happily ever after.

But I can't. Because I don't believe in it anymore myself.

So I do the only useful thing I can think of: I pack up our stuff. I gather our pajamas and dirty clothes, our toothbrushes and toothpaste, Lindsay's contact lens solution. I pick up travel-size shampoo bottles and soaps. I zip up suitcases, turn off lights, and grab our purses, all while Lindsay pours her heart into a borrowed pillow on a borrowed bed in a borrowed room.

———— ∞ ————

After leaving the hotel, we stop at a gas station to fill up the car. When I go in to pay, Lindsay follows me. "I need sugar."

One more thing we have in common.

There's a short line at the counter. By the time it's my turn, Lindsay is standing next to me, her arms loaded with candy bars, a bag of cheddar-flavored kettle chips, a bottle of Dr Pepper, and a bottle of water.

I point at her haul. "Are you planning to share any of that, or should I buy my own?"

"I'll share," she says as she dumps it on the counter.

While the man is ringing us up, she spins a rack of post-cards. She takes one out and shows it to me. "Look at this."

It's a scenic view of the Grand Canyon. The shot is slightly out of focus and the colors are muddy. They don't do justice to what the canyon must really look like.

The cashier pauses with his finger poised over the register keys. "Do you want to buy that too?"

"What? Oh, no." She puts the postcard back in the rack. "Are we near the Grand Canyon?"

"You bet. Take you about ninety minutes or so to get there from here."

"Really?" She turns to me now. "Natalie, we've got to go see it."

"I don't know." That's at least a three-hour round trip, not counting whatever time we'd actually spend at the canyon.

"Oh, come on. How can we not stop there? When are we ever going to have the chance to see it again?" She dips her chin and looks up at me from under her long, pale lashes. "Please?"

Why does she keep doing this to me? And why do I keep falling for it? I know she's only being nice and sweet in order to get her way. The next time I do something she doesn't like, she'll get all snarky again. But times like this are so hard to come by, I hate to ruin it.

I look at the cashier. "Can you tell us how to get there?"

He smiles and reaches under the counter. "I can do better. I have a map."

"Great. Add it to the bill."

Lindsay claps her hands. "You won't regret it, Nat. It's about time we saw something cool."

I frown at her. "We've seen cool stuff."

"Yeah," she says, taking the bag from the cashier. "But this is a natural wonder." We're heading for the door when she stops and thrusts the bag at me. "I better make another pit stop before we hit the road." Then she makes a mad dash for the rear of the store.

I push my way through the big glass door and head for the car. A natural wonder indeed. You know what would be a true natural wonder? If we make it to Illinois without her driving me nuts.

Now *that* would be a wonder.

24

Standing on the rim of the Grand Canyon, I have to admit that Lindsay was right. It was worth the extra time and gas it took to get here, as well as the hassle of finding a parking spot and crowding onto a shuttle bus. I'd do it all over again to be able to take in the grandeur of God's creation.

The majesty of the place is overwhelming. Looking down the sloping rocks, past the jagged peaks, I glimpse the Colorado River snaking below. I think of the power it took to carve this enormous canyon through solid rock. It dwarfs me. It makes my problems seem small and petty. Insignificant in the big picture of life.

Lindsay stands beside me. I keep waiting for her to make some wisecrack, or to do something silly like yell across the void to see if it will echo, but she doesn't. For once, I believe my sister has been awed into silence. Further evidence of the power of the canyon.

"Amazing, isn't it?"

Lindsay pushes a lock of hair behind her ear, but the wind immediately blows it back in her face. "Yeah, it is. And we almost didn't come. You are so lucky you've got me with you."

"Oh, I know just how lucky I am." I press my lips together and turn on the camera. "Wave at Mom and Dad."

She does. Then, in bold, elaborate motions worthy of a game show model, she indicates the vista behind her. I let the camera follow, taking in everything I can, and knowing there's no way a digital recording will render an accurate representation. When I pan back to Lindsay, her expression is noticeably different. She glares past me, her arms hanging straight down at her sides.

"What are you doing here?"

I turn to see who she's talking to and nearly drop the camera. Ben stands there, looking flushed and guarded at the same time. This guy is harder to shake than the stomach flu.

"I need to talk to you, Lindsay." He steps forward. "Since you just yell at me on the phone, I figured we'd have to do it in person."

My blazing cheeks must surely be redder than the rocks in the canyon. "You can't keep stalking her like this."

His expression turns indignant, like he's truly wounded by my opinion of him. "I'm not stalking her. I'm following her. There's a big difference."

"I don't know what your problem is, buddy, but you can't seem to get it through your head. She doesn't want to be with you."

Ben squeezes his forehead and lets out a growl. Finally, I can see the letters tattooed on his fingers. They spell out LOVE. A word that has nothing to do with the kind of person he really is.

"That's not true," he snaps at me. "She doesn't have a problem with me. She has a problem with me not wanting the baby."

"You bet I do," Lindsay snaps at him.

"But what if I did want the baby?"

Lindsay's face softens, her eyes large and full of hope. "You mean you do want the baby?"

"I didn't say that. But if I did, then you'd want to be with me, right? That means you still love me. And I love you. I'm not going to let you go without a fight."

He reaches out to her. Even though his movement is too slow to be meant as anything but a caress, all I can see is his hand getting closer to the spot where the bruise used to be. And I lose it.

"Don't you touch her." I swat his hand away and wedge my body between them. "You think all you have to do is slap a woman around and she'll be yours forever? Think again. You've hurt her for the last time."

Ben looks at me like I'm crazy. "What are you talking about? I've never laid a hand on Lindsay."

"Natalie—"

"Stay out of this." I bark at Lindsay, then push Ben away from her. "Never touched her, huh? Then how'd she get that bruise on her face?"

"She got up in the middle of the night and ran into the bedroom door."

"You seriously expect me to believe that?"

"Yeah, because it's the truth. She can't see a thing without her contacts."

Wow, this guy is good. There's not a hint of remorse in his voice, not a clue that he's making the story up as he goes along. "Sure she did. I'll bet you'd love to take her back with you where she could run into the door again, wouldn't you?"

I give him another shove for good measure. But this time, Ben doesn't move. His feet are planted and he stands his ground. "Lady, I've never hit a woman, any woman, in my life. But I might make an exception for you."

"Excuse me." A booming voice draws my attention to the tall park ranger standing behind Ben.

When Ben turns around, he actually has to tilt his head up to look the man in the eye. "What?"

"I was concerned there might be some trouble here." The man looks from me to Lindsay. "Is this fellow bothering you ladies?"

"No," Lindsay says.

"Yes," I say.

Hands on his hips, Ben drops his chin to his chest and mutters something I'm glad I can't hear. Then he looks back up at the ranger and jerks his thumb over his shoulder at me. "She's crazy. I'm just trying to talk to my girlfriend."

"He's stalking us," I say.

"No, I'm not!"

By now, most of the people at the lookout spot have turned from the grandeur of the canyon to take in the spectacle of the crazy lady, the pregnant woman, and the stalker. Another ranger walks up. I can tell from the way they look at each other, they're eager to remove us and restore a sense of peace and tranquility.

The new guy is shorter than the first one, but what he lacks in height, he makes up in pure muscle. His forearms are so thick, I wonder if he has to have his shirts specially made.

He motions to Ben. "Why don't you come with me, sir?"

"I didn't do anything wrong."

"I'm not saying you did. If you come with me, you can tell me your side of the story, and we'll get this whole thing cleared up."

Ben deflates. He turns to Lindsay, hands out, palms up, and tries one more time. "Tell them I didn't do anything."

Lindsay's wavering. I can almost hear the battle going on in her head . . . *He loves me . . . He promised he'd never do it again . . . But he still doesn't want the baby . . .*

"Please, Ben," she finally says, "just go with him. Go away and stop following me."

His jaw tightens and he blows out a big breath. "Fine. We'll do it your way. For now."

A wave of relief washes over me as I watch him walk away with the ranger. But Lindsay looks like she could burst into tears at any second.

"Are you ladies going to be all right?"

The concern from park ranger number one is all it takes to push Lindsay over the figurative edge. She puts her hands to her face, trying to hide her sobs, which is useless. "I don't understand how he keeps finding me."

"Maybe because you keep telling him."

"I didn't tell him we were coming here."

She had to tell him. Not only did we get off 66, we made quite a substantial side trip. There's no way he could have guessed we'd be here, in this exact spot on the rim. "You've been texting him, though, haven't you?"

"So? I never said where we were going."

"Then how did he know where to find us?"

"I don't know!"

"Ladies. Excuse me." The ranger breaks in. "I think I might have an answer for you." He holds his hand out to Lindsay. "May I see your phone?"

She hesitates, then looks at me. Oh sure, now she wants my opinion. I nod, and she takes it out of her purse and gives it to him.

Most of the people who were looking at us before lost interest as soon as Ben was escorted away. But a few are still hanging on everything we say, waiting for the drama to play itself out.

One guy in the back of the crowd pipes up. "Toss it over the rail. That'll solve the problem!"

Wouldn't it be awesome if Mr. Ranger did just that? It would sure teach my sister a lesson if he pulled his arm back and propelled that silly little phone into the canyon. But it would also be littering, not to mention destruction of personal property. Not likely this fellow would partake in either of those activities.

He grins at Lindsay. "Don't worry. There's an easier solution." He taps on the phone's touch screen, slides his finger across it, taps a bit more, then stops. "Aha. Here we go. You have FindMe installed on your phone."

Lindsay's hand goes to her mouth. "Oh, man. I forgot that was even on there."

I don't know what the big deal is. "What's FindMe?"

"It's a social networking app." He holds the phone so I can see the screen, but there's so much glare I still don't know what I'm looking at. "It's meant to help you meet up with friends. Every time you send a text message, it gives your exact location."

"How exact?"

"Down to the street address and zip code." He hands the phone back to Lindsay. "I'd disable that if I were you."

She nods and starts moving her fingers across the screen. "I'm doing it right now."

So even though Lindsay never told him where we were, she still led him right to us. And it took a trip to the Grand Canyon to figure it out. "Thank you," I tell the ranger. "We'll be going now. Is there any way you can detain that man long enough to give us a head start?"

"No problem. We'll talk to him for a while." He takes a few steps, then stops and says over his shoulder, "You might want to consider taking out a restraining order. Just to be safe."

127

It's a good idea. I put it at the top of my mental to-do list, right below *Get my sister safely to Mom and Dad's house.*

"You lied to me." I say after the ranger is gone.

She looks up from her phone. "No, I didn't."

"Maybe you didn't technically tell Ben where we were, but you still gave him the information. It's the same thing."

"But I didn't know I was doing it. I forgot that app was loaded on the phone. I swear." She stares at me, her big blue eyes as sorrowful as can be, waiting for me to cave. But I don't. I don't tell her I misjudged her and that I'm sorry for getting upset with her. Because I'm not sorry. And right now, I don't trust her. Not one bit.

When it becomes obvious she's not going to get her way this time, her demeanor changes. Her brows furrow and her lips press into a thin, hard line. "Fine. Be that way. I don't care what you think." She stomps off toward the shuttle bus pick-up area.

If I had a choice, I'd go the other way. I'd walk away from the plans I keep making that never turn out how I want. Away from the people I put my trust in only to have them destroy it. Away from this stupid trip.

If only I could walk along the rim of the canyon until the sun began to sink, throwing shadows on the walls and washing the sky in a watercolor of reds and oranges. If I could, I'd crawl right under the railing and sit at the edge of the rocks, letting my feet dangle into nothing as the air grew cool and quiet around me.

But I can't do any of that. I have a sister to watch out for and parents to get home to. So I follow Lindsay to the shuttle, the rubber soles of my sneakers heavy as if they had turned to lead.

25

By the time we leave the Grand Canyon behind, I've made a decision. "We've wasted enough time on side trips. I'm going to find the quickest way to Illinois and stick to it."

"Fine by me." Lindsay doesn't bother looking in my direction. Her nose is to the window, as if she's fascinated by the scrub and rocks zipping by.

I turn on the radio and push the button I programmed earlier for a show tune station. As Patti LuPone's voice fills the car, I glance at Lindsay. In my mind, I dare her to try to change the channel. But she continues ignoring me. Apparently, I have become too insignificant for her even to acknowledge what she considers my bad taste in music.

My stomach rumbles, and I realize breakfast was five long hours ago. I was hoping to make some good travel time today, but thanks to our spontaneous journey and subsequent stalker sighting, we're not much farther than when we started this morning. I consider pushing onward, but guilt gets the better of me. If I'm hungry, Lindsay must be starving. No matter how bratty she's been toward me, I can't deprive a pregnant woman of food.

Flagstaff is a good-sized city right on Interstate 40. But we're still not escaping Route 66. As we drive through town, reminders of it are everywhere. And when I stop to fill up the car with gas, a local at the next pump over calls out to me without any prompting.

"You gals looking for a good place to have lunch?"

I shield my eyes and look in his direction. "Matter of fact, we are."

"You should head over to Granny's Closet."

Now Lindsay sticks her head out the car window. "Sounds like a thrift store."

The man laughs as he takes the nozzle from his gas tank and returns it to the pump. "No, it's a restaurant. They've got a prime rib sandwich that's out of this world. And you can check out Little Louie."

"Who's Little Louie?" I ask.

"Well now, you'll have to go there to find out. But you can't miss him." The man motions down the street. "You just go that way to Five Points, make a right on Milton, and there you go."

"Thanks." I shut the cover on the gas cap and walk around to the driver's side. "I guess we'll give Granny a try."

"All right, then." He gives us a little wave, gets into his car, and drives off.

Lindsay turns to me as I buckle my seat belt. "You sure know how to work your magic on men."

What is she talking about? "Excuse me?"

"Men are always falling all over themselves to help you. This guy, the Oatman dude, the security guard. You don't even have to ask for help. They just seem to know you need it, and there they are."

It's the kind of statement that could come off as negative and judgmental, but the tone of Lindsay's voice is just the opposite. I get the feeling she wishes the same kind of thing would happen to her.

As I pull out of the gas station and down the street, I think back over the last few weeks. I remember the soundman, who was so kind to me and complimented me on my blouse. And the 7-Eleven clerk who gave me a tiny bit of affirmation when I needed it. Maybe Lindsay's right. Maybe there's something about me that brings out the protector in men. Every man except Tony, the one man who vowed to always love and protect me.

It takes us all of five minutes to reach Granny's Closet. As I park the car, Lindsay leans forward, peering out the window. "Holy cow."

"That must be Little Louie." We're looking at a huge, wooden lumberjack standing beside the building. It's an ironic title if ever there was one, because Little Louie is at least ten feet tall.

"Here's hoping the food is better than the decor." Lindsay gets out of the car, slams the door behind her, and walks to the restaurant. I lock up the car and walk in double time to catch up with her.

We're quickly seated and given menus. After I decide what I want, I take a moment to look around the place. Seeing a giant lumberjack outside, I expected the inside of Granny's to be rustic, but it's much homier than that. There's lots of brick, flower boxes full of red and purple silk blooms, and some beautiful stained glass windows. The unique one is an image of Granny playing a banjo.

"What do you think?" I ask Lindsay.

"The barbecued beef looks good."

"I meant the decor."

"Oh." She fiddles with her silverware. "It's nice."

"Yeah. It is." I can't stand it. If we don't break through this icy wall, we're both going to be miserable. As much as I want to hold my ground and wait for her to apologize to me, I know I can't. Someone has to make the first move, and that someone is going to be me.

Casually, I say, "But then again, it's no Road Kill Café."

She keeps her eyes on the table, but one corner of her mouth rises in a hesitant grin. "No, it's not."

"Lindsay." I reach out, stilling her hand. "I'm sorry."

She looks up, but her face is blank. I can't read her.

"I'm sorry for calling you a liar. You said you forgot about that app on your phone, and I should have believed you."

Her shoulders raise and lower with the quick breath she takes in. "It's the truth, you know. I really did forget about it."

"I know. I believe you." Funny thing is, I *didn't* believe her. Not until just now.

"Thank you." She pulls away and clasps her hands together in her lap.

Now it's her turn. I wait for her to tell me how sorry she is for being difficult, for her bad attitude. But the waitress walks up.

"Can I take your order?"

If Lindsay meant to humble herself and say anything apologetic, the moment is gone now. We order. After the waitress leaves, we chitchat about how nice the weather is today. When that topic runs dry in about a minute, I pick up a card from the table.

"Hey, this explains the big guy in the parking lot. Originally, this place was called The Lumberjack Café, and there were two even bigger lumberjacks outside. The Zanzucchi family bought it back in 1974 and renamed it after Granny Ermalinda Zanzucchi."

"What happened to the other two statues?" The fact that she admits to being interested proves she must be as desperate for something to talk about as I am.

I skim the card and paraphrase it. "The family donated them to Northern Arizona University. They're still there, one inside the Skydome and one outside."

"So Little Louie is a replacement?"

"Um hm."

"Why do they call him Louie?"

I flip the card over, then shrug. "I have no idea. It doesn't say."

It's a relief when the food arrives and we can turn our attention to eating. The portions are large, which is a blessing, because the longer we eat, the less I have to talk.

It's a pleasant meal, and when we walk back out to the car, I'm encouraged. She may not have told me she's sorry, but at least my sister is being civil again.

"Hey, Nat."

I turn around to see Lindsay standing next to Little Louie. I cock my head, wondering what she's got in mind.

She shrugs. "Since we're here, you might as well pull out that camera of yours."

It's impossible to hide my surprise. "Seriously?"

"Sure. It'd be a shame to miss a giant lumberjack."

As I dig through my purse for the camera, it feels like a thousand little pins are pricking my nose.

I guess I got my apology, after all.

26

Wake up. We're here."

I open my eyes and slowly raise my head from the uncomfortable position I was in. When Lindsay offered to drive back in Flagstaff, I'd been more than a little surprised, but grateful. Sleep must have come soon after we hit the road because I don't remember most of the trip. "Where is here?"

"The Wigwam Village in Holbrook, Arizona."

"You want to stay here?"

"Yes, I do."

She sounds so proud of herself, I don't dare tell her I was hoping to cross into New Mexico tonight.

We go into the office. I'm still groggy from my unplanned nap, so Lindsay walks up to the front desk and takes charge. "We'd like a wigwam, please."

The man behind the counter smiles. "Let me see what we have." He clicks around on the computer, then looks back at Lindsay. "You're in luck. We have one wigwam available. It only has one bed, though. A double. Is that all right?"

"Sure. My sister and I can share."

Since when? I'm not sure how to take this new side of Lindsay. It's like I woke up in an alternate reality, one where she's happy to take care of me for a change.

"Wonderful." The clerk holds out his hand. "I just need to see your ID and a credit card."

Lindsay looks at me, turning her head fast enough to give herself whiplash. Ah, now that money is a factor, everything's back to normal.

After registering us, the man hands me the key. "It's the third wigwam from the right. If you need anything at all, just let me know."

There are about fifteen concrete wigwams forming a semi-circle behind the office. We walk into ours and Lindsay immediately laughs. "This is so cool."

It's definitely different. While the outside of the wigwam is curved, the inside is made up of flat panels slanted to create a roundish room. The walls go straight up, then angle in toward the middle. But rather than continue up until they meet at a point, they meet a flat ceiling. Because of the shape, nothing along the perimeter is higher than four feet. The window, AC unit, light switches, all are the perfect height for an eight-year-old. Even so, the room doesn't feel cramped. Quite a feat, considering we're inside a giant cone with the top cut off and closed over. But there is a dilemma.

I point at the bed. "Do you want the side closer to the air conditioner or the bathroom?"

Lindsay twists her mouth as she debates. Finally, she drops her purse on the side of her choice. "Air conditioner."

I sit on my side of the bed. "How did you find this place?"

"I saw a sign on the road that said 'Sleep in a Wigwam.' It sounded like fun."

Lindsay's new attitude makes me rethink my decision to stay off 66. If she's starting to enjoy the adventure of our journey, maybe we should see more of the Mother Road after all. I'm about to ask her when the strains of "Love Stinks" play out from my purse. It's the third time Tony's called since we left California. I didn't answer any of those times, and I don't intend to answer now.

"You can't ignore him forever," Lindsay says.

She's right, but is one night of peace too much to ask for? Since she and I aren't fighting right now, the last thing I want to do is get all riled up talking to Tony. On the other hand, I can only handle one conflict at a time. This might be the perfect time to talk to him.

I dive for the purse and answer the call before it can go to voicemail. "Hello."

"It's about time you answered." No doubt about it. He's angry.

"What do you want?"

"I want to know why you're contesting the divorce."

"Because you're trying to sell my home."

"No, I'm trying to sell the house we bought together so we can split the money equally. It's a simple financial decision."

He is so lucky Lindsay's sitting on the other side of the mattress, because that's the only reason I don't tell him exactly what I'm thinking. "There is nothing simple about this," I say slowly. "You have no right to make me sell my home. You're the one who asked for the divorce, not me."

Either there's no one within earshot of him, or he just doesn't care, because he doesn't censor any of his thoughts about the situation.

"Is that language really necessary?" I ask.

Now Lindsay leans over, putting her mouth close to the phone. "Is that jerk bothering you? Do you want me to talk to him?"

"Who's that?"

The demanding tone in his voice grates on me. He has no right to demand anything from me. Not anymore. "It's my sister. Not that it's any of your business."

"What are you doing with her?" He pauses, as if processing this amazing news. "Where are you?"

"In Hollbrook, Arizona."

"Arizona? What are you doing there?"

"We're driving to Illinois to see our parents."

"Why are you driving? Why didn't you just fly?"

"She didn't want to fly."

"Why not?"

"Because she's pregnant."

I hear the quick release of breath on the other end of the phone. "Oh." Then a pause before he continues. "I didn't know she was married."

Something snaps in my brain. How can he say something so stupid? "She's not. But it's not a requirement for conception, is it? You know, maybe that's what you and I were doing wrong all those years. Maybe if we'd skipped getting married and just shacked up, we would have had a herd of children."

The bed shakes as Lindsay gets up and hurries into the bathroom. She slams the door behind her, and I realize what a big mistake I just made. And it's all Tony's fault.

"Look," I tell him, "I don't want to talk to you about this anymore. From now on, if you have anything to say to me, you can do it through my lawyer."

Without waiting for an answer, I end the call and turn the phone off. Then I step to the bathroom door and knock on it gently.

"Lindsay?"

"What?" The way she fires off that one syllable communicates volumes.

"I'm sorry for what I said. Tony made me so angry that I kind of lost my mind. I didn't mean to insult you." I press my palm and the side of my face against the door, trying to hear through the wood, to make out words she's not saying. "Lindsay?"

The doorknob jiggles and I back away right before she pulls the door open. I was all ready for her to be harsh and angry. I'm used to dealing with that. But what I see now throws me. Her face is wet from tears. Her nose and eyes are red. Her lips downturned. I have no idea how to respond to this broken, fragile version of my sister.

"You must hate me." Her words come out in a heartbreaking whisper.

"Hate you? Why would you say that?"

"Because every time you look at me, you must think about Tony, and what he did." Her nose starts to run so she reaches behind her, yanks a length of toilet paper from the roll, and blows into it. "And you must wonder why someone like me got pregnant when you couldn't."

She needs affirmation, and she's looking for me to give it to her. I should tell her that all I've ever seen when I look at her is a beautiful woman carrying the gift of life. But that would be a lie, and there's been enough of that lately. "You're right, I did feel that way at first. But I don't anymore."

"You don't?"

"I don't. Do you know when it changed?"

She shakes her head.

"Back in Oatman, when you washed off that little girl's carrot. It made me think about how you'd be with your own daughter. With my niece."

"Or nephew."

"Or nephew," I say with a laugh. "And it made me happy."

Tears dribble from her eyes, but at least now she's smiling. I step into the tiny space and wrap my arms around her.

"I love you. Even if you are a brat sometimes."

She laughs and returns the gesture. Then, as we stand in the bathroom of a concrete wigwam with our arms around each other and our stomachs pressed together, her baby makes a statement of its own.

"Yowza!" I jump back, looking down at her baby bump. "Did you feel that?"

"Of course I did," she says, wiping her eyes with the back of her hand. "I'm surprised you did, though."

"One thing's for sure. She's got her mother's spunk."

She puts her hand against her stomach. "And his father's sense of rhythm. I think he's dancing a mambo in there."

Interesting how I keep referring to the baby as a girl, and she's convinced it's a boy. I don't want to ruin our sisterly moment by voicing my opinion of Ben, but regardless of what sex it is, I sure hope rhythm is the only thing this little baby inherits from its father.

27

The next morning I wake to find Lindsay already dressed and sitting at the tiny table across from the bed. She chews on a pen as she stares at the maps and travel guides spread out in front of her.

"What are you doing?" I ask, rubbing the sleep-sand from my eyes.

She talks around the end of the Bic. "Trying to figure out the best way to get from here to there."

I sit up and roll my shoulders back, stretching my neck at the same time. "You keep looking. I need a shower."

After I'm done in the bathroom and feeling somewhat human again, I join Lindsay in looking over the maps. While much of Route 66 runs parallel to major interstates, there are several places where it jigs and jags wildly to the north and south. We debate the pros and cons of each way. If we take the interstates, we'll reach our destination sooner, but we'll miss a lot of cool stuff. If we stick to 66, we'll see enough bizarre attractions to fill several memory cards, but it will take us at least a week longer to get to Mom and Dad's. In the end, we decide it's best to compromise: we'll stick to the interstates but take in as many of the Mother Road oddities as we can find along the way.

After we put our bags in the car, I tell Lindsay I want to take one more picture of her in front of the wigwam. A woman smoking a cigarette next to her own teepee overhears me.

"Here, let me take one of both of you." She takes one more drag on the cigarette, then balances it carefully on top of a wooden post.

I hand her the camera and pose next to Lindsay, who immediately puts her arm around my waist. No rabbit ears this time. Just a sideways hug, a tilt of her head toward me, and a wave of her free hand to the camera.

"Thanks," I tell the woman.

"No problem." She retrieves the still-smoldering cigarette and holds it between the sides of two fingers. "You two sisters?"

We both nod, then the lady nods back.

"I could tell. You have the same smile. Have a nice day, now."

So far, we are having the perfect day. It couldn't be better if I plotted it out myself. Mostly, I'm happy, but a tiny part of me, a little slice of my brain, is wary. Yes, Lindsay and I had a breakthrough last night. We connected as sisters in a way we never have before. But I can't help wondering how long our newfound camaraderie will last. How long will it be before I say the wrong thing, look at her the wrong way, and she goes ballistic?

The woman walks away. Lindsay heads for the car. "Do you want me to drive first?"

"Do you want to drive first?" I don't know why I'm questioning her. There wasn't a note of sarcasm in her voice. No reason for me to expect a hidden meaning or agenda. But I do it out of habit.

Calm down, I tell myself. *Don't look for trouble where there isn't any.*

"Yeah. That would be great."

We get in the car, fasten our seat belts, and drive down the road. Our adventure continues.

―――∞∞∞―――

It's probably the best day I've ever had with my sister. We take turns driving. We listen to each other's music on the radio and find common ground in artists like Michael Bublé and Bono. We crack jokes about the kitschy souvenirs we've found, but at every opportunity we buy more of them than we should. We have T-shirts, bumper stickers, refrigerator magnets, bottle openers, shot glasses, even a bamboo back scratcher that I plan to give to Jade. And we shoot lots of video. By the time we arrive at Tucumcari, New Mexico, I'm ready to settle in for the night.

After we check into the Blue Swallow Hotel, we go back outside to explore the town. The sun has disappeared and neon lights blaze on the main strip. There are so many illuminated signs, I don't know where to look first. It's like a mini-Las Vegas, only cleaner and with no casinos.

"What do you feel like eating?" I ask Lindsay.

"I don't know." She's got the camera again, and she seems intent on capturing every shiny thing in sight. "To tell you the truth, I'm not really hungry yet."

"Okay. Let's just walk until something grabs our attention."

Lindsay's not the only camera-toting tourist in Tucumcari. The sidewalks are full of people doing the same thing she is. As we stroll along, we come across a group of Asian college-age girls. They're taking turns recording one another in front of different buildings, but no matter how they run around and reorganize, one of them is always left out, stuck in the role of photographer.

I walk up behind the girl currently holding the camera and tap her on the shoulder. "Excuse me. Would you like me to take a picture of all of you together?"

She glances over her shoulder looking confused. I repeat myself, this time using exaggerated hand motions. Her friends all start talking at once, their language short and clipped. I don't understand a word they're saying, but from the way they smile and point at me, I gather they understand my offer and are happy about it.

Grinning now, the gal hands me the camera. "Thank you," she says deliberately. Then she runs to join her friends. They huddle close to one another, waving and mugging for the video.

A minute later, amid a chorus of thank yous, they continue on down the street. When I turn to Lindsay, she's got her camera trained on me.

"Did you record all that?" I point toward the departing students.

"Yes, I did. It was a very nice cultural exchange." She lowers the camera and hands it to me. "Mom and Dad will be so proud."

If Mom even remembers me. The last time I saw her was Christmas three years back. Her memory was already getting sketchy then. She stayed home when Dad drove Tony and me to the airport. When Dad hugged me and said, "Come back soon, Sugar Plum," it was all I could do not to cry. Because I couldn't bear to see my mother slip away, piece by piece. I knew I wouldn't be back for a while.

Lindsay and I continue walking. "When was the last time you saw them?" I ask.

She blows out a breath and bites her lip. "Right after I left college. So that was, what . . ."

I do the mental math with her. Lindsay attended Illinois State for two years before she decided college wasn't right for her and dropped out.

"Five years ago," we say together.

"How was Mom then?" I ask.

"Not terrible. But I could see where it was going."

So we both chose to avoid our mother rather than face the pain of seeing her mind deteriorate. It's something else we have in common, and I can tell she isn't any prouder of it than I am.

The flashing sign of a Mexican restaurant catches my eye. I grab Lindsay's arm, pull her to a stop, and point across the street. "What do you think?"

"I think it's a great idea." She puts her hand on her side. "So does junior."

Good. The more we eat, the less we have to talk. If we're lucky, we can put off the topic of Mom and how to deal with her a little while longer.

28

Because of the way the highway is laid out, we are able to cover four states in the next three days. From New Mexico, we cut across the chimney top of Texas, through the pot of Oklahoma, over the most southeasterly tip of Kansas, and head up through Missouri on a diagonal. Lindsay and I have spent a lot of time eating, laughing, singing, and talking, and we've managed to sidestep topics too deep or too personal. She doesn't talk about Ben, I don't talk about Tony, and neither one of us mentions our parents. It's a strategy that works well. At least it did until my phone rings and Dad is on the other end.

"Hi, Dad."

"Hey, Sugar Plum." His voice booms. "How are my road warriors doing?"

"We're great. Hold on a second." I turn down the radio and hit a button on the front of the phone. "I put you on speaker. Now you can talk to both of us."

"Wonderful. Lindy Lou! Are you there?"

I'd forgotten about his old nickname. It makes her sound like a Dr. Seuss character. As I hold back my laughter, she squeezes the steering wheel harder and shakes her head.

"I'm here, Dad," she says.

"Whereabouts on the road are you?"

I glance at my watch. "We left Rolla, Missouri, about an hour ago."

"No kidding. When do you think you'll be here?"

"Well . . ." I check the map we went over before starting off this morning. "If we push it, we can probably be home tonight."

Lindsay waggles her fingers at me and I turn to see her shaking her head furiously. "On the other hand," I say quickly, "we'll need to stop for lunch, and there are bound to be some touristy things we'll want to check out. So probably not tonight. But tomorrow for sure."

"Oh." Dad's energy drops just a bit. "Your mother and I can't wait to see you girls. But we want you to enjoy your trip. And to be safe."

"Thanks, Dad."

We chat a little more before saying good-bye and hanging up. I drop the phone in my purse, then turn toward Lindsay. "What was all that about?"

"What was what about?"

"You know. Not wanting to get there tonight."

She shrugs, trying so hard to be nonchalant that it has the opposite effect. "Why rush? Like you said, we might want to see some stuff."

Sure. And I'm the queen of Denmark. I'm tempted to call her on it, but decide not to. With her behind the wheel, it's best to let it rest. I'll wait until we've reached our final destination of the day, then I'll talk to her about it. Whether she wants to talk or not.

We stop for the night when we get to Bloomington, Illinois, a town so close to our final destination it seems silly to spend the money on a hotel room.

"Are you sure you don't want me to keep driving?" I leave the car idling. "Another hour and a half and we can be there."

"I'm sure." She sighs and lets her head fall back against the headrest. "Look, I don't want the first time I see Mom and Dad in five years to be when I'm hungry, tired, and cranky. Okay?"

"Okay." I turn off the engine and pull the key from the ignition. "Let's go get a room."

For our last night on the road, it's a little anticlimactic. No quirky Route 66 lodgings this time. We're staying in a national chain hotel and will probably walk across the street to have dinner at a national chain restaurant. Which is just as well. Lindsay is so distracted, the fun of anything wild and unusual would be lost on her now.

The elevator on our end of the hotel takes so long to come down, we decide to take the stairs. After lugging our overnight necessities up three flights, we find our room. I struggle with the key card, sliding it in and out of the slot at different speeds until the green light finally comes on. After practically falling into the room, I dump my stuff on the nearest bed and call out to Lindsay, "I need to use the bathroom first."

She says something affirmative, which is good, because there's no stopping me now. I probably shouldn't have bought such a large bottle of water at that last minimart.

When I come out of the bathroom, Lindsay is standing to the side of the sink, staring at herself in the mirror.

I walk around her and lean over to wash my hands. "Do you want to talk about it?"

She pulls the rubber band from her ponytail, letting her hair fall free around her shoulders. "What are they going to say when they see me?"

"Who? Mom and Dad?"

"No, Brad and Angelina." She rolls her eyes at my reflection. "Yes, Mom and Dad."

Great. Snarky Lindsay is back. I had really hoped we'd left her somewhere along the road. But I can't be too hard on her. The last time she saw our parents, her hair was normal. Now, it's three different colors: bleached-white blonde, burgundy, and about an inch of her natural sandy-blonde at the roots. She's certainly got enough to think about without worrying how her hair looks.

"It's really not so bad, you know." I smile at her. "In fact, I don't think they'll be surprised at all."

"You don't?"

"No," I say with a shake of my head. "You've always been an artsy kind of person, and that's what artsy people do."

She steps back and cocks her head to the side. "Excuse me?"

"Besides, it's not too late to fix it." There's a drugstore right across the street. We could pick up a box of hair color and touch it up tonight.

"Fix it?"

"Sure. Then they'd never even know. Of course, we have a zillion hours of you looking like that on our travel videos, but that's okay. Everyone makes mistakes, right?"

"Are you insane?" Lindsay erupts, face red, a lava flow of emotions aimed straight at me. "How dare you tell me to fix it. I can't believe you'd even suggest something like that. And then to call him a mistake—"

"Him? I never—"

She pokes her finger at my chest. "My baby is not a mistake. Don't you ever call him that again!"

"That's not what I meant." I try to explain, but she whirls and runs out of the room, slamming the door behind her.

This is terrible. How could she misunderstand me so badly? I rush after her, but in a moment of clarity stop to grab my purse with the room key in it. Then I run outside.

After jogging down the stairs, I look around, but don't see her. How could she possibly be out of sight already? She didn't have that much of a head start. I run out to the parking lot and finally spot her, racewalking down the sidewalk. Of course, in her condition, it's more of a waddle than a walk, but she's still moving pretty fast. She must be furious.

"Lindsay, wait!" I call out as I sprint toward her. She doesn't acknowledge hearing me, but her arms pump a little faster.

When I catch up, I walk beside her, breathing hard. "Lindsay, where are you going?"

"Away from you."

"Can't we talk about this?"

"No. Just leave me alone."

"But you don't understand." I grab her arm, which finally brings her to a stop.

She bats my hand away. "What is your problem? I told you to leave me alone. Who's the stalker now? You know, you go on and on about how awful Ben is, but he never said anything as mean or made me feel as bad as you just did. If you don't leave me alone—"

"I was talking about your hair!" Screaming is my only option. I figure if I scream at her, she'll have to listen.

It works. She takes a step backward. "My hair?"

"Yes. Bleaching your hair and streaking it red. That's the mistake I was talking about."

"My hair? You wanted me to fix my hair?"

"Yes."

"Not the baby?"

"Of course not. How could you even fix—" I gasp and cover my mouth with my hand as I realize what she thought I was saying. "Never. I never even thought that. Not once."

She looks like she's about to fall over, so I lead her to a low wall encircling a raised flowerbed. We sit down and she leans forward, elbows on knees, head in hands. "I'm such an idiot."

"No, you're not." My hand moves in small circles over her back. "You're a little sensitive, but you're no idiot."

"It's just that word, *mistake*. When I thought you called the baby that . . . I lost it."

"I noticed. But why?"

"Because I'm a mistake."

With her face buried in her hands, the words are muffled, and I'm not sure I heard her right. But if I did, I certainly don't want to ask her to repeat it. "You're not a mistake."

She raises her head. "Sure I am. Remember how Mom and Dad always called me their little accident?"

"They were just kidding around." In fact, Mom used to call her their *happy* little accident.

"Kidding or not, they weren't expecting me. And I was never the kind of daughter they wanted. They would have been a lot happier if I'd been more like you."

I plunk my chin down on my fist. "Right. Because I'm such a prize."

"You are. You're a best-selling author."

"I'm an infertile divorcée."

"You're the good daughter."

"Oh yeah? If I was so good, why was I never enough?"

She leans away from me, as if startled by this revelation. Truth be told, I'm a bit startled myself. It's not something I spend a lot of time thinking about, but it has obviously shaped my life and the way I see myself. Now that it's out there, it resonates between us.

"Of course you were enough," she says slowly. "I never meant—"

"I know you didn't." I pat her knee. "You have no idea how much Mom and Dad wanted you. They tried to have another baby for years. Years. And when they finally stopped trying, then you came along. That's what they meant by calling you an accident."

"Wow. I always thought they'd be happier without me. I never thought I could measure up to you, so I didn't try." A tear slips down her cheek and she wipes it away.

"And I've spent my whole life trying to prove that I'm worth something. What a pair we are."

The fact that we're staying in a larger city for our last night on the road has become a blessing. So far, I've chased my sister down the street, we've yelled at each other, and we've had a deep, soul-baring conversation, all without anyone running up to us and welcoming us to town or telling us where we can buy Route 66 snow globes. So when I start to cry, I let the tears come. And when Lindsay pulls a tissue from her pocket and hands it to me, I blow my nose with gusto, not giving a second thought to who might be looking.

29

There's no end to the array of hair colors lining the drugstore shelves. I pick up a box and hold it next to Lindsay's face.

"No," I say, shaking my head. "Too orange."

"What about this one?"

"Closer."

She puts it back and picks up a box marked "Champagne Blonde." "This?"

I wrinkle my nose. "Too yellow."

"This is ridiculous." She plunks the box back on the shelf and walks down the aisle.

"Where are you going?" I call after her.

"To find a baseball cap. I'll just put one of those over my head. Or maybe a paper bag."

I trot up to her, grab her wrist, and pull her back to the hair-color section. "Don't give up now. You'll feel a lot better once we've got you all touched up. You'll see."

"Okay, but let's find something quick. I'm starving."

"Agreed." I look back at the shelf, tapping my index finger against my lip. "What we need is a color that matches your personality as well as your skin tone."

She picks up a box and thrusts it at me. "How about this one?"

Surprisingly, she's picked one that's nearly identical to her natural hair color. "That will definitely work. I just thought you'd want something a little more . . . exciting." I point at one labeled "Red Red Wine." "Like that."

She sighs and wags her head. "That would have been perfect for the old Lindsay."

Withholding the laugh that fights to get out, I take the hair color from her and read the name. "So the new Lindsay prefers 'Toffee Blonde'?"

"Yes. Because the new Lindsay just realized that once the baby comes, she's probably not going to have the time or energy to keep her roots touched up. I need a low-maintenance 'do."

A kernel of pride pops within me. Whether she knows it or not, my sister is exhibiting signs of maturity. This calls for a celebration. I jiggle the box in front of her. "Great choice. Let's pay for it and go get some dinner."

When we get to the register, she reaches for her wallet, but I hand the cashier my credit card first. In response to Lindsay's questioning look, I just shrug. "Don't say I never bought you anything."

"Thanks, Sis."

The softness around her eyes, the lift of her lips, and the total absence of sarcasm are well worth the nine and change I pay for the hair color. Above and beyond.

⸺∞⸺

Back in the hotel room, I volunteer to tackle the dying of Lindsay's hair. It's a risk, I know. If anything goes wrong, it will be all my fault, even if I follow the directions to the letter. But it would be beyond cruel to watch her struggle with it when I'm right here.

After I mix the solution, Lindsay sits on the bed, a towel draped across her shoulders. On my knees behind her, I try to cover the darker stripes in her hair first, then the bleached part, and finally the roots.

"You know what this reminds me of?" Lindsay asks.

"What?"

"That time you helped me get ready for the Valentine's Dance."

I haven't thought about that in years. We sat on the bed, just like we are now, and I arranged her hair in a loose updo. Then we raided Mom's jewelry box and found some cool costume pieces that were perfect with her dress. "How old were you then?"

"Twelve."

She doesn't have to think about it. I, on the other hand, have to do the math. That would have made me twenty-six. Already married to Tony. For the life of me, I can't remember why I was visiting my family that weekend.

"You told me I looked like a princess," she says.

"And you stuck your tongue out at me."

She laughs, her body and head shaking, which throws off my aim. A drop of color formula misses her hair, but I catch it in my palm before it can land on the bedspread.

"I was a little past the princess stage."

"A girl is never past the princess stage." I make a few more squirts with the bottle, rub the solution around with my plastic glove–covered hand, then sit back. "There. You're done. In fifteen minutes, you can finish up in the shower, and you'll be gorgeous."

Careful not to put my hands anywhere that will leave a stain, I scoot off the mattress. Once at the sink, I peel off the gloves and dump them in the trash can.

"Do you really believe that?"

I turn on the water and look at Lindsay's reflection in the mirror. "Of course. You're gorgeous no matter what color your hair is."

"No, I mean the thing about never being past the princess stage."

It seems she and I are destined to misunderstand each other over hair-related comments. After my hands are clean, I pull a towel from the rod and dry them slowly, taking time to think over her real question. "Yes," I finally answer. "I do believe it."

"Even now? After you found out Prince Charming is really a snake and the coach turned back into a pumpkin?"

Well, if she's going to put it that way . . . I blow out a gust of air, toss the towel on the counter, and sit in an uncomfortable straight-back chair near the bed. "Just because I didn't find a true prince doesn't mean it can't happen for you."

She pulls at a loose thread on the bedspread. "What if I already did?"

"You mean Ben?"

"Yes."

"Oh, Lindsay—"

"You just don't know him like I do. If you did, you'd understand."

How can such a smart young woman be so totally taken in by such a slimeball of a guy? "I wouldn't be too sure about that."

"You've only seen him at his worst. But there's a whole other side to him." Her eyes grow wide and she bounds off the bed, grabs her purse, then drops back down on the mattress. She pulls out her phone and starts fiddling with it. "Here. Listen to this."

If she's going to play one of Ben's songs, she's wasting her time. I've already heard what he calls music, and it just solidified my opinion that he's a loser. But the melody flowing from her phone speaker takes me by surprise. It's sweet and haunting at the same time. And when the singer joins in, his voice perfectly complements the instrument. He sings of love and longing, of cherishing his woman and putting her needs first.

She's got to be pulling some kind of joke. "Who is that?" I ask.

"It's Ben." Smug self-satisfaction transforms her face. "That's what I've been telling you. Ben is a sensitive, caring guy. He loves me. *This*," she says, waving the phone between us, "is the real Ben."

As the song continues, I'm swept up in it. She has no idea how much I want her to be loved this way. How I wish the father of her baby was an amazing, tender man. But the fact remains that Ben has anger issues. I've seen him take out his frustrations on his guitar. And I saw the evidence of him taking them out on my sister's face.

When the song's over, Lindsay tosses the phone beside her on the mattress. "What do you think?"

I think it will take more than one love song from a very convincing entertainer to change my mind. All I can do is present her with the truth. "He's a better singer than I thought, but that doesn't change the fact that he hit you."

Frustration rumbles deep in her throat. She picks up the phone, and for a second I'm afraid she's going to throw it at me. But she just shakes it in my direction. "This man would never do that. I told you how it happened. I got up in the middle of the night to get some water. I wasn't wearing my contact lenses. I couldn't see where I was going and I ran into the door. Ben never hit me."

"I'm sorry. I don't mean to upset you. But—" I gasp as I look past her and see the illuminated numbers on the bedside clock. "Twenty minutes."

"What?"

"It's been twenty minutes since we finished the color. You need to wash out the dye!"

With a yelp she jumps off the bed and shuffles into the bathroom. Her phone slips off the bedspread and thumps at my feet. Picking it up, I wonder why she insists on defending Ben. She's been strong in her stance that if he wants her, he has to want the baby too. Why should it matter to her whether I believe he's a good guy or not? Maybe because she's holding on to the fantasized image of him. An image that's reinforced by persuasive text messages and emphatic love songs.

Maybe her phone should get lost. Or maybe the battery could fall out. I turn it over in my hand and realize there's no way I'll ever figure out where the battery compartment is, let alone how to open it. Just as well. If I thought sabotage would really work, I wouldn't be against trying it. But this is something Lindsay's going to have to work out for herself.

My head whips toward the closed bathroom door as the sound of running water stops. I quickly toss the phone back on the bed where she left it and wait for her to come out. When she doesn't, I call after her.

"Is everything okay in there?"

"I can't believe you did this to me!"

Oh, no. Like this day wasn't ending badly enough. Now I've destroyed her hair. "Come out and let me take a look at it. Maybe we can—" I was going to say fix it, but I've learned my lesson.

She pushes the door open and walks out. She's wearing her bathrobe and has a towel wrapped turban-style around the top of her head. With a smile, she pulls it off and her damp hair tumbles down to her shoulders.

I take in a shocked breath. "It looks great."

"I know." Her smile gets bigger when she looks in the mirror. "I can't believe you did it."

Another hair misunderstanding. But this is the best of the day. For the moment, it seems Lindsay has put aside our disagreement about Ben in order to concentrate on how good she looks.

For once in my life, I encourage vanity. And I'll encourage it all the way home to Beaumont if it'll help keep the peace.

30

What should be a ninety-minute drive takes closer to three hours thanks to Lindsay's constant requests to stop. First she has to use a restroom, then she's hungry, then she needs the restroom again. Without a doubt, it's a ploy to drag this out and put off our reunion with our parents as long as possible. The only reason I haven't called her on it is because I know she's nervous, and after our yelling match last night, I'm trying to be understanding and not push her. But when she tells me to stop at a Circle K twenty minutes from the house, my patience flees.

"Whatever it is, it can wait." I drive right past, shaking my head.

"Easy for you to say. You're not pregnant."

I open my mouth, then close it, biting back the cutting retort I was ready to throw at her. Right now, it's best if I say nothing at all.

"I'm sorry," she says a moment later. "I'm just so anxious. I'm not really thinking straight."

"It's okay."

This would be the appropriate time for me to give her some words of wisdom and encouragement. To tell her that Mom and Dad will be thrilled to see her, and that they won't freak out about the baby. I want to tell myself the same thing: that they'll be supportive about my divorce and crumbled career. But I can't. Because I have no idea how any of this is going to play out. How will Dad feel when he finds out the mess both his girls have made of their lives? And Mom . . . how much of this will register with her?

All the unknown factors in this family equation render me speechless. I can feel Lindsay's eyes on me, willing me to say something wise, but I'm all out of bumper-sticker wisdom. Instead, I opt to fill the silence with something innocuous.

"Why don't you find something on the radio?"

She turns on an indie music station she likes. "Is this okay?"

The song that's playing is an odd combination of soft and hard, sweet and sour. The music is full-bodied, with layers of strings, percussion, and wind instruments. But the singer belts out the lyrics in a kind of speak-sing way. Her vocals are loud, bordering on angry. It's a mishmash of styles that makes little sense.

"Perfect."

―――

As soon as we pull into the driveway, I see how much things have changed. The flowerbeds in front of the house, always Mom's domain, show signs of neglect. The roses haven't been trimmed. The woodchip ground cover is uneven and needs replenishing. And, most egregious of all, there are weeds sprouting everywhere.

Lindsay sees it too. "That's not good."

I hope my smile doesn't look as phony as it feels. "Come on. Let's go in."

We're barely out of the car when Dad bounds from the house. "My girls! You're finally here!"

Dad's always been a good-looking man, sort of a senior-citizen version of Brad Pitt. I've never thought he looked his age. Not until today. He still has a full head of hair, but now it's completely gray. The lines on his face are deeper, as though it's a struggle to smile through the weight of his worries. If the last four years have taken such a toll on him, what have they done to my mother? What have I missed?

Why did I stay away so long?

I'm closest, so he hugs me first. I squeeze him tight, clinging as long as I can. "It's good to see you, Dad."

"You too, Sugar Plum."

He plunks a kiss on my forehead, then runs around the car to Lindsay. His eyes drop briefly to her loose top and bulging stomach, but his smile never falters. He throws his arms around her and kisses her cheek. Her eyes bug out as she looks at me over his shoulder. I shrug in return, as clueless as she is. Maybe this will all go much smoother than either one of us thought.

"I'm so glad you two are home." With one arm still circling Lindsay's shoulders, he walks her around the car to me, puts his other arm around my waist, and leads us toward the house.

I glance back at the car. "Shouldn't I get our bags out of the trunk?"

"That can wait. I'll unload it for you later." We get to the porch steps and he stops, turning to face us. "Before we go in, there's something I need to tell you."

My chest constricts and I take a deep breath to loosen it. "How's Mom doing?"

"Good," he says in that way people do when things really aren't good, but they pass for good considering the situation. "But that's not what I need to tell you."

Now he's scaring me. "What's wrong?"

"Nothing. Nothing's wrong, just . . . unexpected." He stuffs his hands in the pockets of his jeans and bounces on the balls of his feet. "There's someone here to see you."

Lindsay and I look at each other. "Us?" I ask.

"No, actually. Not both of you. Just Lindsay."

The earth shifts beneath my feet. If I were still in California, I'd dismiss it as a tremor, but here in Illinois, there's only one thing I can blame on this feeling of shock and dread.

Lindsay's face lights up as she comes to the same conclusion. Then the door behind her opens, a figure filling the frame, removing all doubt.

"You've got to be kidding." I growl the words.

Lindsay shoots me an icy look, then runs up the stairs and into his arms. "Ben!"

I try to reconcile how he figured out where our parents live. Somewhere along the line, Lindsay must have told him our final destination. After that, it would have been easy. There aren't too many Samuelsons living in a town the size of Beaumont.

Standing at the top of the porch, her head pressed against his chest, Lindsay obviously thinks this is the most romantic thing ever. True proof of his undying love for her. I find it just plain creepy. Especially when he looks at me over her head, his expression smug and self-satisfied.

"How could you let him in the house?" I brush past Dad, stomp up the stairs, and grab Lindsay's arm. "Get away from him."

She backs away from Ben, but she pulls away from me too. "Lighten up, Natalie. He came all this way to be with me. Doesn't that prove anything to you?"

"Sure. It proves he's a bigger stalker than I thought."

Ben puts his hand on Lindsay's shoulder, showing me he's in control of the situation. "Are you ever going to give me a chance?"

"Why should I?"

"Your father did."

Wait a minute. I turn to Dad. "How long has he been here?"

"A few days."

Lindsay sighs. I explode. "A few days? He's been here, in this house, for a few days?"

"Yes," Dad says slowly. He doesn't seem to know how to handle the crazy lady I've become. "We've talked, gotten to know each other. He told me all about Lindsay and the baby."

"The baby." I turn to Ben and grab at the one straw I know is a deal breaker. "Have you changed your mind about the baby?"

"I've changed my mind about a lot of things."

Dad is smiling. Ben is smiling. Lindsay is beaming. I'm the only person in this bizarre tableau who doesn't think it's a beautiful sentiment. Desperate for a way to bring sanity to this most insane moment, I jog back down the steps and grab Dad's hand. "You don't know the whole truth. He hit her."

"Natalie!" Lindsay yells and moves toward me, but Ben's fingers tighten on her shoulder, holding her back.

Dad's gentle smile is totally unexpected. "I do know about that. Ben explained it to me. Told me how you thought the bruise was from him, but that she walked into a door in the middle of the night."

"And you believe him?"

"I do. Natalie, I've done the same thing." He gives Lindsay a wink. "Guess you inherited your night blindness from me."

There's nothing left to say. I turn and walk toward the driveway.

"Where are you going?" Lindsay calls.

To get away from you. Because I can't stand here and watch Dad help you throw your life away.

"To get the bags."

31

It's a beautiful day in this picture-perfect, idyllic neighborhood. The sun shines down on the neat rows of well-kept homes, some with yards surrounded by honest-to-goodness white picket fences. A gentle breeze wafts through the trees, rustling leaves, encouraging the birds to sing a little stronger, a little sweeter. The only dark spot in this otherwise pristine scene is the black cloud that surely hovers above my head as I stride down the sidewalk.

Once we were all inside the house, it became obvious to me that I had to get back out. Lindsay and Ben went into the living room together to talk. Mom was upstairs sleeping. And I went into the kitchen with Dad, who looked about as sheepish as I'd ever seen him. After another brief discussion about how insane the situation was—if you could call me ranting and him listening a discussion—he suggested I take a walk and get some coffee. Finally, something that made sense.

It takes about twenty minutes to get to what is now referred to as Old Town. Since the last time I was in Beaumont, they've started a refurbishment and beautification project. With so many of the buildings hidden behind scaffolds and in various stages of repair, it looks more like an anti-beautification project. But most of the shops have big signs proclaiming them open for business, including—Yes!—the coffee shop. There's no physical sign on the building, but the words *Uncommon Grounds* are stenciled on the large front window. Below it, someone has taken glass markers and drawn pictures of a mug of coffee and a dancing muffin. Cute.

A bell jingles as I walk inside. Despite the sad condition of the building's outside, the inside is quite impressive. If the deep red of the brick walls and the warm, honey-toned wood floors aren't enough to make me feel at home, the overstuffed chairs and couches certainly do. Best of all, beyond the coffee area are shelves and shelves of books. I may never leave this place. And since I'm the only customer at the moment, it's not like anybody will shoo me away for the table space.

I look over at the counter and see someone partially obscured by machinery. "Excuse me. Are the books for sale or for reading here?" I ask.

"Either one." A deep baritone calls out, the tone so bright and uplifting, I can tell the man's smiling before I see him. He steps into view, wiping his hands on a blue-and-white striped towel. "You're welcome to read whatever you like. If you enjoy it and want to buy it, even better."

He's young. Not college-student young, but certainly younger than I am by a few years. His dark hair curls up at the ends, as if he's overdue for a trim, and a dusting of stubble shadows his cheeks and chin. Add to that tan skin and well-shaped forearms and he looks like he should be outside with the construction crew instead of serving up coffee and biscotti.

Tossing the towel to the side, he leans over the counter. "What can I get you today?"

There's a loaded question. Several witty remarks come to mind, but I have the presence of mind not to say them. Instead,

I give the chalkboard menu behind his head a quick once over. "I'll have an iced caramel latte."

"Great choice."

After he rings up the total and gives me change, I look for a tip cup to dump it into but don't see one. "We don't do tips here," he says.

I nod as I drop the coins into my wallet. "Apparently, you do read minds."

He laughs, a full-bodied, throaty sound that sends a rush of heat through my chest and makes me glad I ordered an iced drink. "No mind reading necessary. Everybody looks for a tip jar the first time they come in."

"Shucks. Here I thought I'd found someone with super-powers."

"Sorry to disappoint you."

I smile back at him for too long, lost in ponderings about his teeth and whether they're naturally that straight and white or if he's had work done. "Uh, I'm going to find a seat."

Not the best wording, considering that all the seats are available.

"Get a book if you like," he says. "I'll bring your drink over in a sec."

By the time I scan two shelves, I realize that all the books are fiction. Which means I don't have to worry about seeing any of my how-to-make-your-marriage-work books. I do, however, find a few of my novels. Unlike some of the other books with well-creased spines, mine look brand new. Is that good or bad? Has no one picked these up? Or maybe people have picked up other copies, read them while sipping their coffee, and liked them enough to buy them. I choose to believe the latter scenario.

When I've decided on a novel, I take it to the seating area and sink into a hunter-green chair that's so wide I'm able to curl my feet up on it. I open the book and start to read. Rather, I try to read. But I can't concentrate on the words. My mind keeps going back to Lindsay, wondering what she and Ben are doing and whether she'll come to her senses before she's completely taken in by his act.

A moment later, rather than make me come get it, the coffee guy brings my drink to me. "Here you go." He sets it on a table by the chair.

I look up at him and our eyes lock. Wow. Those are some great eyes. It's like God ran out of standard-issue eyeballs and gave him a pair of sparkling topaz gems instead. He glances at the chair next to me, and for a moment, I think he's going to sit down. But the bells on the door jingle and three giggling teenage girls push their way into the store.

Quickly, I read the name on the tag pinned to his polo shirt. "Thanks, Adam."

His smile widens. "I hope to see you again . . ."

"Natalie."

"Natalie." He heads to the counter, then turns around and says casually, "Come back soon."

I pick up my drink, half expecting the ice to be melted from the warmth in his voice. The way he said my name, it was almost like a caress. No one's ever said my name like that. Not even Tony.

Tony.

It's like being drenched in cold water. I'm still a married woman, even if it's only a legal technicality. What am I doing fawning over some stranger just because he was nice to me?

And gorgeous. Don't forget gorgeous.

The giggling from the girls has gotten louder now that they're giving Adam their orders. Seems he has the same effect on all members of the female species. A piece of a Bible verse flits through my head, something about fleeing temptation.

Not wanting to give myself time to rethink or rationalize it, I plunk the book on the table and head for the exit. As the door shuts behind me, I hear his voice one more time. I don't know if he's talking to the girls or calling out a parting message to me. It doesn't matter. My life is complicated enough right now without adding lustful thoughts to the mix.

I head up the street, back to the safety of my parents' house, where all I have to worry about is resisting the urge to attack my sister's no-good boyfriend with a frying pan.

32

When I open the front door, it rams into something solid. Stepping around, I see a suitcase. At first, I think it belongs to Lindsay and wonder why Dad didn't take it to the guest room. Then I realize it's not hers. And it's not mine. There's only one other person it could belong to.

Can it really be true? Has God answered my prayer and made Lindsay see the light? Has she sent Ben packing?

Laughter drifts in from the kitchen, dashing my hopes. I find the three of them sitting at the table, a bag of Oreos between them. Ben twists one open, hands the half with the cream filling to Lindsay, and pops the other half in his mouth.

"Hey, Sugar Plum." Dad waves me over. "Come break cookies with us."

"No, thanks." Oreos will always remind me of the night Tony left and my subsequent sugar bender. And now, they'll remind me of Ben too. I hate that such a delicious treat has been ruined forever.

Lindsay licks the remaining cream off the cookie in her hand. "Where were you?"

I raise my half-full cup. "I walked to town and found a coffee shop."

"Then you must have met Adam." Dad is too excited about the possibility that Mr. Coffee and I made contact. They must know each other.

"Yes, I did." Despite my best intentions, my mind skips back to the moment when he said my name. *Natalie.*

I've got to change the subject. "I saw the suitcase in the living room. Is Ben leaving?"

Ben looks down at his watch. "Wow. It took her less than two minutes to get to that."

Lindsay frowns at me. "Yes, he is. But not for the reason you think."

I look at Dad, hoping we won't have to play twenty questions and he'll simply tell me what's going on.

"Since you two girls are here now, it's not appropriate for Ben to stay too. Plus, we don't have enough room. So I'm taking him to a hotel until we can figure out a better arrangement."

A better arrangement would be him going back to California. "How long do you plan on staying?"

He leans closer to my sister. "As long as Lindsay does."

"What about your apartment? How are you going to pay rent and pay for a hotel?"

"I moved out."

"So you broke your lease."

"No, we didn't have a lease. It was month-to-month." An embarrassed look comes over his face and he fiddles with the napkin in front of him. "Besides, the landlord asked me to leave."

This finally gets something other than a love-struck reaction out of Lindsay. "He did? Why?"

"The guy below us complained. A lot." He looks up and leans in to her earnestly. "But I'm glad. Losing everything made me realize the only thing I really need is you."

This is ridiculous. He can even make getting evicted sound good. "Don't you have a job to get back to? Or did you lose that too?"

"I'm a musician," Ben says. "As long as I've got my guitar, I can find work just about anywhere."

"Just about any bar, you mean."

"If that's where the gig takes me. Yes." His voice is tight.

Dad stands up, the feet of his chair squealing on the worn tile floor. "Natalie, you're not being fair to Ben. Give him a chance."

Give him a chance to do what? To hurt Lindsay again? To beat her to a pulp? And what about the baby? Is no one thinking about how he'll treat the baby? I could ask all these things, but it wouldn't matter. Right now, it doesn't matter how good my arguments are, how valid my concerns. I'm going to be perceived as the bad guy. I'm the one who won't give poor Ben a second chance.

I've got to get out of this room. "You know, I think all that driving is catching up with me. I'm going to go lie down."

As I leave the kitchen, Dad calls to me. "All your stuff is in Lindsay's old room."

"Lindsay's room? Why?"

Dad lowers himself back into the chair. "It's gotten difficult with your mother." He pauses, looking around the table as if weighing just how much he wants to share right now. "She's started sleeping in your old room. So you and Lindsay are going to have to share her room."

Perfect. Just perfect. If my poor father didn't look so defeated, I'd let him know how unhappy I am right now. Instead, I walk back to him and kiss him on top of the head. "Let me know when Mom wakes up."

When I get stressed, it comes out in my dreams. And this one's a doozy.

It's a game show, and I'm standing on a stage between two doors. Off to the side, behind brightly colored podiums, are Tony and Ben. And facing us all, wearing a bright blue, sequin-encrusted suit, is Brad Pitt.

He speaks into a tall microphone. "Ben, which prize are you going to choose?"

Ben doesn't hesitate. "I'll take door number one, Brad."

The door swings open and out steps Lindsay, looking beautiful and petite, holding a cherubic baby in her arms. She runs to Ben, they kiss, then run off together. I have no idea where. They just sort of disappear into the strange, misty void at the edge of the stage.

Now Brad looks at Tony. "There are two prizes left: Natalie, your loving wife of eighteen years, or whatever's behind door number two."

I clench my hands together. He's got to pick me. How could he give me up not knowing what he's getting himself into?

"This is a tough one, Brad." Tony shakes his head. "I mean, I promised to stay with Natalie for the rest of our lives, no matter how tough things got. But darn it, I'm just so bored." He thrusts his fist into the air. "I'll take door number two!"

I can't breathe. The door opens, and there stands Erin. She's tall, perfectly proportioned, her blonde hair cascading down her back in perfect, silky strands. "I've got a surprise for you," she says. Then she slowly turns in a circle. Now she's holding the perfect baby. "It's a boy."

No.

"Are you happy with your choice?" Brad asks.

Tony is grinning like an idiot. "Absolutely. A man's got to worry about his own happiness, right? And this makes me happy." He comes up to the stage to get Erin and the baby. As they walk past me, he gives a sad little shrug. "Sorry about that."

I look at Brad. "What about me?"

"I guess that makes you the big loser. But thanks for playing."

Now I'm all alone.

Natalie.

Who's that calling me? It's a man. Could it be . . .

Natalie.

Where is he?

"Natalie."

I feel the hand on my shoulder and I recognize the voice. Dad.

Pushing myself up off the mattress, I squint at him. "Hey, Dad."

"You really were tired." He brushes a strand of hair from my face. "Maybe I should have let you sleep."

"No, it's okay." I yawn, covering my mouth to block my after-nap breath. "What's up?"

"Your Mom's awake. She's downstairs."

Maybe he should have let me sleep after all. As bad as that dream was, at least I got to look at Brad Pitt. The reality of facing my mother doesn't offer any such distractions. Only cold, hard fact.

I smile at Dad. "Great. Give me a second and I'll be right down."

He pats my leg, then leaves the room. A moment later, I head down the hall with my toiletry bag. I need time to brush my teeth. And to pray.

33

Mom looks . . . normal. I don't know why, but for some reason, I expected her to be unkempt, her hair matted, clothes wrinkled and stained from spilled food. That expectation is ridiculous, because even if she couldn't take care of herself, Dad would never let her live that way.

She and Lindsay are sitting on the couch, talking and laughing. When was the last time they seemed so at ease with each other? Never, not as far back as I can remember.

Dad stands off to the side, his face such a bittersweet mix of emotions, it nearly breaks my heart. "Meredith," he says. "Look who else is here to see you."

She turns her head and for a moment, I see confusion in her eyes. I see her trying to place me, force a remembrance of me to the forefront of her mind. Then there's a spark of recognition, a lift to her lips, and she's off the couch and headed for me with open arms.

"Natalie." She pulls me close, rocking me back and forth with her hug.

"Hey, Mom." Emotion nearly chokes me. She knows who I am. It may not last, but for now she knows. I'm not too late after all.

She steps back, holding me at arm's length. "Let me look at you. You are a sight for these tired, old eyes."

I laugh. Then I catch a glimpse of Lindsay, sitting by herself, watching our mother shower me with attention. "Let's sit down, Mom." We settle on the sofa, and I squeeze her shoulder. "So, have you and Lindsay been catching up?"

"Oh, yes. She's been telling me all about her fella. Such a sweet young woman." She pats Lindsay on the knee. "Your mother must be so proud."

A chill falls over the room, freezing the air around us. A second later, it shatters and a million icy shards of hurt and doubt rain down on my sister.

I look to Dad. How do we handle this? Should we tell her who Lindsay is? Or are we supposed to play along?

Dad kneels in front of Mom and takes her hand. "Honey, do you remember who Lindsay is?"

"Yes, she's a friend of Natalie's." Her words sound normal, but her smile has become too stiff, her eyes too wide.

"Mom," Lindsay says, "don't you remember me?"

Mom looks at her, but doesn't speak. Then she looks back at Dad. She leans forward and whispers, "Joel, why does this girl think I'm her mother?"

"Because you are," Lindsay insists.

I've heard you're never supposed to wake up a sleepwalker, and I'm starting to think this falls into that category. Correcting her delusion is probably the wrong approach. But Lindsay, God bless her, can only see one thing: her mother doesn't remember her.

Beside me, Mom closes her eyes, puts her head down, and starts rocking. She mutters to herself, her voice so low I can't understand what she's saying. Dad reaches out, strokes her hair, tries to calm her, but she just gets more agitated. Her voice gets louder.

"We have a dog. Her name is Peaches."

I named our mutt Peaches because of the color of her fur. We got her when I was eight. Now, she's buried in the back yard under the big tree.

"My husband is Joel. He teaches high school English. On Saturdays, he teaches driver's ed."

Dad used to teach, but he retired five years ago.

"I have one daughter. Her name is Natalie. She goes to Beaumont High School."

No, God. Please, no.

"She's a freshman."

Lindsay bursts into tears, which cuts off Mom's verbal torrent. But it doesn't evoke the sympathy you'd expect. Instead, Mom looks at Dad, her eyes almost completely blank, and says, "Is it time for *Lucy*?"

He doesn't bother to look at his watch and check the time. "Yes, dear. It certainly is. Come on." As he pulls her to her feet, he whispers to me, "Be right back." Then he leads her away.

I scoot closer to Lindsay and she falls sideways on the couch, head in my lap. "She doesn't remember me. Not at all."

I rub Lindsay's back and make shushing noises, but despite my comforting posture, I can't stop thinking about my own pain. Which is worse? Not having your mother remember you, or having her forget everything but the teenage version of you?

By the time Dad comes back in, Lindsay's sobs have turned to snuffles, and my shock has turned to anger.

"I've got her settled in the family room watching *I Love Lucy*. Thank heavens that show came out on DVD. It's one of the few things that always calms her down." He laughs, a sound totally devoid of actual joy. "Of course, she can't remember any of the episodes, so I only had to buy one season."

He wants to shrug it off. Act like this is no big deal. Maybe I have to play along with Mom's delusions, but I don't have to indulge his. "You should have warned us," I say.

He winces. "I told you she'd gotten worse."

"We expected her to be forgetful. To maybe even have moments of not recognizing us, but this? She doesn't even remember having a second child." Lindsay gasps, and I dial back my outburst before she falls apart again. "You should have told us how bad it's gotten."

"You're right. I should have."

"Then why didn't you?"

"Honestly, I didn't expect this to happen." Sitting in the chair beside the couch, he seems smaller than the man I know so well. His shoulders slump forward, his chin falls to his chest, his eyelids droop closed. "It came on so fast."

Lindsay sits up, and I see she managed to use the legs of my jeans as a Kleenex. Lovely. "How long has she been like this?" she asks.

"About a week and a half." He lifts his head and looks at me. "When I first called you, she was so much better. She was excited about you coming home." He turns to Lindsay. "Both of you."

I press a finger against my temple. "We should have gotten here faster."

Lindsay swipes the back of her hand across her nose. "You're the one who wanted to make so many stops."

"Well you're the one who refused to get on an airplane."

"Oh, so now it's my fault?"

"Girls!" Dad's voice cuts between us. "There's enough stress in this house already. The last thing I need to deal with is you two going at each other."

We both hang our heads. "Sorry, Dad," Lindsay says.

"Sorry."

He stands up and moves to the couch, sitting between us. "I understand this is hard for you. It's hard for all of us. The thing you have to remember is that your mother is sick. The love she has for you is still in her heart, even if she can't express it like she used to. That love will never change."

It's a sweet thought, but it reminds me of that old saying: if a tree falls in the woods and nobody hears, does it still make a sound?

If a mother loves you, but she doesn't remember she loves you, does that love still exist?

I don't have an answer. But one look at Lindsay and there's no doubt in my mind what her answer would be.

34

Are you asleep?"

Lindsay calls out to me from her bed. I roll over on the futon, making the wooden slats creak and moan. The contraption is surprisingly comfortable, but with the noises it makes, I'm afraid it's going to collapse beneath me every time I move.

"As asleep as you are."

"What are we going to do?"

That's the question of the day. "I don't know. You have any ideas?"

"I want to leave."

"And go where?"

It's a serious question. She has no job to go back to, and I assume her financial resources are limited. All things considered, this seems like the best place for her, at least until the baby comes.

She sighs. "Some place with a beach. Like Hawaii."

"Sounds nice. But after all my stress eating, there's no way I'm going near a bathing suit anytime soon."

She snorts. "Oh, yeah, no bathing suit for me, either. Okay, where do you want to go?"

With the moonlight coming through the window and my eyes adjusted to the dark, I can make out her shape across the room. She's propped up on one elbow, her head leaning against her hand.

We should probably be having a serious talk right now, but it looks like we've got more than enough serious stuff in our future. For tonight, I want to indulge in a little fantasy.

"I've always wanted to go to Denmark."

"Seriously?" she asks. "Why?"

"I wrote a report about it in junior high and it fascinated me. There are so many amazing things to see there."

"Like what?"

"Like the Little Mermaid statue in Copenhagen." In my mind, I see the picture of her, perched on a rock and gazing across the ocean, waiting for her prince. "And Tivoli Gardens."

"Mmm." She lies back on her pillow and sighs. "What does it look like?"

I shift onto my back, fingers locked together, and hands under my head. "They've got rides, but it's more than just an amusement park. It's beautiful. There are gardens with flowers in every color you can think of. And fountains. And little lights, thousands of them, strung everywhere. In fact, Walt Disney got some of his inspiration for Disneyland from Tivoli."

The more I talk, the more excited I get. Why have I never taken the time to go on a trip like this? It's the kind of thing I always thought Tony and I would do when we retired. That will obviously never happen. So what now? I could go by myself. But it would be more fun with someone else.

"You know," I say, "after the baby is born, if you feel like getting on a plane, maybe you and I could visit Tivoli together."

My offer is greeted by dead silence. "Lindsay?"

Nothing. Until the sound of a gentle snore drifts across the room.

With a smile, I turn over slowly, trying not to make the futon creak too much. It occurs to me that for the first time, I've told my sister a bedtime story and lulled her to sleep. It's a warm, cozy moment, utterly at odds with the cold weight that settles in my chest.

If only someone were here to do the same for me.

———— ∞∞∞ ————

The flimsy curtains on the window above me did little to filter out last night's moonlight, and they're absolutely no match against the morning sun. I pull the covers over my head, but the stuffiness of being trapped with my own hot breath compels me to push them back off again. I lean over the side of the wooden frame and fumble on the floor for my watch. When I find it, I bring it close to my nose and squint at the face. Six a.m.

"Ugh."

I fall back on the mattress, arm flung over my eyes. It's too early. If I get up now, I'll be exhausted by dinnertime. I command myself to get some more sleep, but an image of Tony pops up behind my closed eyelids. And then the questions start. What's he doing now? It's 3:00 a.m. in California, so he must be in bed too. Only he's not alone. Erin is beside him. Or maybe they're spooned together, front to back, his arm flung over her waist, his hand resting protectively on her belly.

I bolt upright. It's no use. I can't go back to sleep. Propelling myself out of bed, I grab some clean clothes and head for the bathroom.

The area around the sink is already covered with stuff. Hairspray, lotion, deodorant, and saline solution, along with several mystery containers, all vie for valuable countertop real

182

estate. We haven't even been here a day yet. I shudder to think what it will look like by the end of the week.

As I step in the shower, my mind goes back to last night and Lindsay's question: what are we going to do? In the beginning, when things were simpler, I expected this to be a visit, nothing more. We'd stay for a week, maybe two, and then we'd head back home. But that was before I discovered that Lindsay was pregnant, unemployed, and essentially homeless. She can't go back to that. At least here, Dad and I can keep an eye on her. Even with Ben hanging around, we can make sure they're not alone. And if they're not alone, he can't hurt her again. Not without getting hurt himself.

What about me? I squirt shampoo in my hand and lather up my hair, pondering my future. I've got to go back, if for no other reason than keeping Tony from selling the house out from under me. And I have a career to salvage. Or to bury.

The doorknob rattles and I jump. Shampoo burns my eyes, and I quickly turn my face to the spray of water.

"Who's in there?" My mother's voice calls out. She sounds mad.

"It's me." I turn off the faucet, stick my head around the shower curtain, and grab a towel. "It's Natalie."

"Oh, good. Come on down. Breakfast is ready."

It's like someone flipped a switch on her. Now she sounds like the Happy Homemaker.

"Okay, Mom. I'll be right there."

Since I don't get an answer, I assume she's not outside the door anymore. I carefully step onto the bath mat and dry myself off. The towel is rough, like someone washed it but forgot to use fabric softener. Something about the abrasiveness of it against my skin feels right, and I rub harder, trying to get dry and dressed before my mother's mood changes again.

When I get to the kitchen, Dad is sitting at the table, his eyes glued to Mom, an untouched newspaper beside his plate. Mom is looking into the refrigerator. Lindsay is not there. Probably because it's barely 7:00 a.m. and she's still snug in her bed. But why didn't anyone bother to get her for breakfast?

Of course. Not only does Mom not remember Lindsay, she doesn't remember she's in the house. She probably wouldn't have remembered me, either, if she hadn't found me in the shower. I wonder if she's already forgotten about that. Just to be on the safe side, I stay in the doorway and call out, "Good morning."

Both my parents turn my way. Dad's smile is tight. Mom's smile is normal. Just the way I've seen it a thousand times before in this same kitchen. She walks toward me, a jug of orange juice in her hand, and kisses me on the cheek. "Good morning, sweetheart."

She goes to the table and sits by Dad. Then she waves me over. "Sit down. Eat."

Mom points at the same spot I always sat in as a girl. Is it because she's mentally out of sync, or just because it's the seat closest to her? I'm tempted to sit in the other open spot, just to see what would happen. But then I remember her meltdown last night and decide not to chance it.

"How did you sleep?" Dad asks.

"Great." It's not a lie. Not really. The three or four hours I was able to snatch did feel great. I ease myself down into my chair. Now that I'm at the table, I notice how it's set. Plastic bowls. Plastic cups. Boxes of cold cereal in the middle. Orange juice, but no milk, which is just as well, since there are only forks by our bowls.

"We've got Special K, Cheerios, and Fruit Loops." Mom motions to them as if she's presenting a gourmet menu. "I hope you like one of those."

184

I grab the box of Special K. "My favorite."

"Oh good. I would have cooked something hot, but the stove is broken."

Dad pats her hand. "We're thankful for whatever you serve us."

"You're so sweet." She smiles at him and points at the paper. "What's new in the world today?"

As Dad tells her about current events that won't matter to her in a few hours, I glance at the stove. It's an older model, the kind with knobs instead of push buttons. And all the knobs are gone. Every one of them.

Now I see the other things that should be in this kitchen but aren't. The knife block. The can opener. Even the toaster. All too much of a hazard to leave where Mom can get to them.

Tears pool in my eyes, but I blink them away and look down at my bowl before they can spill over. I'm glad Lindsay's still upstairs. I wish I was back there too. Back in the rickety futon, burrowed under the stuffy oblivion of the covers where I could sleep and sleep and sleep.

35

By the time Lindsay makes her way downstairs, there's no evidence of our breakfast drama. The dishes have been cleared, the cereal boxes put away. Dad and I sit at the table, each with a cup of coffee and a section of the paper he finally cracked open.

Lindsay shuffles in and sits between us, stifling a yawn with the back of her hand.

"Good morning, sleepyhead," Dad says. "You hungry?"

"Always. What's for breakfast?" She looks around, as if a waitress will magically appear and present her with a combo platter.

"How do eggs and toast sound?"

"Good."

"Coming right up."

Dad starts to scoot his chair back, but I wave for him to stop. "I've got it." After nearly three weeks and innumerable breakfast orders, I know how Lindsay likes her eggs. Besides, if I take care of Lindsay, there's less of a chance Dad will ask me to help with Mom. At least, that's what I hope.

As I stand up, Lindsay reaches over and grabs my mug. "You can't drink that," I say. "It's caffeinated."

"I know. I just want to smell it." Cupping her hands around the mug, she holds it below her nose and takes a deep breath. "Ah, sweet coffee. How I miss you."

"I can make you a cup of instant decaf," Dad offers.

Lindsay makes a face.

I take a carton of milk from the fridge, pour a tall glass, and set it in front of her. "She hates instant."

"Yes, I do. And I'm starting to hate milk too."

"But your baby loves it." I give her a wink, then start opening cupboards. I find a frying pan. I find a plastic plate. I even find a spatula. But there's one very important thing missing. "Dad?"

"Yes?"

"Tell me you still have a toaster."

"It's on the top shelf of the pantry."

The white slatted doors squeak as I slide them apart. Sure enough, there it is on the top shelf, along with all the other questionable kitchen implements.

"Why did you hide the toaster?" Lindsay asks.

"It's funny, really."

As soon as he says that, I know it won't be funny. It will be sad and depressing, and I wish he'd keep it to himself. But he continues.

"You know how your mother likes her toast crunchy. Well, she thought it might turn out better if she buttered it before she toasted it. The way you do with a grilled cheese sandwich." He takes a sip of his coffee. "Of course, the butter dripped off the bread and burned as soon as it hit the coils. The kitchen was so smoky it set off the smoke detectors."

"So you hid the toaster? Because of one mistake?" Lindsay shakes her head. "That's pretty harsh."

"No," Dad answers, fingering the rim of his coffee cup. "I hid the toaster because she forgot what happened and she did it again. And again. After the third time of the siren blaring and her cowering in the corner with her hands over her ears . . . that's when I hid it."

"Oh."

I need to make Lindsay's breakfast quick. The sooner I put food in front of her, the better. But I've got another problem.

"Is there a way to turn on this stove?"

Dad points above my head. "Knobs are in that top cupboard."

"I don't get it," I say, taking a knob down and fitting it back onto the front of the stove. "What's to keep her from taking any of this stuff down herself?"

"Heights make her nervous. To her, those top shelves don't even exist."

I don't know what to say. Instead, I pour all my concentration into cooking. Spray oil in the pan. Turn on the burner. Crack eggs into a bowl and whisk with a little milk.

Behind me, Lindsay does what I can't. She takes Dad's hand in both of hers and looks him in the eye. "I'm so sorry, Dad. I want to be supportive, but I keep saying and doing the wrong things. I just don't understand any of this."

"You're not the only one. I don't understand much of it myself." He sniffs and has to pull his hand back so he can grab a napkin and blow his nose. "Even the experts, the ones who are supposed to tell us what to do, don't have a lot of answers. Mostly, they make educated guesses."

"Then we'll figure it out together." Lindsay says. She looks up at me as I bring her plate of scrambled eggs and toast to the table. "Right, Natalie?"

Together.

"Right."

For better or worse, we're all in this together.

36

Over the next few days, our family settles into an uneven rhythm. Thankfully, Mom is uninterested in cooking anything other than breakfast, so Dad and I take turns. As hard as it must be for her, Lindsay makes a point of eating lunch and dinner with us. I appreciate her effort, so when I realize that Ben plans to come over every afternoon, I don't make a fuss. Besides, I'd much rather have him here where I can keep an eye on the two of them.

What I want most is to sit down and have a long talk with Dad. I want more details about Mom's condition and what we should be doing. I want to know what to expect in the future. And I want to know how he's holding up. He presents a good front, but he's probably a big ball of stress on the inside. Every time I bring up the subject, though, we're interrupted. Usually, it's because Mom needs something, and since we can't talk in front of her, and we can't leave her alone, a lot has gone unsaid.

Out of desperation, I turn to the Internet.

For the first time since we arrived, I venture into the room Dad uses as an office. As I sit in his desk chair, a sense of peace washes over me. Back when I still thought people wanted to read what I wrote, I spent most of my working hours pounding the keys. It's been more than three weeks since I basked in the monitor's artificial glow, so this is almost like a homecoming.

I type "Alzheimer's" into a search engine and am rewarded with more results than I could read in my lifetime. There's certainly no shortage of places offering information. The problem is that so much of it is general. Phrases like *Patients may experience* and *some symptoms may include* fill the screen.

Clicking from site to site, I hope to find something specific. I read about plaques and tangles, which are thought to damage and kill nerve cells in the brain. But then I read that researchers don't really know what role they play with the disease. I find details about the changes that occur in the brain, but also read that scientists haven't been able to pinpoint what causes those changes.

Now I start clicking random links, hoping I'll accidentally stumble across something helpful. It doesn't take me long to follow a rabbit trail of links far away from my original purpose. Treatment turns to diagnosis, which turns to risk factors, which turns to heredity. And that link leads me straight to fear.

A person whose parent, sibling, or child has Alzheimer's is at greater risk of developing the disease. With each affected family member, the risk increases.

Mom has it. Grandma had it. Great-grandma most likely had it. How many generations back does this curse stretch? And how far forward will it extend? Will I get it? Will my sister? And what about her baby? With all my heart, I hope she has a boy, despite my earlier misgivings. Not that males don't get Alzheimer's. It just doesn't seem to work that way in our family.

Discouragement settles around my shoulders like a mothball-infused shawl. All I want to do now is turn off the computer and try to forget everything I've just read. But then I see a link for *Prevention*. If they don't know what causes it, how can they know how to prevent it? It's probably just more bad news, like one sentence in the middle of the page, screaming *There is no way to prevent this! Deal with it!*

I click it anyway. It starts out pretty much like I expected, only nicer. *It's not known whether or not Alzheimer's can be prevented.* But then it goes on to talk about how to lessen the risks. It's mostly commonsense-type stuff, like a healthy diet, exercise, and taking care of your heart. But there are other things I hadn't thought of, like keeping your mind active and challenged, maintaining social and emotional connections with friends and family, and engaging in some sort of community faith experience. I've been falling down on all of that lately.

A strategy starts to formulate in my head, accompanied by abridged bits of Scripture. *I have a plan for you, says the Lord . . . Whatever is good, think on these things . . .*

I click the print button. As pages whir out of the printer, I navigate to another page and click a PDF link. The *Caring for Someone with Alzheimer's* publication is long, but I print it anyway. I can always buy Dad more paper and ink.

"What are you doing?" Lindsay stands in the doorway.

"Research. What's up?"

"I need to run an errand, but Dad won't leave Mom alone, and she's watching *Lucy.* Again." She leans her head against the door frame. "Can I borrow your car?"

I pull the pages from the printer and straighten them out, pounding the edges against the top of the desk. "I was just getting ready to go out myself. We can go together." She doesn't look too happy with my idea, which immediately makes me suspicious. "Where do you need to go?"

"To see Ben."

I should have known. "No way."

"You are such a hypocrite." She shoves away from the door and propels herself into the room. "You talk about forgiveness and giving people a second chance, but you don't do it yourself."

While I used to talk about forgiveness all the time, I haven't done it lately. Not since my husband did the unforgivable. So it's a little surprising to have her throw it in my face. "There's a difference between being forgiving and being stupid."

"I am not stupid."

"I didn't say you are."

"You just did."

I sigh. Are we ever going to get along like real sisters? Or is that what we're doing now? Do all sisters fight like we do? "What I meant was, it would be stupid of me to take you to see a man that I don't trust."

"But I trust him. It's my decision and my life. You can't control me, you know."

"I know. But unfortunately for you, I control the car."

She doesn't argue on that point. Instead, her lip begins to quiver and she looks down at the floor. "Fine."

As she turns to leave the room, a delayed pang of guilt zaps me. She was right about the forgiveness thing. But I was right too.

"Wait."

She looks over her shoulder, ready to keep on going if I don't say what she wants to hear.

"How about a compromise?"

Now she turns completely around to face me. "Like what?"

"Call Ben and tell him to meet you at the coffee shop in Old Town." It's the first place I think of where they can sit and talk but still be around other people. And if we happen to see Adam, that wouldn't be a bad thing. He can help keep Ben in line.

Lindsay considers my offer, then leans over the chair and hugs me. "Thank you." She dashes out, calling behind her, "I'll meet you downstairs."

Just like that, she's happy with me again. I'd like to blame her wild fluctuations of mood on the fact that she's pregnant, but I have a feeling this is just Lindsay being Lindsay.

Picking up my pages, I smile. It's taken twenty-five years, but I'm finally getting to know my little sister. What a challenge. What a blessing.

37

Unlike the first time I was here, the coffee shop is packed. Still, it only takes a second for Lindsay and Ben to find each other. He stands up and motions her to his table. She runs to him, and they embrace as though he's a returning war hero.

They're drawing a wee bit of attention, the oh-isn't-that-sweet kind. To look at them, they could be any young couple, deeply in love and excited about the birth of their first baby. If only. The truth of their relationship sits like cement in the pit of my stomach.

"I knew you'd come back." Adam stands next to me, his hands full of empty cups, paper plates, and napkins.

Blush heats my cheeks. "Oh really? Why's that?"

"We're the best coffee shop in town."

I laugh. "As far as I can tell, you're the only coffee shop in town. On this side, anyway."

"Which is why we're the best." He motions sideways with his head. "Follow me."

He walks behind the counter, throws away the trash, then leans over in my direction. "So what'll it be? Iced latte, or are you in the mood for something different?"

The fact that he remembered my drink both surprises and pleases me. And the fact that it pleases me bothers me. "I'm not staying." When he doesn't answer, I continue. "I just brought my sister here to meet her boyfriend."

Looking over my shoulder, I see they're engrossed in conversation. He laughs at something she said, then reaches out. His palm nears her face and I flinch, my jaw set. But all he does is cup her cheek in a gentle caress. Another move that would look completely innocuous to an uninformed observer.

Adam clears his throat. "I take it you don't approve."

"Is it that obvious?"

"I'm extremely good at reading people."

"Goes with the job, huh?"

He shrugs. "It's a gift. Like mind reading."

"I see," I say with a chuckle. He has a quality about him that's so genuine, so bright, I feel like I'm talking to an old friend. Someone I can trust. "Listen, you don't know me from . . . anybody. But would you do me a favor?"

"Depends. What is it?"

"I've got some shopping to do. While I'm gone, would you keep an eye on them?"

He opens the back of the pastry case and starts moving things around. "What am I looking for?"

There's no way I can go into all the details. "You'll know it if you see it. Just use that gift of yours."

"Okay. But on one condition."

"What?"

"One day, soon, you'll sit down with me and we'll have a conversation."

"Why?"

"I want to get to know you better."

Did he just ask me on a date? It's been so long, I don't remember what it feels like. Hope rises up in me, but I quickly squash it and blurt out, "I'm married."

"Good to know." He closes the case and wipes his hands on a paper towel. "So, do we have a deal?"

Do we? I look back at Lindsay, then at Adam. "Okay." What did I just agree to?

He grins. "Good. Now, if you're going shopping, you should take one of these." He thrusts a sheet of paper at me. "Most of the Old Town merchants have coupons on there. Hopefully, they'll come in handy."

"Thanks." I fold the paper and put it in my purse. Maybe I totally misread him. Maybe he's just a very good salesman. Yes, that's probably all his attention was: a sales ploy.

He smiles and moves down the counter where a customer is waiting to order. That's my cue to go. I stop over at Lindsay's table. She doesn't notice me until I put my hand on her shoulder.

"It's not time to go already, is it?"

"No. I'm going to do my shopping, then come back and get you. I'll be about an hour. Will you be all right?"

She rolls her eyes at me. "Of course."

"Okay. I'll meet you right back here." I catch Ben's eye and hold it. "Right here." I jab the table with my finger. "Got it?"

He leans back in his chair, a smirk twisting up his mouth. "It's a difficult concept, but I think I got it."

Lindsay laughs. So does the man sitting at the table beside them. Gee, I wonder who else in earshot thinks I'm a huge jerk. I muster as much dignity as I can. "Good. I'll see you soon."

On my way to the door, I glance at the counter. Adam's looking at me. He winks and nods his head. We're coconspirators now. But in what?

My shopping takes about half an hour longer than I expected. Entering the coffee shop, I look around at the now mostly empty tables. This shop definitely operates in ebbs and flows.

Ben is sitting at the table where I left him. But Lindsay's not there. I don't see her anywhere. I charge up to Ben. "Where's my sister?"

He raises his head slowly. "Some place where you'll never find her." I feel my eyes bugging out, then he laughs. "She's in the bathroom. Seriously, you have got to relax."

"As long as you're around? Not likely."

"Well, I'm not going anywhere. So you're going to be uptight for a pretty long time."

We stare at each other, neither willing to look away first. Finally, he points across the table. "If you sit down, maybe we can talk about this."

He's the last person I want to sit with. If the world was on the brink of destruction and my sitting with him would stave it off, I'd still have second thoughts. But until Lindsay comes to her senses, I'm going to keep running into him. Maybe now's a good time to draw up some boundary lines.

I sit, pushing the chair back from the table and keeping as much space between us as I can. But I don't say anything.

He leans forward. "I love Lindsay."

"Do you always hit the people you love?"

He presses his lips together, stretches his fingers, then lays his palms flat on the table. "I did not hit her." Each word is said precisely, emphatically, as if each word is its own sentence. "But I understand why you think that. Running into a door is the most clichéd cover there is. But I swear that's what happened. I didn't do what you think I did."

Ben sounds so sincere, I almost believe him. Almost. But then I look down at his hand and see LOVE tattooed across his knuckles. If he had punched Lindsay, that word would have been the last thing she saw before he made contact. Is that his idea of love? Or is Lindsay telling the truth and I've totally misjudged him? How can I be sure? I used to think I was good at reading people, the way Adam talked about. But my own husband cheated on me, and I never had a clue until it was too late. How can I be sure of anything ever again?

"I don't believe you."

He sighs and pushes back in his chair. "Look, I get you. Honestly, if I thought some guy was waiting on my sister, I'd rip his arms off."

This visual doesn't make me feel any better about his temper.

"So there's only one thing left for me to do." He rakes his hand through his hair, spiking it up even more.

"What?"

"Prove myself."

I don't know how he plans to do that, but before I can ask, Lindsay comes back.

She grins as she reaches the table. "Wow, I never expected to see the two of you sitting together. This is a good sign."

Or a sign of the coming apocalypse.

"Did Ben tell you his news?" She sits down and leans her shoulder against his.

There's news? I shake my head, and Ben pushes the cardboard cup in front of him from one hand to the other. "No, we didn't get to that."

"Ben's got a job!"

This is the worst news possible. I was counting on him running out of money and needing to leave town. If he's got a job, he's not going anywhere. "When did this happen?"

"While you were gone." Now she leans across the table and squeezes my arm. "Isn't it great? I'll admit I was kind of ticked when you said I had to meet Ben here. But if you hadn't, he never would have found out about the job."

She might as well slice my finger with a piece of paper and squeeze lemon juice on it. "Who hires someone they don't know after running into them at a coffee shop?"

Adam looks up from the table he's wiping down. "I do."

I stare at him, hoping I misunderstood what I just heard. "You gave him a job?"

"Yes."

"Doing what?"

"Playing his guitar."

"Are you insane?"

The handful of remaining customers looks in our direction. I guess that came out a little louder than I meant it to. Across the table, Lindsay glares at me while Ben looks resigned. Causing a scene doesn't help matters one bit, but that's just what I've done.

I stand up and motion to Adam. "Can I talk to you for a minute?"

We walk behind the bookshelves where I hope no one can hear us talking. "What happened while I was gone?"

Adam looks genuinely perplexed. "I was keeping an eye on your sister, just like you asked. I figured the best way to do that was to talk to them."

"How do you go from chatting with complete strangers to offering one of them a job?"

"Easy. He asked me if we ever hire musicians to play here. I said no, but I know of a band that's looking for a guitar player. He plays guitar." He holds his hands out, palms up. "It seemed like a perfect fit."

"You have no idea what you've done."

"Why don't you tell me?"

Either this man is extremely trusting, or he's playing me. Since I don't see any benefit for him in the latter, I can only assume he hasn't had much life experience. "It's a long story. Let's just say he's no good for my sister. He's dangerous."

"You sound pretty sure of yourself."

"I am."

"What if you're wrong?"

"Believe me, if you knew what I know, you wouldn't ask me that."

"Because of the thing with her eye?"

Wait a minute . . . "How do you know about her eye?"

"They told me the whole story." He smiles softly and puts his hand on my shoulder. "It sounds like you made a snap judgment and you won't consider that you might have been wrong."

Backing away, I shake off his hand. "What makes you so insightful? You don't even know Ben."

"And you do?"

Truthfully, no. I don't know Ben at all. But I know what I saw, and I know what my gut tells me. And that's enough.

He steps toward me. "It's wonderful that you love your sister so much. That you want to protect her. But she's a grown woman. She has the right to make her own decisions."

"Even if they're wrong?"

"You need to have a little faith."

Which is exactly the wrong thing for him to say. Having faith in people hasn't worked out so well for me, especially lately.

"We need to get home."

I leave the bookshelves and collect Lindsay. From the look on her face I can tell she heard every word, but she doesn't argue about leaving. Neither does Ben. Probably because they both know they won a battle today.

But the war's not over. And I intend to win this one, even if I have to fight the whole thing by myself.

38

Lindsay and I don't say a word to each other on the way back home. When I pull in the driveway, I barely have time to turn off the ignition before she jumps out of the car and runs inside. The door slams, and a sigh of relief whooshes from my lungs. I hate that she's mad at me again, but at least I know where she is and that she's safe, away from Ben. Now I can turn my attention to my mother.

Arms loaded with packages, I push my way into the house. Just about everything I bought today is because of what I read on the Internet earlier. I have running shoes and exercise clothes because I intend to take up jogging. I have Sudoku and crossword puzzle books to keep my mind in shape. And I have several bottles of vitamins, which are supposed to delay mental impairment. There's no guarantee any of it will work, but I intend to make my body as unwelcoming a host for Alzheimer's as possible. The rest of the stuff is to help my mom. Again, I don't know that any of it will work, but I'm going to give it a shot.

Upstairs, a door bangs so hard it makes the pictures on the wall rattle. Dad comes out of the hall, looks up the stairs, then looks at me. "Are you two at it again?"

"Things didn't go quite the way I planned."

He takes some of the bags from me and puts them on the coffee table. "What happened?"

"Ben got a job. From your buddy, Adam."

"Really?"

"Yes. He hired him for some band." I dump the rest of my bags and slump onto the couch. "I knew there was something off about that man. Turns out he and Ben are the same type."

Dad scratches the back of his head. "Honey, there's something you ought to know about Adam. He—"

"Stop." I hold my palm out at him for emphasis. If Dad starts defending Adam, I'll lose the shreds of composure I've managed to hold on to. "I get it. He's your friend. No offense, but I don't want to talk about him anymore. Where's Mom?"

"Two guesses."

"Watching *Lucy*?" He nods. I pat his hand. "I've got a surprise for you." I grab one of the bags and plop it in his lap.

A smile lights his face as he pulls out a long box. "Wow. *I Love Lucy*, the complete series on DVD."

"I don't know about you, but I'm tired of hearing the same episodes over and over again."

"Some variety will be nice." He flips it around and reads the back of the box. "Although 'Vitameatavegamin' makes me laugh no matter how many times I see it."

"Agreed. It's a classic for a reason."

He pats my hand. "Thank you, Sugar Plum. This is a very thoughtful gift."

I'm glad he understands why I got it. Not because Mom will tell the difference, but because he will.

He points at the other bags. "What else do you have there?"

"A little bit of everything. Hey, do you still have that old card table we used to do jigsaw puzzles on?"

"Sure. It's in the hall closet." His eyebrows lift. "Are you planning on working a puzzle?"

"Yes. With you and Lindsay and Mom."

His brows fall, along with the corners of his mouth. "Honey, your Mom's not up for that."

"Probably not, but there's no reason why we can't be in the room with her while she watches her show."

"I guess not." He rubs his chin. "What makes you want to do a puzzle?"

"I did some research today on Alzheimer's and I read about nonmedical therapies. One of the things they recommended was to find activities the person used to enjoy, and try to reintroduce them."

"Like the puzzles."

"Exactly. Remember how much fun we all used to have?"

The melancholy twist of his mouth says more than any words.

"I don't expect Mom to jump in and put a puzzle together on her own, but maybe if she sees us doing one it will spark something in her. Maybe she'll even join us. It's worth a try, right?"

Lips puckered tightly, he nods. "Right."

"Great." I push off the couch and grab most of the bags. "Do you need help with dinner?"

"No, I've got it covered." He kisses my cheek. "But thanks."

I kiss him back. "You bet. Let me know when it's time to eat."

I'm halfway up the stairs when he calls after me. "What are you doing until then?"

"Making peace with my sister."

Hopefully, I can convince her to join us for after-dinner puzzle fun. One way or another, that family room is going to live up to its name tonight.

Lindsay isn't interested in talking with me, but she has no qualms about talking at me. Apparently, I am hardheaded, unforgiving, and lame. I'm a lot of other things, but those are the attributes that stick in my head. As tempted as I am to tell her she's soft in the head, naive, and reckless, I don't. Instead, I ask if we can call a truce, for our parents' sake. Then I tell her about my puzzle idea. Wonder of wonders, she agrees to go along with it.

After dinner, we all go to the family room together. The card table is already set up, far enough from the TV so it's not in the way, but close enough that Mom will notice it. While Dad fiddles with the DVD player, I take out the puzzle boxes.

"Think you bought enough?" Lindsay asks.

I did get a little carried away. "I wanted us to have choices. Which one looks good to you?"

Lindsay picks up one after the other, studying the pictures on the front. "This one." She chose a scene of colorful hot air balloons in a robin egg blue sky.

"Nice."

She spills the contents onto the middle of the table. Immediately, we begin sorting out the edge pieces so we can build the frame. The familiar *Lucy* theme music fills the room, and a moment later, Dad joins us at the table, placing the TV remote beside him.

As we work on the puzzle, we talk about the weather, local news, music . . . anything that's light and controversy-free. Occasionally, we respond to jokes we hear from the TV, our laughter blending with Mom's. It's almost as if we're a normal family, enjoying a normal evening.

Almost.

When the episode ends, Dad picks up the remote and turns off the TV. Usually, Mom watches one show, sometimes two. But he always turns it off in between.

I wait for some kind of response from Mom. Finally, it comes.

"I'm tired."

She stands up. Dad pushes back his chair and goes to her. "Bedtime, then."

Threading her arm through the crook of his elbow, she lets him lead her. But before they pass the card table, she stops next to Lindsay.

"What are you doing?" Mom asks.

Lindsay looks up. "We're working a puzzle."

"You remember how we always used to do puzzles together, Mom?" I ask.

She doesn't acknowledge my question. As she stares at the pieces on the card table, her hand stretches out, almost on its own, and strokes the back of Lindsay's head. "You always had such beautiful hair." Her hand drops and she looks back at Dad. "I'm tired."

When they're out of the room, I turn to Lindsay.

"It worked," I say. "She remembered you."

"She remembered." Lindsay lets go of the sobs she's been holding back. "She's still in there. Somewhere, somehow, she knows me."

I pull Lindsay to me, stroking her hair like Mom did. Only I don't stop.

39

Saturday, I attempt to salvage the garden. I considered bringing Mom out to sit on the porch while I worked but decided against it. If she remembers anything about her flowerbeds, seeing them in this shape might make her hysterical. Once I've gotten the weeds under control, I'll invite her to join me. A quick perusal of the backyard shed reveals that Dad didn't get rid of the yard tools, he just hasn't had time to use them. Wearing Mom's wide-brimmed straw hat and her green canvas gloves, I kneel on the edge of the flowerbed, yanking up dandelions. They don't look like difficult plants to remove, but these things must have root systems reaching to China. When mere tugging and pulling gets too strenuous, I grab a trowel and start digging them out.

I've gotten about halfway around the bed when the screen door hinges creak. Dad walks out on the front porch, my cell phone in his hand.

"You've got a call, Sugar Plum."

Sitting back on my heels, I take off a glove and wipe the back of my hand across my sweaty forehead. "Who is it?"

"Jade."

My knees pop as I stand up. I'm definitely not used to so much manual labor. As I mount the stairs, I try not to let on how much my muscles hurt. But it's pretty obvious.

"Looks like you need a break anyway," Dad says.

I take the phone. "Thanks." Then I sit on the porch swing and wave Dad away. After he goes back in the house, I put the phone to my ear. "Jade?"

"Hey there, *Sugar Plum*."

"Very funny." Pushing off with one foot, I set the swing to swaying. "It's good to hear your voice."

"You too. I was afraid you were stranded in the desert somewhere."

"Why would you think that?"

"It's the only reason I could come up with to explain why you haven't called in the last three weeks."

With everything else that's been going on, I haven't had time to miss Jade. But now I do. "Sorry. Life's been kinda crazy."

"I'll bet. How's it going with your mom?"

"Tough. But I'm glad I'm here." And sorry I waited so long to come. "How are things with you?"

"Great. I've been throwing wild parties in your house every night."

Sure she has. Knowing Jade, she's probably spent most of her time reading or doing homework. Right now, I'll bet she's sitting on a chaise, enjoying my backyard. The professionally landscaped, immaculately kept yard that I pay a crew of gardeners to maintain. I look down at the blister beginning to rise on my thumb. How the mighty have fallen.

"Have all the fun you want," I say. "Just make sure it's clean when I get back."

"Speaking of coming back, when are you?"

"I have no idea."

"But you've been gone so long."

"Yeah, but Lindsay and I only got to our parents' a few days ago."

Jade sighs, sending a long hiss of air through the phone. "You can't stay away forever. Sooner or later, you've got to come back to real life."

We talk a little longer and before I hang up I promise Jade that I'll figure out a return date soon. But just thinking about it muddles my brain. True, life as I've become accustomed to living it is back in California. Only nothing there is the way it used to be. Soon, I'll be without a husband, and if Tony gets his way, without a home.

Dad comes back out onto the porch, holding two glasses of lemonade. "I thought you could use a break."

"Thanks." I take the glass he hands me and motion for him to join me on the swing. It groans under our combined weight, but I have no doubt it will hold us.

"Is everything okay?" he asks.

"Yep." I sip my drink. The tart and sweet combination makes me want to smack my lips. "Mmm. That's good."

Beyond the picket fence, two boys zip by on their bikes. Birds sing in the trees, leaves rustle. My father and I sip and sway, the condensation from our glasses sliding across our fingers and falling to make dark splotches on our jeans. The scene is Norman Rockwell perfect, except for one thing: I shouldn't be sitting on this swing. It should be Mom. The two of them should be sitting together, reveling in the simple pleasures of life, enjoying the view from their porch.

"How do you do it, Dad?"

"Do what?"

"How do you get up every day and take care of Mom, when you know it's not going to get any better?"

"I have to. I love her."

His face is so honest, so raw, I have to look away. "You make it sound easy. But love isn't always enough."

"If you ask me, it is. If it's not enough, then it's not really love." He squeezes my hand. "You know the love chapter in the Bible?"

"First Corinthians thirteen." If I didn't know it, I'd be a pretty sad marriage expert. Sadder than I already am.

"The next time you read it, really concentrate on the words. It's all about putting the other person first. There's nothing easy about loving someone that way. It's something you choose to do, every day."

For the first time, I see how truly amazing my father is. "Mom is so lucky to have you."

"We're lucky to have each other. If the roles were reversed she'd do the same thing for me." He pats my leg. "Enough of this. Let's talk about something more interesting."

"Like?"

"Like, how about coming to church with us tomorrow?"

That cross-country drive has me so discombobulated, I didn't even realize today is Saturday. "I'd like to, but what about Mom? Who's going to stay with her?"

"No one. She's coming too."

"Really?" Since we arrived, she hasn't left the house once.

Dad nods. "Church is the one place she still connects to. Not that she remembers who most of the people are, but she still loves to sing. Still loves to hear the sermons." He stands up and takes my empty glass. "I think you've done enough work out here for one day. Why don't you come in?"

I glance at the flowerbed. It still needs plenty of attention, but I made a good dent in it. "Okay. Let me put the tools away first."

Going back and forth between the front of the house and the shed, I think about what Dad said. How love is a choice. Over the course of our marriage, Tony and I made a lot of choices. Like flipping through a card file, I peruse the memories, trying to recall a time when either of us chose to do something purely because it would benefit the other. Nothing comes to mind. Not one thing. And even though Tony committed the biggest betrayal of all, if I'm honest, I have to admit that I didn't love him the way I should have either.

I shut the shed door, but I don't go to the house. Instead, I walk behind a tree in the corner of the yard, fall to my knees, and cry. There's no denying it anymore. I played a part in the death of my marriage. And even though I still can't bring myself to forgive Tony for what he did, the hard shell I've wrapped around my heart begins to crack.

40

As surprised as I am that Mom is going to church, I'm even more surprised that Lindsay is joining us. Not only that, but she's excited about it. She wakes before I do, grabs the shower first, and is dressed and heading downstairs when I'm just stumbling out of bed.

By the time I've made myself presentable and get to the kitchen, everyone else is eating. It's another cereal breakfast, so I look at Mom and smile. "Thanks for cooking."

"Lindsay and I did it together," she says.

That explains why we have spoons today. I look at Lindsay. "Very nice."

When we're done eating, we all pile into the car and head for church. Mom sits up front beside Dad, humming along to the music playing on the radio. Lindsay and I sit in the back, craning our necks to see where we're going.

For the next ten minutes, I let myself pretend our family is perfectly happy and normal. I push away the divorce, the unexpected pregnancy and abusive boyfriend, the Alzheimer's . . . none of that exists in this car. We are four people who love one another. That's all. That's enough.

But when Dad pulls into the parking lot and I see people milling around outside the church, my fantasy crumbles. It's been a long time since I've been here, but I remember some of them. Does Mom? How do they relate to her? What about Lindsay? What will people say when they realize she's an unwed mother-to-be? As my protective instincts go on high alert, I look to Dad, ready to take my cue from him. If he's concerned about anything, he certainly doesn't show it. Just the opposite. He's grinning like a little boy with a frog in his pocket.

Arm in arm, he and Mom walk toward the church. Lindsay comes around to my side of the car and puts her hand on the small of my back, pushing ever so slightly. "Don't worry," she whispers, "I'll bet no one knows about your recent issues. They probably won't even recognize you."

Great. I'd been so worried about Mom and Lindsay, it hadn't crossed my mind there might be gossip about me too.

We're enveloped in a cloud of handshaking and hugging as we make our way to the front door. Apparently, my dad told everyone he could that his girls would be with him at church, and they've been looking forward to seeing us. Thankfully, the greetings are all positive, for both Lindsay and me.

By the time we run the gauntlet of well-wishers, music's already playing inside. As Dad leads us down the aisle to empty seats, a voice booms through the sound system. "Let's all stand and praise the Lord."

There can't possibly be two men in this town with the same melts-like-butter voice. I stop in the middle of the aisle. A woman bumps into my back. She walks around me and mouths the words *I'm sorry*. I make a flapping motion with my hand and hope she knows that means *No problem*.

Dad spots four empty seats. As I follow him into the row, I stretch my neck and scan the front of the church. There he is. Adam from the coffee shop is also Adam the praise team leader.

I tug on Dad's sleeve. He leans down and I put my mouth close to his ear. "Why didn't you tell me about Adam?"

"I tried."

When did he try? The only time he tried to tell me anything was when we talked about Ben, and— Oh, no!

Beside me, Lindsay lifts her hand, but it's not in praise. She wiggles her fingers and waves at her boyfriend. Ben is playing with the worship band.

Dad wasn't kidding. Mom acts like a different person at church. She engages in the worship service, singing out, her bright soprano clear and strong. She follows the responsive reading. She even takes notes during the sermon. Sitting next to her, Dad is different too. He seems more relaxed and happy. Even Lindsay is having a good time. She beams every time the band plays a song. I'm the only sourpuss in the group.

How could they? How could they let me walk in here and see my least favorite person in the world help lead worship? How am I supposed to concentrate on God when all I can do is stew in my anger? It's the worst church service ever.

As soon as the last *amen* is said, I'm out of my seat and race-walking up the aisle. I avoid the smiling folks shaking hands at the door, circumnavigate the doughnut and coffee table, and head straight to the parking lot. Since Dad drove his car, all I can do is lean against the door, arms crossed over my chest, until my family joins me.

"What is wrong with you?" Lindsay asks.

213

"What do you think?" I turn to Dad. "Is there a good reason why you didn't tell me about this when you invited me to church?"

Beside him, Mom looks flustered. "What's wrong?" Her voice has that high, tight quality it gets when she's about to have a panic attack.

Dad shakes his head at me sharply, then gives all his attention to Mom. "Nothing's wrong, dear. Nothing at all." He opens the door and helps her into the car. Once he's sure she's okay, he comes around to my side. "I was afraid if you knew about Ben, you wouldn't come today."

He was right about that. Which is why he should have told me.

"Natalie!" A voice calls to me from across the parking lot. Turning in the direction of the sound, I see Adam sprinting toward us.

Dad opens the driver's-side door and looks over the roof at my sister. "Get in the car, Lindsay."

"But Dad, it's hot." I see right through her whining complaint. She wants to eavesdrop on my conversation with Adam.

"In the car." Dad uses his no-arguments voice. "Now."

She huffs out her disdain but follows his orders.

Adam stops in front of me, hair tousled, grin sheepish. "Surprise."

That's an understatement. "So you're a coffee dude and a worship leader. Are those your only jobs, or is there somewhere else I should expect you to pop up?"

"No, those two are it."

"Good. Then it should be easy to avoid you."

He grabs my wrist as I reach for the door handle. "You can't do that."

I whirl, ready to lay into him. But his eyes are so intense that, for a moment, I'm speechless. All I can do is stare back.

"Ignoring me won't solve anything," he says. And I realize that his interest in me goes beyond that of one friend for another. Not that we're friends. Somehow, we've skipped right over the friend part and landed smack-dab in the middle of forbidden attraction.

Yanking my arm from his fingers, I take a step back. "I told you, I'm married."

"Yes, you did. But that's not the whole truth, is it?"

How does he know? I glare at Lindsay through the car window. Of course. She talks to Ben. Ben talks to Adam. They've probably been encouraging him to pursue me. Maybe she thought if they kept me distracted, I wouldn't watch her so closely. She's got another thing coming.

I turn back to Adam. "My personal life is none of your business."

"I'm sorry you feel that way." He looks down at his feet, and when he looks back at me, he seems more confident than ever. "I truly believe God brought the two of us together for a reason. You may not see it this way, but all I want to do is help you."

"Help me? How does hiring my sister's low-life boyfriend help me? How does it help anybody? What business does a person like Ben have playing in a worship band?"

Now he pulls back, as if truly offended by my words. "A person like Ben? What kind of a person is that?"

"You want the short list?"

"I get it. He's a sinner. So am I." He slaps the palm of his hand against his chest. "So are you. And God loves us anyway. All of us."

I can't believe I'm getting a lecture in basic Christian principles from the guy who makes me coffee. "You don't get it. Of course, he belongs in church. Where he doesn't belong is up front helping to lead worship. I don't even think he believes in God."

"Have you asked him about his faith?"

"No."

"Maybe you should stop assuming and start asking."

I open my mouth to retort but can't. It's as if I'm in an airless vacuum and no sound will come out.

"Take care, Natalie. I hope to see you again soon. Somewhere." Adam walks away, leaving me stunned and speechless.

41

I'm going home next week."

Dad and Lindsay look at me like I've announced I'm going to the moon. "When did you decide this?" he asks.

"Yesterday." After we got back from church, I spent a lot of time thinking about what I've been doing here. Although I've wanted to spend time with Lindsay and my parents, I've also wanted to hide—from Tony, from the failure of my life. The more I went over everything, the more obvious it became that I have to face it. I have to go back.

Lindsay tosses a puzzle piece into the middle of the table. "This is because of me, isn't it? You're mad about Ben being at church."

"I'm not mad." Disgusted maybe. Irritated definitely. But not mad.

"Yes you are. And you want to teach me a lesson."

Elbow on the table, I press my fingertips into my cheek and forehead. "For crying out loud, Lindsay. Not everything is about you!"

"Shh." Dad puts his finger to his lips. In unison, Lindsay and I look toward the couch. Mom is still asleep, her head listing to one side, her breath coming out in occasional short puffs.

"This is about me." I take a deep breath, determined to keep my voice low and calm. "My home is in California. There are things I have to clear up there."

Lindsay frowns, but she doesn't come back at me with anything. Dad squeezes my hand. "I understand, Sugar Plum. But I wish you could stay. It feels like you just got here."

"I'm not leaving yet, Dad. I still have to book a flight."

"You're flying back?" Lindsay asks.

"Of course." One road trip per lifetime is plenty for me.

"Then you're not going to tell me I have to go with you?"

"Would it do any good if I did?"

"No."

"Okay then."

A snuffling snort sounds from the couch. "Oh, dear." Mom's own snoring has woken her up. "Why aren't I in bed?"

"That's just where we're heading now." Dad kisses us on the head, first Lindsay, then me. Mom is so foggy, she doesn't slow down at all as he leads her from the room.

I break up the jigsaw puzzle and dump the pieces in the box. Lindsay stands up. "I'm going to sit outside for a while."

She heads for the door, but I speak up before she gets out. "Ben's coming over, isn't he?"

Her eyes narrow and I suspect she's debating whether to tell me the truth or come up with a cover story. "How did you know?"

The truth. That's a refreshing change. "Why else would you sit outside by yourself?"

Our eyes lock. The silence deepens, the tension grows. We both have something to say, something important. Intuitively, I know this moment will define our relationship. Which one will be the first to speak? Who will be the first to take us to a place we can never turn back from?

It's me. "You're making a big mistake. Why can't you see that?"

She closes her eyes and shakes her head. "You are so blind. Why can't *you* see that you're wrong? You misjudged Ben from the start but you won't let it go."

"No, I won't. Because he's no good. You think you can trust him, but you can't." I don't want our parents to hear us fighting, so I struggle to keep my voice down. The result is a low, almost menacing tone, not at all what I want to project. But I can't stop myself. "No man is worth that kind of pain."

Her eyes narrow, her jaw juts forward. "This isn't about me at all, is it? You're jealous."

"Jealous? Of what?"

"Ben dropped everything and followed me across the country because he loves me. What has Tony done?"

The words are like a slap in the face, and I take a step back. What's Tony done? Left me for another woman. Broken my heart. Hurt me more than I thought possible.

"Natalie." Lindsay's voice is soft and gentle, laced with an empathy I didn't think she possessed. "This is a terrible time for you, and I'm so sorry. But Ben is not Tony. We've had problems, yes, but he loves me. I know he does. And I love him. You have to accept that."

I watch as she leaves the room and goes out the front door, pulling it closed softly behind her. Is she right? Have I really been envious of Ben's dogged determination to be with the woman he loves? I told myself I was over Tony—that we were done—but do I really believe it? Is there a part of me still waiting for him to change his mind, to tell me how wrong he's been and to beg for forgiveness? And if he did, what would I do? Would I take him back? Could I?

Lindsay's not an expert in the field of relationships. She hasn't studied Scripture down to the roots of the original Greek and Hebrew texts. She didn't even graduate from college. Yet she identified and exposed a major issue in my life. Two things are now abundantly clear: I need to sort out my feelings for my husband, and I owe my sister an apology.

When I go outside, I find her sitting on the porch steps. "Mind if I join you?"

She looks up at me, her face impossible to read in the shadows thrown by the porch light. "Be my guest."

I don't know where to start, so I say something safe and general. "I'm surprised you didn't choose the swing."

"I don't trust it."

"Dad and I both sat on it the other day and it held our weight." I look at it over my shoulder. "It's perfectly safe."

"Probably." She rubs her stomach thoughtfully. "But I'm not taking any chances."

One thing I'll say about Lindsay, she's extremely serious about her health and taking care of her baby. No caffeine, no flying, no porch swings . . . Which is why it's so odd that she wants to be with Ben. Why would a woman who's normally so conscientious about her well-being and safety willingly put herself in such a dangerous situation?

She wouldn't.

The truth hits me like hail from the sky. I look into the darkness of the night, the inky blackness dotted with splotches of illumination from streetlamps and porch lights, and I wish it would swallow me up.

"Ben never hit you, did he?"

"No."

I hang my head, not able to look at her. "I've been such an idiot."

She puts her arms around me, squeezing so tight I can barely gasp in a breath. "Not an idiot. A concerned sister."

I lean my head against hers, letting a tear drip down my cheek and into the hair I helped her color. I'm so sick of crying, and even more sick of hurting. "I'm sorry."

When we pull apart, her expression reminds me of when she was a little girl. When she was five, I took her to a circus. She had that same look on her face when I bought her cotton candy and took her picture with an elephant. Like her big sister had just given her the most precious gift imaginable.

"What changed your mind?" she asks.

Staring at my clasped hands, I shrug. "You're an intelligent woman. You're capable of making your own decisions and taking care of yourself. Granted, they're not always the right decisions, but nobody's perfect."

"True."

There's more to say, but the sound of whistling drifts to meet us. Lindsay plants a kiss on my cheek, struggles to rise from the step, then runs down the path to meet Ben. As he enfolds her in his arms, my heart aches. He loves her. Why couldn't I see that before?

She says something to him, motioning wildly with her hands. He looks over her shoulder at me, surprise evident on his face, even in the murky light. I force a smile and wave. He waves back.

I stand and brush off the seat of my jeans. "I'll leave you two alone."

Back in the house, I find Dad waiting for me in the front room.

"Did you hear any of that?" I ask.

He nods. "Most of it. If you wanted privacy, you should have shut the door." He puts his arm around my shoulders and pulls me close to him. "You did a good thing."

"I hope so."

Leaning into him, I soak up as much of his strength as I can. Because my apologizing isn't over yet. Tomorrow morning, there's another portion of humble pie waiting to be swallowed. And I intend to wash it down with a cup of the best coffee in Beaumont.

In the spirit of killing multiple birds with one shot, I decide to jog to Uncommon Grounds in the morning. I've been meaning to start an exercise regimen, and now seems like the perfect time.

Two blocks into my run I realize what a bad idea it was. By the time I reach Old Town, I'm breathing hard and sweating even more. I'm tempted to turn around and try again tomorrow, but then I see Adam through the window. He's standing on a ladder, putting books on one of the high shelves at the rear of the store.

The bells jingle as I walk in. He looks over his shoulder, smiling to welcome a new customer. When he sees me, his smile slips. And so does his foot. Right off the ladder step. His arms flail and he goes down with a thud.

"Adam!"

There are only three other people in the shop, all senior citizens, so I run to offer aid. Kneeling beside him, I try to remember everything I've seen in medical dramas on TV. "Lie still. Don't move. Something could be broken."

"You okay over there?" a wavering voice calls out.

Adam groans and pushes up on one elbow. "I'm fine, Mr. Jordan," he calls. Then he looks up at me. "I'm fine."

"Are you sure?" I touch his arm. "Did you break anything?"

"The only thing broken is my pride." He sits up and I notice a splotch of red on the carpet where his elbow had been.

"You're bleeding."

He looks down but seems unconcerned. "It's just a nick."

Ignoring protocol and probably violating several health department rules, I run behind the counter, grab a paper cup, and fill it with ice. I pull some paper towels off a roll and turn to run back to him. Except that he's standing right behind me, so I run into his chest, spilling ice all over him and the floor.

"Woman, you are a danger to yourself and others."

Don't I know it. "I'm sorry."

"It's okay. I'll live." He opens a cupboard and pulls out a first-aid kit.

"Can I help you with that?"

"No, I've got it." He swipes an alcohol swab across his elbow, hissing at the sting. Then he looks back at me. "You can't be here."

What did I expect? I was rude to him at church, and now I nearly made him break his neck. Why would he want to have anything to do with me? "Of course. I'll leave you alone."

I'm halfway to the front door when he calls out. "Natalie, I meant you couldn't be in the food prep area. I don't want you to leave the building."

"You don't?"

"No." He smirks. "At least not until I find out why you came. After Sunday, I didn't expect to see you again."

"That's why I'm here." Should I order a coffee? Make this a more professional meeting? No, I just need to say what I came to say. But it's so hard. "Can we sit down?"

He looks around. "I don't know if I should. I'm on duty."

Mr. Jordan rustles his newspaper. "When a beautiful young woman asks you to sit with her, you'd best do it."

I look down at my running clothes. Mr. Jordan must be nearsighted.

Adam smiles and whispers to me, "Guess I've got to honor my elders, right?" He sits on a couch and waits for me to join him. Settling at the other end, I angle in his direction, careful not to let our knees accidentally touch. "Okay, what did you want to talk about?"

"About Sunday . . . I was wrong."

"About what? Me or Ben?"

"About all of it. You were right. I was so convinced that Ben was bad for Lindsay, I never gave him a chance."

"You were worried about your sister. If I'd been in your shoes, I probably would have done the same thing."

"I doubt it. You didn't even know Ben, but you saw something in him I didn't. You gave him a chance. And I blasted you for it."

"Your reaction was a little strong." He looks down at the seat cushion then looks back at me. "Why do you think that was?"

My breath catches in my throat. I know, but I don't want to put my feelings into words. I want to hide them away, keep them in the dark where they can't hurt me. I've learned, though, that the things I ignore and push to the side are the things that hurt me the most in the end. "Because you scare me to death."

His fingers reach for mine, but he stops himself, draws back. "You scare me too."

"I'm leaving at the end of the week."

At my announcement, his eyes widen. "Because of me?"

He sounds like Lindsay. Doesn't anybody think I have a mind of my own? "No. Not because of you. Because that's where my home is."

"Are you sure?"

I laugh and try to make a joke out of it. "Last time I checked."

His expression turns serious. When he reaches for my hand this time, he takes it, his grip firm and certain. "Do me a favor?"

My throat is now completely devoid of moisture. "What?"

"Consider that maybe God has a new path for you. Maybe there's a road leading out of California to someplace new."

"Someplace like here?"

"Maybe."

Looking down at our hands, the way his strong, warm fingers protect mine, I'm struck by the beauty of it. The rightness of it. The wrongness of it.

Slowly, I pull my hand away from his. "I'll consider it. But you have to remember, I'm still married."

"I think you ceased to be married as soon as your husband broke your vows and cheated on you. The rest is a legal technicality." His jaw clenches and he forces a smile. "But I know you're a married woman. Believe me. I know."

For just a moment, I let myself look into his eyes. They're deep and full of things I wish I could know better. I've got to get out of here, before I do something really stupid.

"I should go now."

He stands with me. "Will I see you before you leave?"

"I don't know. I haven't even booked my flight yet. And I want to spend as much time with my family as I can."

"How about if I come to you?" I open my mouth to object, but he holds up a hand and stops me. "I can bring you some iced coffee after I get off work. Just as friends. Promise."

The idea of talking to someone outside of my family is too good to pass up. "Okay," I say. "Just as friends."

What harm can there be in that?

42

Now that I've decided to return home, I figure it's also time to reconnect my techno-umbilical cord. For the first time in weeks, I sit down at a computer and log on to my e-mail. The amount of unread messages makes me slightly dizzy. I didn't know my inbox would hold so much.

Scanning the first few pages for anything marked urgent, I pause. Several of the subject lines contain the word *divorce*. I know I've decided to stop running away from painful truths, but I'm just not ready to take a cyber-scolding from well-meaning strangers. The e-mail has waited this long. It can wait a few more days. I type in a new Web address and hit enter before I have time to change my mind.

While I'm searching for the best nonstop flight from O'Hare to LAX, my phone rings. I hit the speaker button so I can talk and surf at the same time. "Hello?"

"May I speak to Natalie Marino, please?"

"This is she."

"Ms. Marino, I'm calling from the Santa Monica Police Department."

I snatch up the phone and press it against my ear. "Yes. Do you have news about my car?"

By the time our conversation is done, I'm left with a mish-mash of emotions. I take a few minutes to complete my airline reservation, then I call Jade.

"Hey," she says. "When are you coming back?"

"In five days."

"Really? I was just joking, but that's great. If you give me your info, I'll come pick you up."

"I added your e-mail address to the reservation. You should have a copy of the itinerary."

"Okay. Is something wrong? You sound kind of down."

"The police found my car."

"That's good. Isn't it?"

"It was stripped and chopped."

There's a long pause. "Oh." Then another pause. "What does that mean?"

"Pretty much what it sounds like. All the parts were removed, and if they couldn't be removed, they were cut out." I take a deep breath and try to put an upbeat lilt into my voice. "Want to hear the good news?"

"I can't imagine there being anything good after that. So yeah, I want to hear it."

"They found some of Lindsay's boxes."

"No way."

"Yes way. They were in the back of the garage they used for their operation. Apparently, thieves have no use for almost-new maternity clothes."

Jade bursts out laughing. Despite my best attempts, I join her. Even though part of me wants to throw something, a bigger part is glad to experience some resolution. Once I contact my insurance company, return the loaner car, and get the recovered boxes from the police station, I can put this whole irritating situation behind me.

Speaking of irritating situations . . . "Jade, have you taken a look at my e-mail lately?"

"I've been watching it for anything that needs immediate attention." She sounds positively breezy. Too breezy.

"Nothing from my agent or editor, then?"

"No, but that's not a bad thing. They probably just want to give you space."

"Probably." Or they want to distance themselves from me. Never a good thing. "There sure are a lot of unread messages in my box."

She makes a noise. It's either a grunt of approval or a groan. I don't want to know which. "I was going to read them, but then I changed my mind. We can go through them when you get back." Before I can reply, she rushes on. "Too bad it's not sooner, but at least you're finally heading home."

Home. I think of Tony, and I think of the house. Then I push those thoughts away. "I can't wait to see you, Jade."

After I hang up, I swivel the desk chair so it's facing the window, looking out on the yard. The grass needs mowing. Weeds crowd in among the tulips ringing the base of the elm. Even the fence is looking shabby, the white paint on the boards cracked and peeling. So much needs to be done. Five days may seem like a long time to Jade, but I wonder if it's long enough to accomplish everything I want to do before I leave.

Pushing myself from the chair, I go in search of Lindsay. She's not in the guest room. Not in the kitchen. When I poke my head into the family room, I find Mom and Dad sitting on the couch together, reading. He's reading a novel; Mom is flipping through a magazine, most likely only looking at the pictures.

"Dad? Have you seen Lindsay?"

He takes off his reading glasses as he looks at me. "She's out with Ben."

I frown. Just because I don't think he's abusive doesn't mean I'm excited about their relationship. Not the way it is right now. "Did she say when she'd be back?"

"In time for dinner."

"Okay." I turn to leave but then grab the door frame and pull myself around. "What would you think about inviting Ben to join us?"

"For dinner?"

"Yes."

He considers it, twisting his lips to the side. "I think it's a good idea. Looks like he's going to be a part of this family one way or the other. We should get to know him better."

Exactly what I was thinking. We need to know him, and he needs to know what kind of a family he's getting into. It will also give me a chance to make a few things clear. To both of them.

"If you need me, I'll be outside." Waggling my fingers, I leave my parents to their reading and head for the garden. If I don't do anything else, I'm determined to whip Mom's flower-beds into shape before I leave Beaumont.

———— ∞ ————

"Mary, Mary. How does your garden grow?"

I'm on my hands and knees, wrist deep in a topsoil and mulch mixture, when Adam's rich voice singsongs behind me.

"Are you calling me contrary?" I ask, looking over my shoulder.

"Depends on the day." He motions with the two icy drinks in his hands. "How does taking a break sound?"

Brushing off my hands, I raise myself straight up on my knees, feeling a bit like a prairie dog. "Sounds perfect."

He heads to the porch and I'm relieved when he sits on the top step. Something about the porch swing would be a little too intimate for two friends.

Putting the straw to my lips, I take a slurp of the cool, creamy coffee. "Mmm. This is exactly what I needed."

"Glad to be of service." He points to the corner of the yard. "What are you planting there?"

"Pansies in the front. Behind that, I'm putting in marigolds."

"Annuals. Interesting."

"How so?"

He shrugs his shoulders so quickly, it looks more like a hiccup. "Just that they'll die at the end of the season and need to be replaced next year."

I hadn't considered that when I bought the plants at the nursery. My main focus was what looked pretty. "Guess I'll have to hire someone to do that next year."

"Or you could do it yourself."

"I could. If I'm here."

"Or you could hire me."

I laugh. "Yes, because you desperately need a third job."

His lips quirk into a sad little smile. "I may be down to one job pretty soon."

"Really? Why?"

"The coffee shop's for sale."

"I'm sorry to hear that, but I can't say I'm surprised. Half the time I've been in there, it's been empty or nearly so."

"Yeah. It's hard to meet operating expenses when people are cutting back on luxuries."

"The renovation probably hasn't helped either."

"No. Which is ironic, because the whole idea of the renovation is to attract more people." He moves his cup in a circle, watching the liquid and ice cubes swirl inside. "I just hope the new owner decides to keep the apartments upstairs, or else I'll be out of a home too."

"There are apartments?"

He bobs his head. "Yep. Four of them."

"Are they all rented out?"

"Only two. The other two are empty." He grins at me. "Why? Are you in the market for an apartment?"

"Maybe. But not for me." If Lindsay decides to stay in Beaumont long-term, she's going to need a place to live. Hanging out in the spare bedroom is great now, but not after the baby comes. And if she and Ben are serious and end up getting married. . . . Another slurp of my coffee produces a loud sucking sound as the straw encounters nothing but air. Making a sad face, I jiggle the empty cup. "Looks like my break is over. Thanks for the drink."

"Thanks for sharing a step with me. See ya." He pats me on the shoulder, quick and firm, the way a friend would when saying good-bye. But as he walks away, I can't help wondering about God's timing, why things happen the way they do, and how a person's life can become so complicated so quickly.

43

Maybe it makes me a small, petty person, but I have to admit, I get a zing of pleasure out of how uncomfortable Ben looks at our dinner table. My sister, however, is almost euphoric. To her, the sharing of a meal signals our family's total acceptance of her relationship. Ben knows better. He's a little older, has seen a bit more of the world. He knows that being the only player without home-field advantage is rarely a good thing.

I wasn't sure how Mom would handle having a stranger for dinner, but I guess most people are strangers to her. Tonight, she dug deep and pulled out her company manners. Even though Lindsay introduced her to Ben, whenever she speaks to him she calls him *young man*. Probably because she forgot his name shortly after she heard it. I find it cute, but it rattles Ben. I don't bother correcting her.

"So Ben," Dad spears a piece of chicken from the platter before passing it on to me, "you must be racking up quite a bill at the hotel. Have you thought about your living situation?"

"I'm not at the hotel anymore. I found a roommate."

"Really?" After I take my chicken, I hold the platter in front of Mom so she can take a piece. "Who with?"

"One of the guys in the band has a friend with a spare room, so he's letting me crash there."

"For free? Wow, that's nice of him."

Ben nods. "It's just temporary. Hopefully, I'll be in a more permanent situation soon." He and Lindsay smile at each other, and I pounce on the moment.

"Does that mean the two of you are planning to stay in Beaumont?"

The platter has made it all the way around the table to Ben. He sets it down gently as he looks me straight in the eye. "It does."

"Why?"

"Why not?" Lindsay jumps to his defense, but he puts his hand on her wrist and squeezes it.

"It's a nice town. A great place to raise kids. And Lindsay wants to be closer to her parents."

Mom looks up from her plate and smiles. "Oh, they'll love that."

Confused, Ben looks at Lindsay. She whispers in his ear. I move the conversation forward as if nothing odd just happened. "Sounds good. I'm surprised playing in the worship band pays enough to support a family."

Lindsay kicks me in the shin. My knee jerks up and hits the table, setting the dishes to rattling.

Ben grabs the tottering salt shaker and shakes it vigorously over his food. "I'm looking for a second job, something full-time with health insurance."

Dad points his fork in Ben's direction. "That's very ambitious of you."

"If Adam can do it, so can I."

Adam is certainly a good influence on Ben. I'll have to tell him so the next time I see him. If I see him.

Mom leans back in her seat. "I'm full."

It's not unusual for Mom to break into a conversation with whatever's on her mind. Nor is it unusual for her to proclaim she's done eating even though we've all just started.

Leaning over, I turn her plate a bit. "Have you tried the potatoes, Mom? They're really good."

Without acknowledging me, she picks up her fork and holds it poised over her food. Then she says, "When is the wedding?"

She succeeds in stopping all activity in the room: eating, talking, breathing. Lindsay is the first to find her voice. "What wedding?"

"Yours, of course." She looks back and forth between Lindsay and Ben. "I've never seen two young people so much in love. You are meant to be together." She laughs, the sound a little too tight, a little too loud. "I've been telling you that for years."

She's got them confused with another couple, but I have no idea who. Dad and I look at each other. He shrugs, clueless as the rest of us. Lindsay's lips are pressed tight, lower lip clamped between her teeth, eyes wet and shiny. There's no way she can talk and keep from crying at the same time.

I struggle to find something to say that will help, or at least change the subject. "Who wants dessert? We have cake."

"Not until you clean your plate," Mom says. She looks across the table, her expression dreamy and far off. "We had such a beautiful wedding, didn't we, Joel?"

Dad nods. "Yes, we did."

"The cake was so big. It was . . . " Her eyes drift to the side as she searches her mind for the answer.

"Lemon." Dad fills in.

Her attention snaps back to him. "Lemon chiffon. With cream cheese frosting."

One of the mysteries of Alzheimer's is how it riddles a person's memory with so many holes and gaps it's turned into the mental equivalent of Swiss cheese. There's nothing fair about the fact that Mom can remember the frosting on a cake she ate forty years ago, but she doesn't recognize her own daughter who sits right beside her.

It would be hard enough for Lindsay to handle if she wasn't pregnant, but now, it's all too much. She drops her face in her hands and the tears come, hard and fast, along with gulping sobs.

The crying agitates Mom. Her hands start to shake and she bunches up her napkin in her lap. "What's wrong? Why's she crying?"

"They're happy tears." Ben jumps in, putting his arm around Lindsay and pulling her close. "We're just so excited about getting married."

"Oh." Mom relaxes. "Oh, yes. Of course you are."

Ben looks directly at my dad, his expression serious. "Sir, there's nothing I want more than to marry Lindsay. Nothing."

"That's good to hear." Dad's voice is so thick, I'm afraid he may start crying too. But he clears his throat and carries on. "Why don't you and Lindsay get that cake now?"

"Good idea. Come on, babe." He helps Lindsay out of her chair and they walk quickly from the room.

I toss my napkin on the table. "I think I'll give them a hand."

Once in the kitchen, I shut the door behind me. Ben and Lindsay stand in the middle of the room. He presses her against his chest and she clutches the back of his shirt in her fists. They look as if they're holding each other up, and if you removed one of them, the other would fall.

"Are you okay?" I ask.

Lindsay sniffs and nods. "Yeah. I just . . . frosting. She remembers frosting."

"I know." There's no tissue anywhere in sight, so I rip a paper towel off the roll and hand it to her.

"Thanks." As she dabs her eyes and blows her nose, she steps back from Ben. "That was some pretty quick thinking back there."

"Did you mean it?" I ask him.

"What if I did?" He asks back, head slightly tilted, eyes narrowed.

"I asked you first."

"Yes. I meant it." He looks down at Lindsay and reaches for her hand. "It's not the way I wanted to ask you, but I meant what I said. I want to marry you, more than anything."

I shouldn't be here for this moment, but I'm not leaving unless someone asks me to. So far, they only have eyes for each other. Lindsay stares at him, her mouth open, jaw slack.

Ben looks worried. "You're not saying anything."

"Wow."

"Is that a good wow, or a bad wow?"

"A good wow. A very good wow."

"Does that mean yes?"

"What do you think?" When he doesn't answer, she throws herself at him. "Yes! Of course. Yes."

That's enough for me. I turn to the counter and busy myself with setting out plates and cutting the cake. When Tony asked me to marry him, it was very romantic. He took me to a restaurant overlooking the Pacific Ocean. Afterward, we walked along the shore, carrying our shoes. He rolled up the cuffs of his dress pants to keep them out of the briny water, but he ruined them anyway when he went down on one knee and proposed. The surf, the moonlight, the ring he removed from his jacket pocket, every bit of it was perfect.

Ben's proposal has been anything but perfect: in a kitchen, surrounded by dirty dishes and old Formica, illuminated by the harsh glow of overhead lights, and witnessed by the bride-to-be's often cranky sister. There isn't even an engagement ring to slip on her finger. But none of it matters to them. Set apart in their own bubble of love, this kitchen has just become the most romantic, special place on earth.

As I put slices of cake on the small plates, I say a little prayer for my sister. She and Ben are starting out all wrong. Neither of them has a good job, their spiritual life is shaky, and they have a baby on the way. Marriage is hard enough without so many strikes against you. It's hard to imagine how they can possibly make this work.

Then again, Tony and I did everything right and look how we ended up. Maybe Lindsay and Ben have a shot after all.

44

I can't sleep. On the other side of the room, Lindsay lies motionless, her breath even and rhythmic. No matter how hard I try, I can't shut off my brain. There are too many thoughts vying for my attention, tangential threads that are crowded and tangled up with one another. But the more I try, the more knotted it all becomes.

In three days, I have to face whatever waits for me back in California. After a month of ignoring my career, it's time to figure out what to do with it. Is there anything left to salvage? What about Tony? What about my house? What about Lindsay? She and Ben are going to have a baby together, so getting married seems like a good idea, the next logical step. But is it really? Can I trust Ben to keep his word?

Flopping onto my side, I squint at the alarm clock on the dresser. Two a.m. This is ridiculous.

As quietly as I can, I get out of bed and head downstairs. Maybe a cup of tea will help. Or a piece of that cake.

When I reach the foot of the stairs, I notice the light in the family room. I could have sworn I turned it off before we all headed to bed. As I get closer to the room, I hear something. A faint slapping and the muffled tones of someone talking under his or her breath. The sight that greets me when I step into the doorway breaks my heart.

My mother sits at the card table. Empty puzzle boxes litter the floor and a mound of pieces cover the table. She picks up two pieces, tries to fit them together, but when it doesn't work, she throws them aside. She does it again. And again. And now that I'm closer, I make out what she's saying. "I can't find it. I can't find it."

"Mom?"

She doesn't look up. Just shakes her head violently and continues her useless task. "I can't find it. It's here somewhere. I know it is. I just can't find it."

Picking my way around the cardboard mine field, I sit in the chair beside her and reach for her hands. "This is a really hard puzzle."

She stills, looks at our hands, hers holding two pieces and mine enfolding them. Then she lifts her head, and I know she's with me. My mother, the woman who's been lost for so long, is right there with me. But this moment of clarity costs her, the emotions so raw and painful in her eyes they cut like jagged shards of glass. "I used to be able to do this."

"I know."

"I used to be able to remember."

"I know."

"What's happening to me?"

My chest feels empty and full at the same time, as if someone sucked out all the air and replaced it with concrete. "It's not your fault. You're sick."

The light in her eyes flickers, and I know she's starting to slip back into that lost place. But she fights back. She pulls her hands from me and cups my face. "I love you."

The block in my chest breaks. Tears fall, rolling across her fingertips. "I love you too, Mom."

In the distance, I hear the sound of feet clomping down the stairs. Dad appears in the doorway a moment later, his eyes as wild as his hair. "Meredith. What are you doing down here?"

Her hands fall from my face and her gaze looks through me. The spell is broken. She looks up at her husband. "I couldn't sleep."

"Neither could I." Drying my eyes with the cuff of my pajama top, I smile at Dad. "Sorry we woke you."

"That's okay. I'm glad I found the two of you together." He walks to Mom and helps her up. Then he turns to me. "Are you all right, Sugar Plum?"

I take in a shaky breath, my lungs expanding, my heart thumping. No matter how difficult this episode was, it was also amazing. Now I know that my mom is still in there, and she loves me.

"I'm great, Dad. Good night."

He nods. Silently, they walk out of the room.

I doubt this is the first time he's found her missing in the middle of the night. But they sleep in separate rooms now, which means he must get up to check on her. When was the last time he had a good night's sleep? When was the last time he did something for the sheer pleasure of it?

Dad told me to read about love in the Bible, and I have. I've read it so many times I can practically quote the entire chapter. But I've never really lived it, not the way my father lives it every single day.

I pick up a puzzle box. With the side of my arm, I swipe the pieces into it until it's full. Then I grab another and do the same. As I clear up the mess, mixing together puzzles that none of us will ever work on again, the tangles of my mind start to sort themselves out.

The next day, I'm back in the garden, tackling a new section. And again, Adam stops by. But this time, he's brought along more than just a drink carrier with two iced coffees in it. There's also a plastic bag dangling from his elbow, and a can of paint in his other hand.

I stand up and push back the brim of my hat. "You look like you've come ready to work."

"I have. If that's okay with you."

"More than okay." As much as I hoped to make the garden perfect before I leave, it wasn't looking like I'd have time to paint the fence. Adam doesn't know it, but he's almost an answer to prayer.

"Great. But first, it's break time."

We sit on the step and sip our coffees. "Has anyone bought the store yet?" I ask.

He laughs. "It's a little soon for that. In this economy, it'll be a miracle if it sells at all."

"No, it's not the best time to sell." Which makes me think about my house. Even if I agreed with Tony and wanted to sell it, we probably wouldn't be able to.

"How about you?" Adam asks. "Are you all set to head back West?"

"Almost. Thanks to you, the garden will be finished today."

He smacks his forehead with his palm. "You mean I'm helping you leave with a clear conscience? Me and my great ideas."

"Actually, there is something I could use your help with."

"Putting up a scarecrow? Finding the yellow brick road?"

I bump his shoulder with mine. "I'm serious."

"Sorry. Ask away."

"It's about Ben and Lindsay. They got engaged last night."

"Really?" He looks surprised. "That's good, right?"

"I hope so. I think it is. Anyway, that's what I'm concerned about. While I'm gone, would you keep an eye on Ben?"

"I'll do what I can. But other than rehearsals and Sunday mornings, I don't see him much."

"But you do see him. And he respects you. Maybe if you talked to him, it would help."

"What am I supposed to talk to him about?"

"I don't know," I say with a shrug. "Man stuff."

He laughs. "That's a pretty broad topic."

"Very funny. I'd feel better if Ben knows that even though I'm gone, there are still people watching out for Lindsay."

"I see. But you are coming back."

"I am?" Does he want me to come back? Or does he expect me to—out of a sense of duty to my family?

"Of course. There's no way you'd miss your sister's wedding."

Family duty it is. Disguising my disappointment, I take a final sip through my straw.

He puts his empty cup in the cardboard carrier and holds it out for me to do the same. "You know what I think is going to happen?" he asks.

"What?"

"I think you're going to go back to California, and you're going to miss it here. You're going to realize all the great things Beaumont has to offer."

The air around me feels thicker, and I need to take a long, deep breath in order to fill my lungs. "Like?"

"Like family. Friends." His face inches closer to mine. "Maybe even your future."

How do I respond to that? I've borrowed library books longer than I've known this man, but he affects me in a way that throws me completely off balance. And—here's the kicker—I'm still married. It doesn't matter how amazing I feel when he looks at me, how my insides feel all warm and tingly, how I'd like nothing better than to sit on this porch with him for hours just talking. I can't act on any of it. I can't even think it. Because I'm still married, even if it is in name only.

I lean away from Adam. Yet even as I put physical distance between us, there's something I need to know. "Why me?"

He shakes his head, his lips quirking up into a wry grin. "I've been asking God the same thing. Why her?"

"Gee, thanks."

He pushes himself off the step and starts pacing in front of me. "You know what I mean. You're the most unattainable woman I know, but I can't stop thinking about you."

"But you barely know me."

"That's the thing. I can't wait to know more about you. What's your favorite color? Do you like dogs or cats? What kind of movies do you like?" He stops in front of me, one hand on his hip, the other squeezing the back of his neck. "All I know is that God brought you into my life for a reason. Right now, it's to be your friend. Maybe later, it will be more. I don't have the answer, but I want to find out."

"Me too."

The friend part I understand. But something more . . . it makes no sense. If that's the case, then why would God bring him into my life now, when neither of us can act on these feelings? Are we being tested? And there's one more thing nagging at me.

"How old are you?"

He laughs. "Seriously? You're worried about my age?"

"Not worried," I say with a shrug. "Curious."

When he doesn't answer right away, I do start to worry. "Come on, you can't be that much younger than me. Can you?"

"No. I just don't want to give you another reason to push me away." He pauses, then shakes his head. "I'm thirty-four."

"Really?"

"Yes." He takes his wallet from his back pocket. "Want to see my driver's license?"

He holds it out to me, but I shoo it away. "No, I believe you."

"And what do you think?"

He's five years younger than I am. Not a big deal, especially if we're just friends. "I think if we don't get to work, this yard will never be done."

"Come on." He grins and holds his hand out to help me up. "Let's go paint a fence."

Adam walks across the yard and I follow him. He hands me a paintbrush, and when I take it, our fingers meet. We pause, both of us holding the handle, and I say, "Purple."

"What?"

"My favorite color. It's purple."

A slow smile blooms on his lips. "Good to know."

45

Are you trying to tell us something?" Lindsay points to the box in the middle of the card table.

"Yes. It's time for us to stop concentrating on what Mom can't do and focus on what she can."

"And you think she can do this?"

"With our help, yes." The new puzzle is a picture of Snoopy, Charlie Brown, and friends. It has bold lines, bright colors, and just twenty-five chunky pieces.

She lowers herself gently into one of the folding chairs. "You really must believe in miracles."

"Don't you?"

"Sometimes."

It's the opening I've been waiting for, a time to talk to Lindsay about her faith without her feeling like I'm pouncing. But then our parents walk in, and the moment is gone.

"I got a new puzzle today, Mom. Do you want to join us?"

Her expression is a mixture of confusion and fear. "No, thank you, dear."

Dad frowns as he walks past me and gets her settled on the couch and her *Lucy* DVD playing. When he joins us at the table, he's still frowning.

"What made you say that?" he asks. "You know she can't do puzzles."

"She might be able to do this one. We won't know until she tries."

"No." Dad jerks his head to the side. "If she tries and fails, she'll fall apart. You can't put her through that."

"She's already going through that." I put my hand on Dad's arm. "When I found her down here the other night, she was trying to put the puzzles together. She knows she's not like she used to be."

"Oh, Lucy!" Mom calls out from the couch a split-second after Ricky does on the TV. She looks so proud of herself.

I open the box and spill the huge pieces on the table. "We're going to put most of the puzzle together. If she wants to come and help us finish it, great. If not, that's okay too."

Lindsay snorts. "This thing will take five minutes to do."

"If we take our time," Dad says.

My heart sinks. They're not even going to try.

"We're going to have to take turns." Lindsay puts a piece in the middle of the table, then turns the rest of them upside down. "There, that should challenge it up a bit."

I reach over and give her a one-armed hug. "Thanks."

For the next twenty minutes, we alternate between playing with the puzzle and making small talk. When *Lucy* is over, Mom stands up.

"I'm tired."

Dad turns off the TV. He takes her by the arm. "Time for bed, then."

I've seen them do this every night since we've been here, but it's never discouraged me until right now. There's one puzzle piece left on the table. I turn it over and push it toward Lindsay with my finger.

Mom and Dad stop between our chairs. "Good night, girls," he says.

Mom looks down at the table. "There's a piece missing."

Lindsay's eyes bounce from me to Mom. "There is. Do you want to help us?"

Wordlessly, Mom reaches for the stray piece. Her hand is shaking, but she picks it up and moves it to the empty spot in the puzzle. It's upside down, so when she tries to place it, it doesn't fit. Holding my breath, I wait for the meltdown. But it doesn't come. Instead, she moves it around, jiggling it until it finally slides into place.

Dad, Lindsay, and I all exhale at once. Mom grins. "I did it."

"You did it." I rise from my chair and kiss her cheek. "Good night, Mom."

She smiles at me. Then she turns to Lindsay and kisses the top of her head. "Good night, sweetheart."

We watch them leave the room, then I slump down in my seat. "Wow, that worked out better than I thought."

"I'll say." Lindsay shakes her head. "Sorry I doubted you, O wise one."

"Wisdom has nothing to do with it. I'm just winging it."

"Well, it was a good call. Maybe this is your new field of expertise. Alzheimer's therapy."

"Not on your life."

I break up the puzzle and put the pieces in the box. One lucky guess doesn't make me an expert. It just means we had a good night. But it looks like that's how we have to take things: one day at a time, one night at a time, one success at a time.

Which might not be a bad philosophy in all areas of my life.

While I'm packing the next night, Lindsay offers to stay with Mom so Dad can drive me to the airport.

"Are you sure you're up to that?"

Sitting cross-legged on her bed, she waves off my concern. "Absolutely. We'll watch TV, nap on the couch. It'll be a breeze."

I agree, but make a mental note to corner Dad and get his approval too. As I put the video camera and extra memory cards in the suitcase, she stops me.

"Would you mind leaving the camera here?"

"Sure. Why?"

"I thought I could work on editing some of our videos together. If I burn a DVD, I might be able to sneak it into Mom's *Lucy* rotation."

"Good luck with that." I laugh and hand her the camera case. "We'll want it here when I get back for the wedding, anyway."

Lindsay sighs. "I wish you didn't have to go."

"Seriously? I figured you'd be happy to have the room to yourself."

"Weird, huh? Nothing about this trip turned out like I expected."

Looking over my shoulder, I grin at her. "You mean it wasn't totally lame?"

She tosses a pillow at me. "No. Not totally."

"I'm glad to hear that."

"In fact, it's been nice getting to know you."

"Getting to know me? You make it sound like I was a stranger."

"You kind of were."

"And whose fault was that?"

We both say "yours" at the same time, then we exchange looks like the other sister is crazy.

"You were never around," Lindsay says.

"That's not true. We did a lot of stuff when you were little. And when you were bigger I tried to hang out with you, but you were so . . ." There's no other word for it, so I say it. "Bratty."

"Do you think it was easy having you for a sister?"

Frustration curls my fingers up into fists by my sides. "What was so hard about it?"

"You were a sex expert."

An appalled exclamation escapes my lips. "I was a romance novelist. A Christian one. There were no sex scenes in any of my books."

She blows a long breath out through her teeth. "Yeah, and then you wrote your first marriage book. Remember that?"

"Yes."

"What was the title?"

Uh-oh. I think I see where she's going now. "It was *Between the Sheets: A Christian Gal's Guide to Romance After Marriage*."

"I was in fifth grade. How do you think it feels to have all your friends asking if you know as much about sex as your sister does?"

"But it was a book for adults. Your friends shouldn't have been reading it."

"They weren't. But their mothers were."

It never occurred to me that my writing might cause problems for my sister. "Why didn't you say anything before now?"

"What could I say? Please give up your career because it embarrasses me? Besides, Mom and Dad were so proud of you. I just didn't know how to handle it."

My fingers relax as all the fight drains away, and I sit on the edge of her bed. "I am so sorry. I had no idea."

She uncrosses her legs and scoots over so she's beside me. "I know. And that made it worse. I felt exposed at school and invisible at home."

All those years, when she was acting out and getting into trouble, was it from a desire to prove she was nothing like me 0r that she was better than me? The prospect of what she might have done in order to put space between herself and my professional image makes me shudder. There's still so much I don't know about my sister, and here I am, getting ready to leave her again.

"What was your dream, Lindsay?"

"What do you mean?"

"After you left college. You must have had a dream, a goal for your life. What was it?"

She puts her hands on the edge of the mattress and kicks her heels against the bedframe. "You'll think it's stupid."

"No, I won't. What was it?"

"I wanted to be an actress." She looks up at me, waiting for the response she's sure is coming, but I surprise her.

"Really? That's so cool."

"You think so?"

"Sure." We're not so different, Lindsay and me. She wanted to create characters through acting. I did the same thing, only through writing. "So, what happened? Why did you give it up?"

She looks down, picking at the edge of the sheet. "I went on auditions, got some jobs doing extra work. But it's a tough business. Lots of rejection."

I can relate to that.

"One good thing came out of it."

"What's that?"

"Ben. We met each other on cattle call for a music video."

"What's a cattle call?"

She laughs. "Pretty much what it sounds like. As many actors as you can find herded into one audition. It's madness, and you have to wait around a lot. So Ben and I got to talking. Neither of us got a job, but we got each other."

It remains to be seen just how good a thing that was, but for now, I'm giving Ben the benefit of the doubt. I put my arm around her and she leans her head on my shoulder. There's only one thing left to say. "I love you."

"I love you too."

46

It's about a forty-five minute drive to the airport. Normally, I'd be itching to get there as soon as possible, but this is the first time Dad and I have been completely alone since I got home. There's so much I still want to talk to him about, I don't know where to start.

"I'm really glad you and your sister came home, Sugar Plum. It's meant a lot to me, and your mother too."

"I'm not sure how much it's really meant to Mom."

He rubs his thumbs against the steering wheel. "I don't have scientific proof, but I truly believe she picks up more stuff than we think she does."

"I hope so."

"You know how coma patients will sometimes say they heard things while they were unconscious? That's how I think it is with her. There's a part of her subconscious that's collecting information and storing it away. That's why I'm so careful about what I say in front of her."

"And why you still take her to church?"

He nods. "I want her surrounded by positive, uplifting experiences as long as possible."

The door is now wide open for a topic we've both been avoiding. I can't put it off any longer. "How long do you think that will be?" He doesn't answer, so I rephrase the question. "How long can you care for her by yourself?"

"As long as it takes. There are challenges, but we can manage."

It's a beautiful, self-sacrificing sentiment. It's also naive and a sign that he's in denial. "You're doing a great job with her. But it's not always going to be like this. It's going to get worse."

"I know. And when that time comes, we'll deal with it. But not today." He sniffs hard and musters up a smile. "Now, unless you want me to go to pieces and run us up a telephone pole, I suggest we change the subject."

He's right. This subject is much too emotional for a moving car. "What do you want to talk about?"

"I want to know how you and Tony are doing."

"Didn't you hear?" I pull out my old friend, sarcasm. "We're getting a divorce."

"Sugar Plum." The way he says it turns my old nickname into a gentle rebuke.

"Sorry. But there's nothing new to tell. Tony's girlfriend is still pregnant. He and I are still getting a divorce. And I'm still trying to keep him from selling my home."

"I see." He puts on his blinker, glances in the rearview mirror, then changes lanes. "How do you feel about all that?"

"Like a failure. An idiot. The punch line of a lousy joke."

"You're angry."

"I have a right to be, don't I?"

"Yes, you do. But that kind of anger, the kind that smolders under the surface, will only hurt you." He looks quickly in my direction, his smile sad, then turns his eyes back to the road ahead. "You need to forgive him."

Of course, Dad would think that. He's the type of man who keeps his promises, no matter what. And he expects me to be that kind of woman. "I'm sorry I've disappointed you."

A frown twitches on his lips. "Where did that come from? I never said you disappointed me."

"No, but I'm sure you don't agree with this divorce."

He doesn't respond for so long that I think he's done talking. But then he finally speaks up. "I am disappointed, but not in you. I'm disappointed in Tony and the choices he made. Normally, I think divorce should be a last resort. But in this case, not only was he unfaithful, he fathered a child. Now there's another innocent life involved in all this."

"So you don't think it's wrong to end my marriage?"

"Honestly, I think Tony ended it already. All that's left now is the legal part."

It's almost exactly what Adam said to me. Which makes me appreciate my new friend's wisdom even more.

Dad gives my knee a quick pat. "Honey, I'm so sorry this happened. But you have to know that God has a plan for you. A wonderful, amazing plan. Hold on to your faith, look to Him, and you'll be all right."

How in the world can God use any of this mess to give me something amazing? Still, I want so much to believe my father. "You promise?"

He makes the sign of a cross over his heart. "I promise."

Getting back to California is much easier than leaving it was. My flight takes off on time. Not only do I snag an aisle seat, but the seat next to me is empty. And because the flight is only half full, the attendants let everyone have two bags of mini-cookies instead of one.

For reasons unknown, we land ten minutes ahead of schedule. As I go down the escalator to baggage claim, I wonder if my early arrival means I'll have to wait for Jade. Then I hear her screeching.

"Natalie! Natalie, over here!"

She jumps up and down beside a row of black-suited, card-holding limo drivers. I weave my way through the crowd and throw my arms around her. The way we're laughing and talking at the same time pulls smiles and a few snickers from the professionals.

"Come on." I link my arm through hers and lead her to the right baggage carousel so we can wait for my luggage. "How was the traffic?"

"Crazy. Typical LA traffic. How was your flight?"

"Great. Very untypical." Overcome by a wave of happiness, I sandwich her face between my palms and give her a good squeeze. "It's so good to see you."

She pulls back and rubs her cheeks. "Okay, now you're scaring me. What happened to grumpy, down-on-life Natalie?"

"I left her somewhere between here and there. She may still be hanging out on Route 66."

"Good. I want to hear everything about your trip."

"Of course. Oh, I've got a surprise for you." I rummage in my carry-on bag and pull out the back scratcher.

She takes it and reads what's printed on the back of the handle. "I've got the itch to travel 66." Her mouth quirks to one side and she shakes her head. "Thanks. I'll think of you whenever I use it."

A buzzer sounds and the blue light atop the carousel begins to flash and spin as bags spit out onto the moving belt.

"Let's find my luggage and I'll tell you all about it on the way home."

It takes another twenty minutes to locate both my bags, drag them to short-term parking, and make our way out of the lot. Once we're on the freeway, Jade orders me to talk, and I comply. I tell her about the drive, our adventures in Oatman, the Grand Canyon, the Wigwam Village. I tell her about Ben and how he stalked us—only he wasn't stalking us—and how he turned out to be an okay guy after all. I tell her about my parents. I tell her about Lindsay—how much better things are between us. The only thing I don't tell her about is Adam because I'm confused enough about him as it is, and I'm fairly certain Jade would encourage me to pursue the relationship and confuse me even more.

An odd feeling comes over me when we turn onto my street. Nothing's changed while I've been gone, yet it's foreign. And when we pull into the garage and she says, "Welcome home," I don't feel like I'm home. It's almost like looking at someone else's house.

Each of us carries a bag in through the kitchen. It doesn't even smell the same. "Have you been baking?"

"That'll be the day." She points at a tiny vase full of bamboo reeds on the counter. "It's a vanilla oil diffuser. Smells good, huh?"

"Delicious." It's a nice, homey touch. Only it doesn't make this house feel like home. Instead, it reminds me of the way my parents' house used to smell when I'd come home from school to find a plate of freshly baked Toll House cookies sitting on the kitchen counter.

Jade carries my suitcase toward the stairs, but I call after her. "Not up there."

"You don't want to sleep in your own bed again?"

Not that bed. I shake my head. "I'm going to hang out down here in the guest room."

"Okay." Thankfully, she doesn't press the issue.

As we walk down the hall, I change the subject. "Did you have a chance to read any of that e-mail?"

"I did."

Her omission of any details makes me nervous. "And?"

"And it wasn't at all what I expected."

Terrific. If it was worse than she expected, it must be pretty bad.

"And there's so much of it. You've probably gotten more mail in the last month than in all the time I've worked for you."

I groan. "Don't remind me. That inbox is overflowing."

"It's not just the e-mail. It's snail mail too."

"Really? Actual letters?"

"Yep." We walk in the bedroom and she motions to the suitcase. "Where do you want this?"

"Against that wall is fine. Who sent me letters?"

"A lot of people. You won't believe it unless you see it." She walks past, crooking her finger for me to follow.

At my office door, she stands aside and waves her hand for me to enter. "There you go."

I take one step into the room, then freeze. I've gotten reader mail before, but never anything like this. Stacked beside my desk are six white plastic tubs with *United States Postal Service* embossed in blue on their sides. From what I can tell, they're all full.

The edges of my vision blur, most likely because I haven't eaten anything but cookies in the last eight hours, but possibly from shock. I grab Jade's arm, afraid I'll pass out.

"What's wrong?" she asks.

"That's an awful lot of hate mail."

"It's not hate mail."

I blink, clearing my vision. "It's not?"

"No." She wobbles her head from side to side. "Okay, some of it was. About ten letters. But that's just because there are

256

crazy people in the world. I got rid of those. But the rest, they're all good."

"What do they say?"

"Oh, no. You've got to read them for yourself. The e-mails too."

It's going to take me forever if I do it all by myself. "Will you stay and help me get started at least?" Jade considers it, and I know just the thing to bring her over to my side. "We can order pizza."

With a smile, she whips out her cell phone. "I've got the pizza place on speed dial. And you have a deal."

47

Listen to this."

I pop a piece of pepperoni in my mouth as Jade reads from one of the letters.

> When my husband left me I felt like my world had ended. It's bad enough he broke my heart but my life as I knew it was torn apart too. None of our friends know how to talk to me anymore and I'm starting to think they were more his friends than mine. It's the same way at our church. One woman actually said I needed to fix what I'd done wrong and save the marriage. Even though he had an affair, it made me wonder, did I do something wrong? Was it my fault somehow?

Jade staples the page to the envelope it came in, then sets it on top of a stack of already-read letters. "I had no idea there were so many scumbag husbands out there."

"Neither did I." It's overwhelming. We've only gone through a fraction of the letters, and almost all are from women with the same story.

Jade rises from her cross-legged position on the floor and picks up the dirty plates and cups. "It's enough to make me want to swear off men entirely. Isn't there a convent somewhere nearby?"

The idea of Jade as a nun nearly makes me choke on my last swallow of soda. "Don't give up hope. Not all men are like this."

"Oh yeah? Like who?"

I call after her as she carries the trash into the kitchen. "Pastor Dave. My dad. Your dad. Other guys." Guys like Adam.

She comes back in and plops beside me on the couch. "Your dad sounds like an amazing man. I'd like to meet him."

"Want to come with me to Lindsay's wedding? Then you could meet the whole crazy family."

Looking up at me from beneath sooty lashes, she smiles. "As tempting as that sounds, I don't think Lindsay would be very happy to see me."

"She's grown a lot in the last month. And not just because she's pregnant. I think she'd surprise you." I yawn and look down at my watch, which is still set to Illinois time. No wonder I'm so tired.

"And that's my cue to go." Jade gives me a hug, then stands up. "Do you want me to come by tomorrow?"

"Yeah, if you can. Since I'm carless, you could help me with some errands."

"Cool. See you then."

After she leaves, I look at the Post Office tubs we moved into the family room. So many letters. So many women. I wish

I could reach out to every single one of them. But right now, I'm so tired, the only thing I can reach out to is my bed.

There's time enough to deal with all this tomorrow.

There's not enough time in the day to take care of everything. The list I made during breakfast fills up two entire legal pad pages. Every time I wrote down one task, I'd think of three or four others associated with it.

"That's what you get for running away from your problems," I grumble to myself.

At least I don't have to worry about grocery shopping. God bless her heart, Jade made sure there was food waiting in my pantry and fridge. Smiling, I stir a few soggy pieces of Special K around in the milk puddle at the bottom of the bowl. Mom would love this meal.

A high-pitched ding sounds from my phone. It takes me a second to realize it's signaling a text message. Since I'm not big on texting, I rarely get them. After tapping the screen, I discover the message is from Adam.

How are you doing?

Clamping my lower lip between my teeth, I type back.

Good. How did you get my number?

The answer comes quicker than I expected.

From your dad.

Great. I wonder what Dad thought when Adam asked him for it? But more important, what do I do now? I feel like a teenager passing notes in class, and I'm afraid of being caught by the teacher.

I miss you.

Three words from Adam, and my insides turn to mush. I'm in trouble. As quickly as I can, I type a response.

Will call you soon. Gotta go.

Not exactly poetry, probably not the response he wanted to read, but it's all I've got right now.

OK. Am praying for you.

"That's good," I say looking at his last message. "Boy, do I need it."

Twenty minutes later, Jade arrives. When she sees my list, she turns on her heel and walks back outside. Once we're both in the car, she asks, "Where to first?"

"The police station."

She looks behind her as she backs out of the driveway. "Didn't I warn you about making me go to the police station?"

"Yes, but this is important. Now that they've found what's left of my car, I need to get a copy of the final report for the insurance company, and pick up Lindsay's boxes."

"I'm surprised they're letting you take them. Don't they need to hold them as evidence?"

"If there was going to be a trial, maybe. But the guys that did it pleaded guilty."

"Interesting. They probably made a deal in exchange for a lighter sentence."

I shake my head. "You've been watching way too much *Law and Order*."

"Hey, it taught me everything I know about our legal system. So, what did they recover at the scene?"

"I don't know for sure. The officer I spoke to could only tell me it was personal property."

"That could mean anything."

"I know." Which is precisely why I didn't tell Lindsay about it. I'm hoping the car thieves threw all her boxes in a corner without opening them. Then I can be the hero and return her possessions to her unscathed.

When we get to the police station, my hopes are dashed. It turns out only three boxes were recovered, and all of them were torn opened and rifled through. From the looks of them, by someone with filthy hands. It's a safe bet I'm not going to find an iPod in there.

"What a mess," Jade says.

The clerk behind the counter pushes a form in my direction. "Before I can release any property to you, you need to sign this statement that you recognize it and it does belong to you."

As far as I can tell, it's all maternity clothes. Using only the tips of two fingers, I move aside the garments to look below. There are a few books, some cheap knickknacks, and a photo album. I pull out the album and thumb through it. There's Lindsay. There's Ben. That's good enough for me.

"Yes. It's mine. Actually, it's my sister's but it was in my car when it was stolen."

The clerk looks at Jade. "Then she can sign it."

Jade elbows me and we both crack up. "Sorry," I say to the clerk. "This is my friend. My sister's in Illinois. Can I just sign for her?"

"Sure." After I scratch my name on the bottom of the form, she tears off the yellow copy, hands it to me, and says, "Have a nice day." Her tone clearly conveys her irritation with us for being so silly.

Jade eyes the three boxes. "Do you think you could help us carry these to the car?"

"I can't leave the office, but I've got something you can use." She goes to a closet and comes back a minute later. "Here you go."

Taking the metal handle of the two-wheeled cart, Jade grins. "Well, hello, dolly."

The clerk is old enough to get the joke, but not happy enough to go with it. I quickly pile the boxes on the dolly and push it down the hall before the woman can change her mind. Behind me, Jade hums and I try my hardest not to sing along.

"This is weird," I say as we load the boxes into the trunk.

"Yeah, I didn't think you'd get anything back."

"That's not what I meant." I slam the lid and turn to her. "I'm happy. I'm enjoying myself. And I think that's really weird."

"Why?"

"Because my life is a mess. What do I have to be happy about?"

Jade puts her hand on her hip, shifting her weight to one side. "Can't you just be happy and enjoy it? Do you have to analyze everything and figure it all out?"

The funny thing is that I haven't figured anything out. Nothing at all. If today's any indication, that seems to be working for me. Maybe that's an answer to a question I haven't thought to ask.

"Do you think I'm a control freak?"

"Yes."

"Wow. You didn't waste any time on that one."

She tilts her head to the side. "Am I amazingly talented?"

"Yes," I say with a laugh.

"See. When you know, you know." Her hands drop to her side and the wisecracking stops. "Seriously, you do like to orchestrate things. Which is good when it comes to running your business."

"But not so good when it comes to relationships," I finish for her.

"If you ask me, and you did, you need to step back and let God steer the ship."

Now that's dirty. She's quoting from one of my own speeches. But she's right. After years of giving advice on how to trust God, I guess it's time I tried it myself.

48

The next few days are the most gut-wrenching and satisfying I've experienced in a long time. Typically, Jade and I spend the mornings going through letters and e-mails. We separate them into three piles: women who need encouragement, women who are encouraging me, and men who've been left by their wives and want a woman's perspective as well as encouragement. We also keep a shredder nearby for the occasional ugly letter. Thankfully, there aren't many of those. I intend to write back to these people eventually. Just as soon as I have something worth saying.

After lunch, Jade goes home and I spend time reading my Bible and praying. You'd think, given my career and area of expertise, this would already be a normal part of my daily routine, but it's not. At first, it shamed me to think how much time I've spent over the years reading my own notes, examining my own thoughts for speeches and books, all the while neglecting the words and thoughts of my heavenly Father. Soon, I realized that shame was simply another barrier between me and God, so I pushed it aside and chose to move forward. Ever since, my study time is richer, my prayer time deeper and more intimate.

Adam hasn't contacted me since the day he sent those text messages. I've thought about him, but I still don't feel right pursuing any kind of a relationship with him, even a purely platonic one. The truth is, I don't know if I can keep my feelings for him platonic. When it comes to Adam, the only thing I know for sure is that maintaining my distance is the best thing for both of us right now.

Around four o'clock every day, Dad calls. At that time, they've just finished dinner in Beaumont, and Mom and Lindsay are usually together in the family room. He tells me how they're all getting along. Then I talk to Lindsay and she fills me in on wedding plans. Every time I hang up, a sweet sadness floods me, and the loneliness in my empty house grows a little heavier.

Tonight, it's more difficult than usual. It could be because of a particularly poignant letter I read from a mother of two whose husband left her for the kids' twenty-three-year-old piano teacher. Or maybe it's because when I talked to Dad, I could hear Mom and Lindsay singing together in the background. *I am the queen of the gypsies . . .* I know exactly which episode of *Lucy* it's from, and now the tune is stuck in my head, a constant reminder of the family bonding that's going on without me.

The doorbell rings, and I jump. Who could that be? I pull the door open, and standing there is the last person I expect, or want, to see.

"Tony."

"Hello, Natalie."

"How did you know I was back?"

"Mrs. Hernandez called me."

Ah, our sweet little neighbor is trying to play matchmaker and fix our broken relationship. Her intentions are good, if misplaced.

Tony shifts his weight from one foot to the other. "Can I come in?"

No, I want to say. You can't. You left, remember? You can never come in again. Instead, I step aside. "Sure."

He looks around, almost like he expects the entryway to look different. It doesn't, but he does. His tie is askew. His hair needs a trim, his face needs a shave. He looks tired. Unhappy.

"Why are you here?" It's blunt, perhaps even rude. But I'm too emotionally strung out to play games.

"I made a mistake."

"You what?" He's got to be talking about the house. Please God, please let him be talking about the house.

"I never should have left you. It was a mistake."

For the love of Pete. "Does Erin know you're here?"

"This isn't about her. It's about us."

"It most certainly is about her. She's the mother of your child."

That shuts him up. For half a second. Then he plows forward. "I know. But you're my wife. I never should have left you."

That's the second time he's said he never should have left me. Not *I never should have played around* or *I never should have hurt you* or *I never should have broken my vows*. Just that he shouldn't have left.

"I'm not your wife anymore. Not since you cheated on me."

Rubbing his hand across the stubble on his cheek, he stares at me, as if he can't believe what he's hearing. "You make it sound like it was easy. You don't understand how hard I fought it. I didn't want to be with someone else, but you and I . . . I felt so far away from you."

"And you thought sleeping with another woman would bring us closer?"

"No, of course not. But she made me feel special. Like I mattered. You have no idea what it's like to discover that someone else wants you that way, especially when your spouse doesn't seem to want you at all."

Actually, I do. I've been fighting those feelings with Adam for weeks. Fighting and winning. So not only can I empathize with him but I also recognize what a load of bull he's throwing at me.

"Forgive me, Natalie. We can work this out. We can." He grabs my wrist and pulls me up against his chest.

There was a time not so long ago when I would have given almost anything to be in this spot, so close to him that we can feel each other's heart beating. But it's not his heart I'm feeling now. It's his desperation. I see the fear in his eyes. Smell the remnants of liquor on his breath.

"Have you been drinking?"

"Just one beer. But I'm not drunk." His words come out faster, almost frantic. "I swear. I meant every word I said."

"Okay." I push him away and take several steps back. "Look, Tony. I know I'm not perfect. And I'm sorry if I did anything to make you feel like I didn't want you. If you'd talked to me instead of jumping into someone else's bed, you would have known it wasn't true. That's when we could have worked it out. Not now."

"But Erin—"

"*But Erin* nothing. Don't blame this on her. Love is a choice. So is breaking a promise. When you had your affair, you chose to ignore our vows, to ignore me. You chose another life. *You* did that."

He shakes his head, and I get the feeling this is the first time he truly understands how life-changing his actions were. Strange, but I actually feel sorry for him. The barrier around my heart cracks again and, finally, the protective shell falls away. Now I'm able to do what seemed impossible just a few days ago.

Stepping forward, I put my hand on his cheek, make him look me in the eye. "You hurt me, Tony. Our marriage is over. But I forgive you."

This is the closest I've ever seen him to tears. "What do I do now?"

"First you pray. Square things with God. Then you go back to Erin. When our divorce is final, you marry her and you be the kind of husband and father I know you can be. You choose to love them. Every day."

His eyes squeeze shut. When he looks back at me, I see resolve in them. "And what are you going to do?"

"Follow a new path, wherever that leads."

I open the front door and as he walks out, I take in a deep breath of clean night air. "Tony."

He turns, and smiles, although his eyes still brim with sadness. "Yeah?"

"We can sell the house. I'll call my lawyer in the morning."

It's final now, and he knows it. He nods, turns, and walks down the driveway.

As I shut the door and lean my back against it, tears begin to flow, but not because of anger or sorrow. Not because of pain. They flow from an overwhelming sense of relief. Because for the first time in months, I am free.

49

When Jade gets to the house the next morning, she finds me sitting at the patio table in the backyard, pounding away at the keys on my laptop.

"This is new," she says, closing the sliding glass door behind her.

"It's a beautiful day. I thought I'd enjoy the yard while I can."

"While you can?" She sits in the chair to my left. "What does that mean?"

"I'm selling the house."

"Wow. What made you change your mind?"

"Tony stopped by last night." The horrified expression on her face brings a smile to mine. "It's okay. There were things we both needed to say. And by the time he left, I was able to forgive him."

"That's nice, but what does forgiving him have to do with selling the house?"

"Turns out I was only holding on to it to torture him." I lean back, elbows on the armrests of my chair, fingers steepled in front of me. "I don't feel the need to do that anymore."

"I see. Well, you're a bigger woman than I am. I'm still fantasizing about ways to torture him." She leans over to look at the laptop screen. "What are you working on?"

"A proposal."

Her eyebrows lift. "For a new novel?"

"Nope." I shake my head. "A nonfiction project."

"Let me guess. How to survive a divorce?"

"Oh, no," I say with a shake of my head. "I'm not qualified to write about that. Not yet, anyway. This book's about mothers and daughters. How we see ourselves, how we see each other."

"Does your agent know about it?"

"I called her this morning. She likes it, especially with all the aging Boomers out there."

She hits the Page Down button and scrolls through my morning's work. "You sure have gotten a lot done so far."

"That's not all." I push my legal pad in front of her. "I also sketched out a rough game plan for my life."

Drawing her brows together, she gapes at me. "Good grief. You did all this today? How early did you get up?"

"With the proverbial chickens," I say, grinning.

While Jade reads over my scribbling, I sip my coffee, cradling the mug between my hands. Across the yard, a group of little brown birds hop and peck around the blooming flower border. I wonder how the garden is doing back at my folks' place. I hope Dad is remembering to water all the new plants.

"You're leaving me."

I look back at Jade. "No I'm not. I'm going to something new."

"It's the same result. I'm losing a friend and a job."

Reaching over, I give her hand a quick squeeze. "You're welcome to come with me if you like." It's an empty offer, really. There's no way she would leave college, and I wouldn't let her. But I want her to know how important she is to me.

"Thanks, but no. I couldn't handle those Illinois winters."

"Well, you can at least come to visit. In the spring or summer, when it's warm."

She jabs the paper with her finger. "Are you sure you want to do this?"

"Absolutely."

The corner of her mouth turns up in a half-hearted smile. "Okay. While this stinks for me, I'm happy for you."

"Good. But you're not out of a job yet." I stand up and gather my laptop and papers. "I'm going to work you like a dog as long as I'm here."

She grabs my coffee cup and follows me into the house. "What's first?"

"Letters," I sing over my shoulder. "We've got letters."

⸙

That afternoon, I'm too impatient to wait for Dad's call, so I call him.

"Great timing, Sugar Plum. We just finished dinner."

"Good. I've got a question for you. Are you someplace you can talk?"

"Just a second." There's a muffled rumbling, like he's talking to someone and holding his hand over the phone's speaker at the same time. A door bangs shut, then he's back. "Okay. What's the super-secret news?"

I tell him about my conversation with Tony and my decision to sell the house. And then I tell him my plans for the future.

"What would you think about me living with you and Mom for a while?"

When he doesn't have an immediate answer, I worry I may have miscalculated. Maybe he doesn't want to have another female under foot. Or he might think I'm questioning his ability to take care of Mom.

"I think it would be wonderful," he says, sounding slightly mystified. "But are you sure you want to do that? Wouldn't you rather have a place of your own?"

"Eventually I will. But for now, I want to help you out and spend as much time as I can with Mom. Then you can take some time for yourself. The best way to do that is to stay at your house. But if you don't want me there, I'll understand."

"Sugar—" His voice cracks, and he has to clear his throat before going on. "You have no idea how this makes me feel. It's an answer to prayer."

"For me too, Dad." I should have been there sooner. Fear kept me away, and as a result I missed precious, coherent time with my mother. I don't want to miss any more. We'll walk down this mysterious road of Alzheimer's together. And when the time comes when she does need full-time care and can't live at home anymore, at least I'll know I've done all I could.

"When do you plan to come back?"

"As soon as I wrap things up here. A couple weeks, I think."

"That's just great." He coughs a few times. "Do you want to talk to your sister?"

I picture him sitting on the porch swing, rubbing his eyes before any of the neighbors walk by and catch him being emotional. I sure do miss him.

"I do, Dad. But one more thing first. Do you know the name of the Realtor that's handling the Uncommon Grounds sale?"

"Let me think . . . It's Roy Gerard. Why?" His volume goes up by one excited notch. "Are you looking to buy a business?"

"Possibly. Right now, I'm on a fact-finding mission. But don't mention it to anybody yet."

"You've got it." Now his voice drops, becoming whisper-soft. "Mum's the word."

I laugh. "Okay, I'm ready to talk to Lindsay now."

My sister is excited when I tell her about her recovered boxes, until she finds out what condition they're in. At first, she tells me to toss the clothes but then she changes her mind.

"Do you think they'd be okay if I washed them?" she asks.

"Sure. They're not torn, just dirty. If you want, I'll throw them in my washer for you."

"That would be great. Who knows, I might need them again later if Ben and I have more kids."

"More kids?" It took him long enough to want the one they're expecting. "Have you talked to him about that?"

"Yeah, I have. It came up during counseling the other night."

"Counseling?" This is a surprise.

"I know. Who'd have thought, right? But Pastor Wade won't marry us unless we have counseling first."

This is even better than I hoped. "Does that mean you're getting married in the church?"

"No. We want to get married before the baby comes, which doesn't give us a lot of time. We decided a small ceremony at home would be the best thing."

"Oh, you should have it in the backyard." I can already picture it, the grass emerald green and freshly cut, new flowers blooming and swaying, tree branches festooned with silk ribbons. "I can do all the decorating for you."

"Does that mean you're coming back soon?"

My heart warms at her hopeful tone. "Yes. And not just for a visit. I'm coming to stay."

If everything goes according to plan, not only will I have a new business to run, but I'll be the landlord of four nice apartments. One of which I'll offer to Ben and Lindsay at a discounted rate.

"I can't wait till you get back," Lindsay says. "And I'm not the only one."

"Dad sounded pretty excited, didn't he? I'm sure he'll enjoy having some help so he can take a breather every now and then."

"I wasn't talking about Dad. I meant Adam."

"Oh . . . uh . . ." I sputter like a malfunctioning faucet.

Lindsay laughs. "Oh, boy. You've got it for him too."

"No, I don't. We're friends. That's all."

"Well, your *friend* has been stopping by a few times a week to keep up the garden."

"He has?"

"Yes. And every time he's here, he asks about you."

"That's sweet. But seriously, we're just—"

"Friends. Yeah, I know." She sighs, and I can imagine her shaking her head at me. "Natalie, no one's judging you. Adam's a good guy. You both deserve to be happy."

Yes, we do. But that doesn't mean we're going to be happy together. Not now, anyway. And if God does mean for Adam and me to be together eventually, I'm not going to risk messing it up by moving too fast.

Of course, if I buy the coffee shop, I'm going to become Adam's boss and his landlord, which means we'll be spending an awful lot of time together. It should scare me silly, but instead, I get a tiny glimpse of my future, and it makes me smile.

"Hey, Sis, I've got to go," Lindsay says. "It's time for *Lucy.*"

"What's tonight's episode?"

"Lucy and Ethel get jobs."

I recall the scene with the two women stuffing chocolates into their mouths as they struggle to keep up with the conveyor belt, and I laugh. "Have fun."

"Okay. See you soon."

A warm flush spreads out from my chest, and I savor each word as I reply, "See you soon."

50

We've hit a snag."

For the first time since my return, I ventured into the master bedroom today with one very clear goal: empty out my closet. Halfway through the daunting task of deciding if each piece should go in the keep, donate, or throwaway pile, my lawyer called. Now I sit on the side of the bed, a denim jacket in my hands, the cordless phone wedged between my ear and shoulder.

"What kind of a snag?"

"Tony's lawyer contacted me today about the house."

Is that all? "That's okay. I told Tony we can sell the house, remember?"

"He doesn't want to sell anymore."

Eyes closed, I propel myself backward on the mattress. The only thing that keeps me halfway up is a mound of sweaters that are most definitely going with me to Illinois. "After all that hassle? What does he want to do?"

"He wants to keep it."

My eyes pop open. "He wants to live here now?"

"Yes."

That's weird, but not a deal breaker. "Okay. How do we handle that?"

I hear papers rustling on Wendy's side of the call. "We'd have the house appraised and then Tony would pay you half of what it's worth. Basically, he'd be buying you out of it."

"Okay."

The paper rustling stops. "You're all right with that?"

"Why wouldn't I be?"

"Let me put it this way," she says slowly. "I've handled a lot of divorces, and I've never yet seen a case where the soon-to-be ex-wife was okay with the mistress living in her home."

Last week, I wouldn't have liked it at all. In fact, I would have fought to the death to keep Tony and his girlfriend from starting their new life here. But now, it doesn't seem all that important. "Look, I'm moving out anyway, so it makes no difference to me who lives in this house. I expected it to be a family I didn't know, but if Tony wants to buy my half, that's fine too."

We talk a little longer about the papers she'll be sending me to sign and about how long the entire divorce process should take. By the time we hang up, I'm feeling quite proud of myself. Like a very turn-the-other-cheek, seventy-times-seven forgiving woman.

How silly that Wendy thought I'd be upset. What do I care if another woman is living in this house, eating at my old kitchen table, sleeping in my old bed . . . with my old husband. Below the piles of clothes, I get a peek at the bedspread we picked out five years ago. It took so long to find something we both agreed on, we swore not to replace it until it was worn out. Heat rises to my cheeks as I'm bombarded by memories of intimate times we spent under that spread. And then, I picture my husband slipping beneath the bedspread, snuggling up against the body on the other side of the mattress. Only he's not my husband anymore, and that's not my body.

Maybe I'm not so well adjusted after all. I honestly don't mind the idea of Erin and Tony living together in this house. But the thought of them sharing this bed . . . that's something else altogether.

Jumping up as though the mattress caught fire beneath me, I hit the call button on the phone and punch in 411. After I request my listing and ask that the number be dialed for me, I wait for the call to be answered.

"Good afternoon. Salvation Army."

"Yes," I say, sounding overly chipper. "I'd like to donate a king-size bed set. And do you know anyone who hauls away mattresses?"

It takes me a week and a half to tie up all the loose ends.

My insurance company cut me a settlement check for my stripped car, which I put straight into my bank account. No sense buying a replacement until I get back to Bèaumont.

I went through everything in the house, packed up the things I wanted to keep, and shipped them on ahead. In the end I decided that Tony could have all the furniture— with the exception of the hastily donated bed. I have no room for it at my parents' house, and when I get a place of my own, I'll want to start fresh.

Change-of-address forms have been filed. My agent, editor, and other business associates have been contacted. I've said good-bye to Pastor Dave and my church family. And Jade threw me a small going-away surprise party. There's only one thing left to do.

Standing in the front yard, I allow myself one last trip into the past. Ten years ago, after we closed escrow and the house officially became ours, Tony picked me up and carried me through the front door for the first time. Only he didn't turn quite sharp enough and he ran my shoulder into the door frame. He almost dropped me, but I just laughed and clutched his neck tighter, holding on with all my might.

I remember birthdays and holidays, celebrations and quiet evenings. Dinners with friends. Anniversaries. So many good times. But also hard times. Times we lost someone we loved. Times when we prayed for a baby who didn't come. Times we cried and held each other. Times we suffered alone, in too much pain to come near another human being.

All of it, all the memories, the emotions, they all come down to this singular moment. This is it. The final good-bye. To my home. To my marriage. To my old life.

Closing my eyes, arms slightly away from my sides, I open my hands and let it all go. "Help me, God. Help me. Help me."

It seems so long ago when I sat in a miserable huddle on the kitchen floor, calling out that same prayer after my husband left me. Then, it was a cry of despair, of yearning to fix what was broken. But now, that simple prayer is full of surrender, full of hope. Now, it's a prayer of promise.

"Are you ready?" Jade's voice is soft behind me.

I turn and take a deep breath. "I am. Let's go."

We get in her car and she backs out of the driveway. As we head down the street, I look in the rearview mirror for one more glimpse of the house. It gets smaller and smaller and smaller, until finally, it's part of the greater landscape, too small to see anymore.

When I get to the baggage claim area at O'Hare International Airport, I look around for my dad, but don't see him. I pull out my cell phone to call and see where he is when I hear a woman's voice calling.

"Nat! Over here."

There sits Lindsay on a bench against the wall. She pushes herself up as I trot over to her.

"What are you doing here?" I ask as I hug her. "Why didn't Dad come? Is something wrong? Is it Mom?"

"Calm down. Everything's fine. Can't a girl pick up her sister without anything being wrong?"

"Sorry. It's just, in your condition . . . you know."

Her eyes roll up toward the ceiling. "Again, I'm pregnant, not an invalid."

True, but she's gotten considerably bigger in the last few weeks. "Sorry, I stand corrected. And I'm so glad to see you."

Since I have three bags—and I am not asking Lindsay to carry anything—I rent a luggage cart. Then I tell her to sit down and wait for me while I collect my things. For once, she follows my directions without argument. It doesn't take long before we're on our way to the parking garage.

As soon as we've paid the fee and driven out onto the highway, I ask Lindsay, "How's Mom?"

"She's good. I've been spending a lot of time with her."

"How's that going?"

"You could say we're getting to be pretty good friends."

I hate to ask my next question, but I need to know. "Does she remember you at all now?"

"Not really." She shakes her head. "Sometimes, I think she remembers having two daughters. But it's never strong enough that she realizes I'm one of them."

"I'm so sorry, Lindsay." Watching her profile, I try to make out any sign of hurt or anger, any clue that I need to back off. "I can't understand why she remembers me and not you."

"The doctor thinks it could be because of the age difference."

"What does that have to do with it?"

"A lot of times, Alzheimer's does the most damage to short-term memory. That's why she remembers stuff like her wedding and when you were little. They're farther back. But being that I'm so much younger than you—"

"Watch it."

She grins. "Anyway, my birth and childhood are newer, fresher memories. So that could be why she doesn't remember me."

"That's a pretty out-there hypothesis." Lindsay's twenty-five, so I wouldn't classify her birth as a short-term memory item. Then again, Mom doesn't seem to remember much of me beyond high school, which is right before Lindsay was born. "How do you feel about it?"

"To tell you the truth, after I heard that from the doctor, I felt better. Made it feel less personal and more of a medical fact. I approach Mom differently now. Instead of trying to make her remember me, I come to her like a new friend. I even call her Meredith."

"And that works?"

"Yeah, better than trying to force her to come up with memories that are probably gone forever."

"But if her problem is short-term memory, then doesn't she forget you by the next day?"

"Pretty much. In a way, it's a good thing. If I make a mistake one day, I get to start over fresh the next." She huffs out a breath. "This would have come in handy when I was a teenager. Might have saved us all a lot of grief."

Every day a fresh start. I think she's making it sound a lot simpler than it really is. Still, if she's found a way to make peace with Mom's illness, who am I to contradict her? Maybe I can even learn something.

"So, how are things with you and— Hey, wait a minute." I twist my neck, trying to read the road sign that just whizzed by. "We're going the wrong direction."

"No, we're not."

"Yes we are." I point behind us. "Beaumont is that way."

"We're not going to Beaumont."

"We're not?"

"No."

"Are you going to tell me where we're going?"

"No."

Oh, fine. Now my sister is kidnapping me. *You know, Lord, when I said I was ready to go down whatever path you chose, this isn't exactly what I had in mind.*

Turns out she's taking me into downtown Chicago. She maneuvers through the late afternoon traffic and pulls into a lot near Jackson Park. After she succeeds in finding a parking spot, we walk down Lake Shore Drive. It's not as crowded as it would be on the weekend, but there are still plenty of folks out riding bikes down the cement path, jogging, pushing strollers, and splashing in Lake Michigan.

"Are you ready to tell me what we're doing here?" I ask.

"I'm surprised you haven't figured it out already." The breeze off the water tousles her hair and she brushes it from her face.

"I blame it on jet lag."

"Of course you do." We walk a little farther, then she stops and turns to face me. "Now I can tell you. We're here for that."

I have to squint to see the sign she's pointing at across the street. It's a Route 66 marker.

Obviously proud of herself, she links her arm through my elbow and pulls me to the curb. "I've been working on editing our road trip videos, and I realized they're not complete. We've got a picture of us at the beginning, but not at the end."

The signal flashes a white *walk* stick man. I'm in a state of semi-shock—not just because she located this marker, but because she thought of doing it at all. "Did you see that?" I point at the big capital letters on top of the sign that say BEGIN.

Fishing the camera out of her purse, she smiles at me. "Well, this is the traditional beginning of the Mother Road. It's exactly right, don't you think?"

I look at my sister, so happy, on the brink of becoming a wife and mother. Then there's me: ending a marriage but starting a new life; heading down a new road, excited about where God will take me. We've come so far. We have so far yet to go.

"It's perfect."

Note to the Reader

I'm so glad you traveled this fictional journey with me. Natalie's story started with one simple question: What would a marriage expert do if her own marriage failed? As the story grew, and I learned more about Natalie, her sister, and what they both faced, it seemed natural to send them on a trip down the Mother Road.

About Route 66

Because I grew up in Southern California, Route 66 is quite familiar to me. In fact, for about ten years I lived on Huntington Drive in Duarte, which is part of the historic highway. But I never ventured any farther on 66 than the California border. Research was in order.

The Mother Road is a fascinating American relic, and I didn't want to tamper with its charm and history by making up locations. So, every place that Natalie and Lindsay visit along the way is real. Today's road warriors can still see the wild donkeys of Oatman, eat at the Road Kill Café in Seligman, and take a picture with Little Louie standing guard outside Granny's Closet in Flagstaff.

Those who check out the Oatman Hotel can see the room where Clark Gable and Carol Lombard are said to have spent their honeymoon. But a bit of controversy surrounds that particular spot. While all the guidebooks and the majority of websites I checked support the honeymoon story, I found a few Internet claims that it might be a hoax. The most convincing came from a fan site and quoted Gable from several 1939 magazine articles. So, did the famous couple stay there? I don't think there's a soul alive today who knows for sure. But since the story has become such a big piece of Oatman lore, I decided to let Natalie and Lindsay experience it as any other tourists would.

The only location in the novel that's not real is Beaumont, Illinois. I wanted the flexibility of a small town where I could create the details I needed, such as the Old Town renovation and the coffee shop, so I took the liberty of making it up.

There's so much more to the Mother Road than I could include in one novel. If you're interested in learning more, or in plotting a trip of your own, you might find these books helpful:

EZ66 Guide for Travelers by Jerry McClanahan (Lake Arrowhead, Calif.: National Historic Route 66 Federation, 2005)

Route 66: The Mother Road by Michael Wallis (New York: St. Martin's Griffin, 2001)

Route 66 Adventure Handbook by Drew Knowles (Santa Monica Press, 2006)

Let's Go Roadtripping USA (Cambridge, Mass.: Harvard Student Agencies, 2010)

I hope you enjoyed visiting all the locations as much as I did.

About Alzheimer's

I was eight years old when my great-grandmother died, but since she lived with us, I remember a lot about her. Toward the end, she didn't know who I was, and she thought her daughter and my mother were her sisters. Although she wasn't diagnosed, I'm pretty sure she had Alzheimer's. Regardless of what name you put on it, seeing your loved one slip away is an experience no family should have to go through.

I did a lot of research on the disease before writing this story. Natalie's mother, Meredith, actually has early-onset Alzheimer's, which means symptoms began to manifest before the age of 65. There is a perception that this form of Alzheimer's progresses at a faster rate, but there's no scientific proof to back it up. It's more likely that, because people in their fifties are more active and social, their friends and families are more apt to notice changes in behavior.

Alzheimer's is a strange and mysterious disease. While there are common markers, each affected person behaves in his or her own unique way. If someone you love has Alzheimer's or another form of dementia, I urge you to build a support system. Reach out to other family members, your church family, and support groups. Please don't try to travel this road alone.

In our electronic age, the first place most of us look for information is the Internet. There's a wealth of information there, but proceed with caution. Look for legitimate sites with solid information, backed up by accreditation or the endorsement of experts in the field. Here are a few sites I found particularly helpful:

Alzheimer's Association (www.alz.org). This is the best place to start. This site provides information and support for not only those afflicted by Alzheimer's but also those who care for the patient or family member.

Mayo Clinic (www.mayoclinic.com/health/alzheimers-disease/DS00161). Click on the "In Depth" tab for a good look at early-onset Alzheimer's. Also, check out the "Resources" section for many more links to helpful information.

Everyday Health (www.everydayhealth.com/info/v1ss/alzheimer's). This site has a nice section on Alzheimer's, including information on nontraditional therapies such as music, pet therapy, art, and other recreational activities.

Family Caregiver Alliance (www.caregiver.org). This is an organization dedicated to the support of those who care for loved ones with chronic, disabling health issues.

Discussion Questions

1. When Natalie's husband demands a divorce, he not only crushes her spirit but also destroys her career. At least, that's how she sees it. Could Natalie have continued speaking and writing about happy marriages after her own fell apart? How would you advise her?

2. Natalie and Tony tried without success to have a baby. Tony thought if God wanted them to have a baby, they would, without any outside help. Natalie was determined to do whatever it took. What do you think? Which viewpoint makes the most sense to you?

3. When Natalie sees Lindsay for the first time in years, she assumes her sister has a black eye because her boyfriend is abusing her. Why do you think Natalie jumped to that conclusion? In that type of situation, is it better to assume the worst and apologize later? What would you have done?

4. The whole idea of the trip down the Mother Road comes from a clerk at the Automobile Club. Natalie sees it as a kind of divine inspiration. Have you ever been in a similar situation? Has God ever used a stranger to point you in the direction He wanted you to go?

5. The sisters stop at a lot of quirky places along the way, making it a trip they won't soon forget. Have you gone on a trip like that with friends or family? Do you want to? What's your idea of the perfect road trip?

6. When they arrive at their parents' house, Lindsay and Natalie are shocked by their mother's lack of recognition. Natalie wonders, If a mother loves you, but she doesn't remember she loves you, does that love still exist? What do you think?

7. Natalie hopes to prod her mother's memory by reintroducing a favorite old pastime: jigsaw puzzles. In

this case, there was some success. But Alzheimer's is different for every person who deals with it. Have you had any experience with someone suffering from Alzheimer's? What advice would you give someone whose loved one was recently diagnosed?

8. There's an almost immediate attraction between Natalie and Adam. What do you think about the idea that Natalie's marriage was over as soon as Tony cheated and that the rest was a legal technicality? Does that give her the freedom to pursue a new relationship? Or is she right in thinking that, until her divorce is final, anything beyond friendship with Adam is wrong?

9. When Natalie returns to California, Tony makes a last-ditch effort to get her back. Why do you think he did that? Was Natalie right to forgive him and send him back to Erin, or should she have chosen to take him back and try to make the marriage work?

10. The book ends with Natalie and Lindsay coming to the last stop on their trip down the Mother Road. Except it's not the end at all. What do you think happens next? How would you continue their stories?